THE NIGHT OFF

What Reviewers Say About
Meghan O'Brien's Work

"[O'Brien] knows how to write passion really well, and I do not recommend reading her books in public (unless you want everyone to know exactly what you are reading). *Wild* is no different. It's very steamy, and the sex scenes are frequent, and quite erotic to say the least."—*Lesbian Book Review*

"Meghan O'Brien has given her readers some very steamy scenes in this fast paced novel. *Thirteen Hours* is definitely a walk on the wild side, which may have you looking twice at those with whom you share an elevator."—*Just About Write*

"Boy, if there was ever fiction that a lesbian needs during a bed death rut or simply in need of some juicing up, *Thirteen Hours* by Meghan O'Brien is the book I'd recommend to my good friends. …If you are looking for good ole American instant gratification, simple and not-at-all-straight sexy lesbian eroticism, revel in the sexiness that is *Thirteen Hours*."—*Tilted World*

"In *The Three* by Meghan O'Brien, we are treated to first-rate storytelling that features scorching love scenes with three main characters. …She hits her stride well in *The Three* with a well-paced plot that never slows. She excels at giving us an astounding tale that is tightly written and extremely sensual. I highly recommend this unique book."—*Just About Write*

By the Author

The Three

Infinite Loop

Thirteen Hours

Battle Scars

Wild

The Night Off

THE NIGHT OFF

by

Meghan O'Brien

2012

THE NIGHT OFF

ISBN 10: 1-60282-673-0
ISBN 13: 978-1-60282-673-1

This Trade Paperback Original Is Published By
Bold Strokes Books, Inc.
P.O. Box 249
Valley Falls, NY 12185

First Edition: July 2012

Credits
Editor: Shelley Thrasher
Production Design: Susan Ramundo
Cover Design By Sheri (graphicartist2020@hotmail.com)

Acknowledgments

I want to thank the entire Bold Strokes Books family for their friendship and support. And specifically, thanks to Radclyffe for all she does for her authors and LGBTQ fiction in general; Shelley Thrasher for her incredible editing assistance; and all the designers, editors, and web/marketing gurus who work so hard to package my words in the best way possible.

I also need to thank my partner Angie for all her support and for giving me the time and opportunity to write despite our parental responsibilities and generally chaotic life. Thanks to my friends and beta readers, Ty Justice, K.E. Lane, and Sandy Lowe, for their support and feedback. A shout out to my sister Kathleen for being awesome, and for my parents for always being proud of me even when I'm writing books I forbid them to read (like this one... seriously. Shut the book now, Mom and Dad. There's nothing else for you here.)

Finally, thanks to all my readers. I do this for you, and you make it so very worthwhile!

Dedication

To my readers—especially the ones who like dirty books.
And to my partner Angie, who definitely likes dirty books.

CHAPTER ONE

Emily Parker nearly dropped her car keys when a strong arm caught her around the waist and a hand clamped over her mouth, muffling her surprised yelp. Heart hammering crazily, she struggled to reach her driver's side door handle, then froze when her attacker's lips brushed against her ear.

"Unicorn."

The nonsense word immediately turned her body to jelly as fear of real injury dissipated. Anxiety and anticipation remained. She had known to expect that this could happen at any time, and now that the big night had arrived, she hoped she could go through with it.

The woman behind her spoke again. "Unicorn, darling." She removed her hand from Emily's mouth.

"Unicorn," Emily repeated in a voice that quavered more than she preferred. "Understood."

"Good." The arm around her waist tightened, jerking her back against a body that felt taller, leaner, and stronger than her own. "Now we're going to get in your car and you're going to drive us where I tell you to go. Then we're going to have some fun together." The woman moved the hand that had covered Emily's mouth to her breast, kneading her roughly through her shirt.

Her heart rate, which had steadied somewhat, took off again. It had been more than four years since anyone had touched her so intimately. The caress felt foreign and almost unbearably personal.

But this was her fantasy scenario down to the most exacting, minute detail—exactly as she had described it to Janis at the Xtreme Encounters agency. She was about to live out her dirtiest, darkest desires with a stranger, to give up the control she held on to so tightly in her daily life.

It was one thing to masturbate to this fantasy and another to actually experience it. She hadn't known how she would react to this brand of real-life make-believe, but she couldn't deny the flood of arousal that her pseudo-abductor's hands had unleashed.

The woman seized her nipple and twisted sharply. "Get in the goddamn car."

Gasping, Emily stepped forward and opened her driver's side door. She eased onto the leather seat, grateful that none of her colleagues had stayed at the office late enough to witness this scene. The last thing she needed was to have someone call the police. She couldn't imagine being forced to explain that this was consensual—that she had, in fact, paid for the privilege of being accosted. Choosing to be abducted from her workplace had been a risky decision, but the heightened sense of danger sharpened her arousal.

The passenger door opened and her abductor folded herself into the seat. Nervously, Emily chanced a sidelong glance, curious about the woman with whom she would be spending the night. She had requested a butch, if possible, definitely someone tough—a woman she could honestly believe might steal her away for an evening of rough, dominant sex. A woman confident enough to say the crude words Emily knew would make her wet.

This woman looked to be all that and more. With dark hair shaved close to her head, she wore a form-fitting T-shirt that showed off her defined arms and the bottom half of a pinup-girl tattoo. Butch was an understatement. Tough—maybe even a little dangerous—those words also described the woman sitting next to her.

She was perfect.

Emily inhaled sharply when the butch gripped her upper thigh, squeezing hard. "Start the car, sweetheart."

Hands shaking, she fitted the key into the ignition and turned it to bring the engine to life. "Where are we going?"

"Don't worry about that for now, good girl." The woman moved her hand between Emily's thighs, cupping her gently through her pants. "Go ahead and get on 101, heading north. I'll tell you when to get off."

Emily eased out of her parking spot without looking over at the woman who touched her so possessively. It took every ounce of her concentration to drive them out of the lot and onto the freeway. Teasing fingertips played along the seam of her pants, making it hard to concentrate on navigating through the dark. She had no clue where they were going, but she had a very good idea what would happen when they got there. Janis at the agency had asked her to write out the sex acts and dirty talk she wanted her escort to include in their encounter. Emily squirmed as she mentally reviewed that list.

Eager to see what the butch would say, she asked, "What are you going to do to me?"

"Make you beg me to fuck you." The hand between her legs retreated, leaving her cold with its absence. She tried not to let her face give away her disappointment. Chuckling, the butch said, "Tell me the truth—does that frighten or excite you?"

Emily didn't want to answer. Admitting her excitement would work against the nature of her fantasy. Instead she said, "What's your name?"

"Nat."

She snuck another glance at the gorgeous butch. Nat. It suited her. "How do you know that I don't have a husband at home waiting for me, who'll call the police when he realizes I've gone missing?"

Clearly amused, Nat forced two fingers into Emily's mouth. Startled, Emily pulled away, but Nat gripped her arm with her free hand, keeping her still. "Concentrate on the road," she commanded.

Emily tightened her hands on the steering wheel and stared straight ahead, mortified by how much Nat's rough handling turned her on. The fingers in her mouth swept over her tongue, then retreated.

"To answer your question, I refuse to live in a world where this beautiful mouth of yours is used for anything except eating pussy." Nat dropped her hand to fondle Emily's breast, pinching and twisting her nipple hard enough to force a whimper from her throat. "So no, you don't have a husband at home waiting. You're all mine tonight."

Emily swallowed, amazed by the wetness soaking her panties. She hoped Nat wouldn't make her drive too far. The sooner they could find a bed, the better. After four years without sex, she felt as though she couldn't wait another five minutes. Still, her fantasy required her to be a not-so-willing participant, at least at first. "If you wanted me, you could have just asked."

Nat grinned. "More fun this way." She continued to caress Emily's breast as though she owned her. "So have you eaten pussy before? Or will tonight be your first time?"

Emily's face burned—part embarrassment and part arousal. "That's none of your business."

"Oh, I think it's very much my business." Nat moved her hand back to Emily's mouth, tracing her lips as Emily pulled away in mock anger. "I need to know whether I'll have to teach you how to pleasure a woman, or not." She seized Emily's chin firmly. "So tell me, are you a good little pussy-licker?"

Emily kept her attention locked on the road and didn't allow her gaze to stray to Nat. She had nothing to fake now. Her humiliation was real. "Yes."

Nat released her chin. "Good. You have no idea how badly I need to come." She pointed at the exit sign. "Get off here and take a left."

That Emily knew what would happen tonight didn't diminish her excitement in any way. The memory of her written fantasy made her so eager for the first touch of Nat's hand on her bare skin that it took all her willpower not to just ask for it. She gripped the wheel tightly and followed Nat's directions as she navigated them into the parking lot of a Spanish-style building.

"Turn off the car," Nat said after Emily pulled into a marked spot.

Emily did so, then withdrew the key and moved to slip it into her pocket.

"No." Holding out her hand, Nat said, "Give it to me."

Emily blinked in surprise. "My car key?"

"Don't want you going anywhere, do I?"

This wasn't part of her script, but Emily appreciated the improvisation. It worked well with the overall tone of her fantasy. She handed her keychain over. "Fine."

Nat pocketed the key, then released Emily's safety belt. "I want you to hold my hand as we walk inside. Can I trust you to behave?"

"Yes."

Sitting back, Nat grasped Emily's chin and stared into her eyes. "You'll address me as mistress from now on."

Emily fought against her instincts, which urged her to yank away from Nat's grip. That was her need for control coming to the front, and tonight she'd promised herself that she would surrender completely. Besides, Nat's forcefulness had all but destroyed any notion of feigning resistance. "I understand, mistress."

"Good." Nat ghosted her lips over Emily's, drawing a whimper from deep in Emily's chest. She sounded so wanton and needy she didn't even recognize herself. When Nat abruptly released her and got out of the car, Emily had just enough time to take a few measured, calming breaths before the driver's side door opened. "Come on."

She took Nat's hand, grateful for the support as she clambered out of her car. Her legs were shaking so badly she had to lean against Nat to stay on her feet. Without missing a beat, Nat pressed the key fob to lock the doors, then led them across the parking lot toward the building's entrance. Emily stayed close to her side and said nothing, focused only on the sensation of Nat's strong fingers curled around her own. Soon those hands would take her places she'd never been. Her stomach fluttered in nervous anticipation.

The trek into the building seemed to take forever. Relieved that they didn't pass anyone on the way, Emily schooled her breathing and tried not to stumble over clumsy feet. She didn't want Nat to know just how anxious she suddenly felt. It didn't matter that Nat was a professional—Emily wanted so badly to satisfy her, and she was scared to death that she wouldn't.

Nat tugged Emily into the lobby elevator, then pushed the button for the penthouse. She shot Emily a cool smile when the doors slid shut. "Tell me your name."

"Emily." She kept her gaze downcast, sensing that eye contact wouldn't be encouraged.

"Emily," Nat repeated, in a low rumble. "And what do you want?"

Uncertain how to answer, Emily lifted her eyes and searched Nat's handsome face. "Uh—"

"You want to please me."

She understood. "Yes, mistress."

"Tell me."

"I want to please you, mistress." Face on fire, she tried not to fidget beneath Nat's heated scrutiny. Nobody had ever looked at her the way Nat was doing now—like she was a particularly savory treat.

"How?"

Emily's cheeks burned hotter as she remembered Nat's words in the car. "Eating your pussy."

Nat's hand shot out and tweaked her left nipple. Hard.

"Mistress," she gasped, correcting her lapse.

The elevator doors slid open and Nat stepped out, dropping Emily's hand as she let them into the penthouse. Nat nudged her forward, encouraging her to enter first. Emily took a few steps inside, then strained to peek into the large room just beyond the front hallway. She'd nearly reached the end of the hall when Nat closed her hand around her upper arm, dragging her back a few steps.

"No," Nat said simply, then folded her arms and raised an eyebrow. "Take off your clothes."

Despite the fact that this was *her* fantasy, Emily blanched at the thought of willingly baring her body to a complete stranger. Nat stared at her with dark, predatory eyes, making her feel vulnerable in a way that bordered on uncomfortable. Swallowing, Emily shook her head. "I can't, mistress." She made sure to address Nat properly, aware that her refusal would be considered transgression enough. "I'm sorry."

Nat tilted her head, but otherwise betrayed no reaction. "You *can't?*"

Eyes tearing up, Emily studied her feet. For a moment, she considered using the safe word. To hell with the money she'd spent on tonight, which had taken months to set aside. Now that the moment had come to truly surrender control, she couldn't seem to do it. Perhaps her fantasies were meant to stay safely within the realm of make-believe.

Nat's work boots came into view, then her slightly spicy scent filled Emily's nostrils as she brushed her lips against Emily's ear. "You're a beautiful woman. That's why you're here. And this is the honest truth, Emily—I want you so badly it *hurts.*" A beat. "Now take off your clothes so I can admire what's mine."

It was as though Nat had known exactly what she needed to hear. The words triggered a welcome burst of confidence, chasing away her doubts. She wanted this. Hell, she *needed* it. And she'd never been so wet. If she gave herself over to this experience, it could change her. At the very least, it would provide her an escape from the burden of always feeling responsible for everything around her. That's all she wanted. A night off.

Emily nodded, determined. "Yes, mistress."

Nat drew away with a gentle kiss on her cheek. "That's my girl."

Emboldened by Nat's praise, Emily brought her hands to the hem of her shirt and, after a brief hesitation, pulled her top over her head. She watched Nat's gaze sweep over her chest, glad that she'd worn her lacy black bra. It was a favorite, and the hunger in Nat's eyes made it clear that she liked it, too.

"Show me your tits."

Biting her lip, Emily gave up her fight against her embarrassment. She'd told Janis that dirty talk was essential for this fantasy, the cruder the better. Now she couldn't believe she'd helped write this script. Couldn't believe it, but for the fact that she was dripping with excitement. With a meek nod, Emily reached behind her back and unclasped her bra, then shrugged it off and let it fall to the ground.

Nat's quiet inhalation seemed very real. "Gorgeous." She met Emily's eyes. "Pinch your nipples for me. Nice and rough. Get them hard."

Emily stared at a spot on the wall over Nat's shoulder as she complied. She groaned at the pressure of her fingertips squeezing her nipples, then hissed as she tugged them sharply. Seeing approval in Nat's eyes, she kept up the harsh treatment until Nat held up a hand to stop her.

"Now your pants. Go slow."

"Yes, mistress." Still trembling, Emily unbuttoned her pants, then slid them down her legs as slowly as she could manage. She doubted she looked very sexy. More likely just scared.

"Perfect." Nat waited until she'd kicked her jeans to the side, then gestured at the lacy black panties that matched her bra. "Very pretty. Slutty."

Emily said nothing. Standing almost completely naked in front of a woman she'd just met, she couldn't disagree with Nat's assessment.

"Turn around," Nat said, twirling her hand lazily in the air. "Let me see that sweet ass."

Relieved that she would no longer have to watch Nat's face during this evaluation, Emily did as asked. She hung her head, very aware of the heat of Nat's gaze burning into her back.

"Bend over, Emily."

Emily hesitated.

A slapping sound came from behind her, loud enough to make her jerk in surprise. Nat didn't make contact with her skin, but the noise alone did the trick. "Do I need to force you to obey?"

"No, mistress." Not eager to test Nat's patience, Emily carefully bent at the waist, aware of how the position left her so very exposed. "Like this, mistress?"

"Very good." Nat's voice deepened. "Now lower those slutty panties to the ground. Put on a show for me."

Closing her eyes, Emily grasped the waist of her panties and dragged them deliberately down the length of her thighs. The cool air hit her abundant wetness, sending a shiver up her spine. She couldn't imagine how she must look: obviously excited, inner thighs and pussy slick with proof that she enjoyed being dominated, belying any protestations she might make.

"Look at that swollen, pink cunt. Dripping wet. Ready to be fucked." Nat's arousal permeated her husky words. "You tell me no again, I won't let you come for a *very* long time. And that wet pussy *needs* to come, doesn't it?"

"Yes, mistress," she whispered.

"Stand up and face me."

Emily straightened. Her heart thundered as she turned around, and she didn't dare meet Nat's eyes. She watched as Nat used her foot to gather her clothing in a loose pile in front of her before beckoning Emily forward.

"Down on your knees, right here," Nat said.

Understanding that Nat intended for the clothing to ease the pain of kneeling on the wooden floor, Emily sank down onto it gratefully. "Yes, mistress."

"What do you want?"

This time she knew the answer. "To please you." And it was the truth. "Mistress."

Nat gave her a grin that made her grateful she wasn't standing. It would've taken out her knees. Dragging a fingertip along Emily's jaw, Nat murmured, "Excellent. Unbutton my jeans."

Emily reached for the button, cursing her shaking hands. It took a fair amount of fumbling before she managed to work it open. When she lifted her face, ready to receive her next instruction, Nat pushed a single finger inside her mouth.

"Suck," Nat said.

At first she was confused, but then Nat wiggled her finger and she realized what she was being asked to do. Self-conscious, she sucked on Nat, who tasted faintly of hand sanitizer. Emily raised her eyes, seeking approval.

"Show me what you can do with that mouth." Nat withdrew her finger slowly, then slipped back inside with a lewd smirk. "Besides getting smart with me, that is."

Emily had long since abandoned any pretense of resistance. Nat's dominant energy rendered her wholly subservient and eager to obey. She sucked harder, swirling her tongue in circles over the pad of Nat's finger.

A low groan rumbled deep in Nat's throat. "Unzip me."

Emily continued to lave Nat with her tongue as she lowered the zipper on her jeans. She gasped when Nat's finger left her mouth, then watched breathlessly as Nat pushed her jeans down her legs, taking her black boxer briefs with them. Rapt, she stared at the neatly trimmed triangle of hair only inches from her face. She inhaled deeply, salivating at the thought of tasting her mistress.

"Oh, you want this, don't you?" Nat ran a hand over her pussy, spreading her labia and exposing slick, pink flesh. "Do you want to kiss me here?"

"Yes, mistress."

Nat slid her fingers through her wetness, then smeared them across Emily's lips. Shocked, Emily flinched away, but Nat stopped her with a hand tangled in her hair. Nat gathered more of her juices with her free hand, this time pressing her shiny fingers directly into Emily's mouth. It was the first time in four years that she'd enjoyed a woman's flavor. She couldn't remember either of her former lovers being so sweet.

"You like how I taste?" Nat tightened her grip on her hair.

Nodding, Emily mumbled around Nat's fingers, "I love it, mistress."

Nat withdrew her fingers, then roughly shoved Emily's face between her legs. "Then eat me like you need it to survive."

Emily opened her mouth on instinct, moaning at the way Nat's flavor went straight to her head. Dizzy with her scent, she drank Nat in, pushing her nose and lips into her folds and lapping at her opening.

"There you go." Nat stroked her cheek tenderly, full of affection. "That's my nasty little slut."

Emily closed her eyes, ashamed by how much she enjoyed the lewd praise. The hand on her face stilled before slapping her lightly. The contact wasn't painful, but she instantly snapped to attention.

"Look at me." Nat's words were clipped, her voice steady. Except for the slight trembling of her thighs, she was in total control. "I want you *here*. Present."

Solid pressure from Nat's hand on her head kept her in place, forcing Emily to struggle to look up into Nat's eyes as she continued to lick her. What she saw there turned her on in a way that shook her very foundation. She had wondered whether she would actually enjoy her dirty little fantasy come to life, but now she knew.

She fucking loved it.

"Funny, you don't *act* very unwilling." Nat chuckled. "Not anymore."

Emily pulled away long enough to say, "No, mistress," then got back to work. Nat set her feet apart and tilted her hips slightly, giving Emily better access. Angling her head, Emily circled her tongue around Nat's opening, thrilled by the way Nat groaned and shook in response.

"Glad to hear that." Nat took a breath, then exhaled. "Because I have big plans for you tonight. I'm going to fuck you, Emily. Spank you. Use and abuse that beautiful body of yours. And I'd love to think that you'll enjoy it just as much as I will." She tugged on Emily's hair, until she met her gaze again. "I don't *need* to think that, mind you. But I'd love to."

Emily nodded, hoping her response was acceptable. She didn't want to stop what she was doing—not when she sensed Nat teetering on the edge of climax. Like magic, all her usual stresses and worries vanished from her mind, replaced by a single-minded focus on pleasing the woman who towered over her.

"Fuck," Nat groaned, fisting her hand in Emily's hair so she could guide her mouth to her clit. "Suck me. Make me come."

Complying with a happy murmur, Emily planted her lips around Nat's hot, swollen clit and sucked gently. Nat shot out her hand and braced herself on the wall, drawing a smile from Emily even as she continued her ministrations. Despite her uncertainty, Nat's reactions made it clear that she was doing a good job.

Nat released her hair and gave her another gentle slap on the cheek. The contact wasn't intended to induce pain, but to degrade—

exactly as she had requested. With only a slight waver in her voice, Nat said, "Harder, slut. Suck it harder."

Emily increased her suction, drawing Nat deep into her mouth. Almost instantly Nat stiffened, then her body quaked in release. She didn't vocalize her pleasure, but it was obvious from the flood of wetness that soaked her lips and tongue that the orgasm had been strong. Wary of stopping before she was told, Emily kept licking until Nat yanked her away with both hands in her hair.

"Enough."

Sitting back on her heels, Emily remained silent and waited for further instruction. Her own juices were pouring from her throbbing pussy, but she wasn't likely to find relief soon. A big part of her fantasy had been the idea of having her orgasm denied until she could hardly stand it. Now she wished she'd thought that one through.

Nat exhaled and took a step back. "That took the edge off."

Emily wished she could say the same. Taking a chance, she murmured, "Thank you, mistress."

"For what?"

"For allowing me to pleasure you."

Nat's eyes sparkled with what looked like approval. She grasped Emily's upper arm and hauled her to her feet. "You're welcome, slut." Taking her hand, Nat led them deeper into the penthouse. "Come on. Now we can begin."

CHAPTER TWO

Nat ushered her into an immaculate bathroom and closed the door behind them—most likely to prevent Emily's escape, since they were alone in the penthouse and clearly long past the issue of privacy. Still naked, heart racing, Emily stood by the sink and watched dazedly as Nat sat on the edge of the tub and turned on the faucet. Lean, well-muscled arms flexed as Nat tested the water with her hand. The easy confidence in her movements made Emily's throat go dry. She tore her gaze away when Nat plugged the drain, nervous about what would happen when the focus returned to her.

Nat didn't seem to be in any hurry. She uncapped a bottle of bubble bath and squirted a generous dollop into the steaming water. "Come tell me if this is too hot."

Strangely touched by the offer, Emily took a tentative step forward. "Yes, mistress." She held her hand beneath the flow of water. It was hot, but not hotter than she liked. "That feels wonderful." She startled when Nat's hand caressed the curve of her bare ass.

"So do you."

Emily straightened, at a loss for words. A sharp slap on her bottom tore a gasp from her throat and prompted a hasty response. "Thank you, mistress."

"You're very welcome." Nat slid her hand lower, stroking gently. She traced patterns with blunt fingernails, teasing ever closer to the juncture of Emily's thighs. "Are you wet?"

"Yes."

Tapping the inside of her thigh, Nat murmured, "Open."

Emily set her feet apart, obeying the command as though she had been trained to do so. Nat made a quiet, approving noise, then dragged her fingertips through the abundant wetness between Emily's legs. Whimpering, Emily closed her eyes. It was overwhelming to be touched so intimately. It had been far too long.

"Oh," Nat said softly, "So, so wet. You like being told what to do."

She considered the statement. For years she'd gotten herself off on fantasies about being taken by a dominant lover. So far her desires had easily translated into real life. "Yes, I do. Mistress."

"That's good." Nat pushed her fingers deeper into Emily's folds, making her gasp. "You looked so *put together* in your work clothes—like such a good girl. But you're not, are you? You're not a good girl. No, sweet, innocent Emily wears sexy black lingerie beneath her business casual attire. Her pussy drips with excitement at the thought of being fucked by a stranger. Worse than that, *taken* by a stranger."

She'd expected the verbal humiliation, the degradation. After all, she'd written it into the script. She'd paid for it. The words made her cheeks burn even as her desire spiked. Conflicted, she avoided meeting Nat's eyes and simply enjoyed the sensation of lightly callused fingers exploring her labia.

Nat withdrew from between her legs. She brought her hand to her lips, meeting Emily's eyes as she used her tongue to clean her fingers. "Delicious," Nat murmured.

"Thank you, mistress." Emily's knees wobbled. She reached back with one hand, desperate for something to hang onto. She found the sink and took an inadvertent step away from Nat, resting on the cool porcelain with a grateful sigh. Waiting for another admonishment, she held her breath and met Nat's gaze.

Nat stared at her, blank-faced. Almost cold. "Do you like being fucked?"

It was difficult to maintain her composure under such blunt questioning—far more difficult than she'd ever imagined. Her face was on fire. Her hands were shaking. "I…" An unwelcome thought flitted into her mind—could she handle what Nat was going to dish out? Her fantasy was hard-edged. Rough. She'd never played this dynamic before in real life, and though the thought sure as hell got her off, she couldn't deny that she was already shaken, and they still had a long way to go. Fantasy-Emily was always so fearless when she submitted to harsh treatment. Real-Emily couldn't seem to relax. "I think so."

Nat raised her eyebrows. "You think so?"

"Mistress," she said quickly, hoping to avoid punishment. Standing, Nat closed the distance between them with a predatory smile on her face. Emily braced herself for whatever she had planned.

Without breaking eye contact, Nat took off her shirt and tossed it onto the floor. "Do you like being fucked?" she repeated, watching Emily's reaction.

Inhaling, Emily whispered, "Yes." Unable to hold Nat's intense stare, she lowered her gaze and promptly lost her breath at the sight of Nat's bare breasts. Surprisingly full and feminine, they stood in stark contrast with the hard masculine lines of the rest of her body. The urge to take one of those pebbled pink nipples into her mouth overrode her fear briefly, throwing her into further uncertainty.

"Yes?"

Emily flinched at Nat's amused tone. "Yes, mistress." She dragged her attention back to Nat's face, relieved to see no anger or frustration in what she suddenly realized were very kind brown eyes.

"So Emily likes getting fucked." Nat's smile belied her blunt words. "There's no reason to be shy about that. Not with me." She placed her hands on Emily's chest, sliding them down to cradle her sensitive breasts. Pleasure rippled through Emily's body as gentle thumbs brushed over her turgid nipples. "Because I'm going to enjoy fucking you. Very much."

Emily held her breath. She was fiercely attracted to Nat, more than she'd ever been to a prospective lover. It made true surrender feel almost impossible. She didn't want to disappoint this sexy butch or embarrass herself by being unable to act out her own secret desires. A familiar fear of failure threatened her composure for what felt like the countless time since their session began.

"Hey."

Nat's quiet murmur broke through her inward focus. She moved her hands from Emily's breasts to her shoulders, then gave her a tentative squeeze. An unspoken question lurked in her eyes.

Emily could use her safe word at any time. One *unicorn* and everything would stop. But then what? Colleen was at a friend's parents' cabin for the weekend. With her younger sister gone, the apartment would feel depressingly empty. And she would still be sexually frustrated.

She would also be out an embarrassing amount of money.

More than that, she would regret not seeing this through. Nothing had happened yet that she didn't honestly enjoy, so walking away would only make her feel stupid later. She had revisited this scenario time and again in her head for a reason—it was what she wanted, what she *needed*. Guilt-free surrender, the thrill of having a stronger partner take her. She didn't have to be a psychologist to understand why an evening like this was the perfect vacation from her control-freak ways. Hell, it would be good for her.

Taking a steadying breath, Emily laced their fingers together and moved Nat's hands back to her breasts. She managed a tentative smile. "It's just…been a while."

Nat said nothing, just stroked her nipples—first with her palms, then her knuckles. Emily shivered and drifted closer, whimpering when Nat pulled away. Then she inhaled swiftly as Nat took her by the arms and walked her backward until her shoulders pressed against the closed bathroom door. Without speaking, Nat captured her mouth in a deep, soulful kiss that curled Emily's toes and erased all doubt from her mind—along with her ability to form a rational thought.

Strong, assertive hands were everywhere, skimming over the curve of her breasts, along her sides, gripping her hips. Nat pinned her against the door, her solid body heavy and warm and electric on Emily's bare skin. The kiss was passionate, unrestrained, and utterly convincing. It was as though they were no longer escort and client, but simply two women who wanted each other. It was obviously a professionally delivered reassurance, but damn if Nat wasn't brilliant at it.

Nat pulled away, panting. She stared at Emily's mouth as though she wanted to go back for more. Instead she blinked and refocused, searching Emily's eyes. "Okay?"

Emily responded automatically. "Okay."

"Good." Nat didn't release her from her spot against the door. She slipped a hand between their stomachs, combing her fingers through Emily's trimmed curls.

Emily moved one foot to the side, opening herself to Nat's gentle exploration. She shuddered at the sensation of roughened fingertips gliding over her labia. Raising an eyebrow, Nat circled her opening sensuously, then pushed up into her. Slow. Deep. Emily moaned.

Nat brought her mouth to Emily's ear. "Do you like being finger fucked?"

Closing her eyes, Emily whispered, "Yes, mistress." Pleased that Nat had once again known how to reassure her without breaking the scene, she was finally ready to get back into character. And stay there, she hoped.

"You make me so goddamn hard." Nat added a second finger, spreading them apart slightly, stretching her open. "I hope you're ready for my butch cock."

Of course she was. Emily had to bite her lip to stop from crying out. "I am, mistress."

Chuckling, Nat removed her fingers, leaving her so empty she ached. "Not until you *beg* me for it."

As much as she craved to surrender control, Emily wasn't going to let go so quickly. Half the fun was in making Nat push her to submit. "Understood," she ground out. "Mistress." She nearly collapsed when Nat backed away suddenly, leaving her standing alone on weak legs.

Nat walked across the small room to turn off the faucet. Fragrant, enticing bubbles rose above the edge of the tub, beckoning Emily closer. "Get in." Taking the lead, Nat stepped into the steaming water. "I'll wash you."

Emily climbed into the tub, sitting across from Nat with a grateful sigh. She pulled her knees to her chest and wrapped her arms around them as she watched Nat settle opposite her.

Nat shook her head and beckoned Emily closer. "I can't reach you over there."

Recognizing that Nat had gentled her tone slightly, Emily scooted forward without hesitation. She didn't want Nat to soften all the rough edges of this encounter. Though a single word could transform this evening into a more traditional lovemaking session, she refused to succumb to the comfort of the familiar. This was a once-in-a-lifetime opportunity to act out her dirtiest fantasy with her dream lover. She didn't want momentary doubt to ruin months of planning.

Aware that presumption might lead to punishment, Emily took a chance and straddled Nat's hips. She didn't rest her weight on Nat's thighs, choosing instead to hover over her and offer easy access to her body. With an approving nod, Nat snaked an arm around her waist, holding her in place.

"*Now* you're obedient." Craning her neck, Nat licked the tip of her breast, then took an erect nipple between her teeth and applied exquisite pressure. Emily sucked in a quick breath as pain mingled with pleasure, but took care to remain perfectly still. Eventually Nat released her nipple with a soothing kiss. "Maybe you *are* a good girl after all." Without warning, she penetrated Emily again.

Emily struggled to stay on her knees. Nat's fingers felt so good, and her masculine beauty made it hard to concentrate. Gritting her teeth, Emily fought to stay silent. She didn't want to give Nat the satisfaction of moaning out loud. Not yet.

Her resolve weakened when Nat circled her anus with the tip of her thumb, sending shock waves deep into her belly. She collapsed heavily onto Nat's thighs, unable to bear her own weight any longer.

Nat chuckled. "Oh, you nasty thing. Do you like being fucked in the *ass*?"

Cheeks burning, Emily hurried to rise back up, but Nat held her down upon her lap. Her hand continued to pump slowly between Emily's thighs, fingers thrust deep. Emily squirmed around, wishing for more direct stimulation to her g-spot. But she knew Nat wouldn't reward her that easily.

Aware that Nat required an answer, Emily spoke honestly. "I don't know, mistress."

"You don't know?" Nat looked skeptical.

"Mistress, I've never…done that before." It was the truth. After a fair amount of internal debate as she filled out her questionnaire, she had requested some light anal play. She was nervous about the prospect, but also excited. The act figured heavily into her fantasies, though she'd never felt comfortable enough to ask for it in real life. "So I honestly don't know if I like it."

Desire darkened Nat's eyes. She pulled out of Emily's pussy, maneuvering so that the pads of her fingers brushed over the sensitive pucker of Emily's anus. "Well, you're about to find out."

Shivering, Emily whispered, "Yes, mistress." She kept her head down as Nat squirted soap onto her hand, then continued to massage her in a way she'd never experienced before. Greedy for more contact, she lifted up subtly, tilting her hips to give Nat better access. At first Nat seemed content to apply light pressure to her tight opening, but when Emily rocked against her with increasing urgency, she growled and pushed slightly inside. Emily choked out a gasp, surprised by how foreign it felt to have Nat there.

"Relax, darling." Nat pressed an open-mouthed kiss to her throat. "I want this to feel good for you, too." She wiggled her fingertip. "Relax and let me inside."

Emily took a deep breath and willed her body to loosen up. Unfortunately, being cradled on the lap of the hottest butch she'd ever seen in reality didn't exactly inspire calm. Inspiration struck. "Mistress, may I rub my clit?"

Sharp teeth scraped over her neck. "Yes, you may." She continued to move inside of Emily, but didn't attempt to push deeper. "But do *not* make yourself come." Nat raised her head and met Emily's eyes. "That's something only I can give you. And you haven't even come close to earning it yet."

The words alone made her rock harder against Nat's hand, causing Nat's long finger to slide deeper inside her ass. "Oh," Emily murmured, then quickly brought her hand to her clit and rubbed herself unselfconsciously. Warm pleasure spread through her lower body, stoking the flames of her lust even higher. She hoped Nat wouldn't make her stop touching her pussy anytime soon. It had never felt so good.

Nat brought her thumb up to play with Emily's labia, then down to tease the opening of her pussy. Emily bit her lip and rode Nat's fingers, moaning, in awe of how quickly she was peaking. Just as she decided that she was actually approaching orgasm, Nat went still.

Emily was instantly, undeniably frustrated. Why had she ever asked to have release withheld? "Please, mistress." She ground down on Nat's hand. "Just a little more, please."

Nat carefully extracted her finger from Emily's ass, then removed her hand from between her thighs. She pushed gently on Emily's shoulders, forcing her to back off. "No, that's enough. You're nice and clean now."

Clean was the last thing she felt. At this point, she wanted to come so badly she would do anything Nat asked. Anything. Taking another chance, she touched Nat's firm thigh beneath the bubbles. "Mistress, please. Just—"

Nat seized her upper arm in an iron grip. Her free hand lashed out and slapped one tender breast, then the other. The blows weren't overly painful, but the harsh punishment startled Emily into stunned silence. "Enough."

Nat radiated a calm, self-possessed confidence that allowed Emily to adjust to the escalation in intensity with ease. She had asked for this—and it was definitely turning her on. Her pussy ached, her nipples were tight, and her entire body trembled in anticipation. Slight anxiety remained, but her fear was gone. Nat would do everything she could to make sure that Emily felt safe— she was sure of it.

Nat smoothed her hand over the stinging flesh surrounding Emily's nipple. "I told you I'd make you beg for it. Funny, I didn't realize you'd get there so *quickly*. You really are a dirty, fucking slut." She ran her gaze down the length of Emily's naked, soapy body. "It's going to take more than moaning 'please, mistress' like a bitch in heat to convince me to let you come. You're going to have to do as I say. *Everything* I say."

"Yes, mistress." Chest heaving, Emily fought to regain control. They still had a ways to go with this fantasy, and Nat wouldn't grant her release anytime soon. Her only choice was to enjoy the journey.

"Of course."

"Get out of the tub."

Emily immediately stood up, then froze when she realized that Nat wasn't following. She remained seated, staring up at Emily's body in an unflinching appraisal. Unnerved by the scrutiny, Emily quickly stepped out of the tub before Nat could reprimand her for disobeying. Since Nat hadn't told her what to do next, she stood, dripping on the rug. Waiting for instruction.

"Towels are next to the sink." Nat reclined against the back of the tub, looking utterly relaxed. "Get them."

Shivering, Emily hurried to pick up two fluffy towels. She desperately wanted to shake one out and wrap it around her exposed flesh, but that would be a mistake. When she'd laid out this encounter, she had intended for orgasm denial to function as punishment. That was back when she'd imagined she would be tempted to test limits. But she wasn't. Right now Nat held all the power, and Emily wanted only to please her.

She offered a towel to Nat. "Would you like me to dry you, mistress?"

Nat chuckled. "She learns fast." She stood, sending water to sluice down her hard-yet-soft curves. "Sure."

Hands shaking, Emily unfolded a towel and smoothed it over Nat's body. She kept her touch light, thrilling at the way Nat's throat tensed when she brushed over tight nipples. Her breath hitched as the urge to drop the towel and simply touch Nat's skin threatened to overwhelm her.

"Thank you." Nat caught her wrist. "That's enough." She stepped out of the tub and took the other towel, spinning Emily around to dry her.

Emily bit her lip at the delicious friction created by the plush fabric against her sensitive flesh. Nat's brusque rubdown made it difficult to stay on her feet. She swayed slightly, then gasped when Nat dropped the towel and wrapped her in a possessive embrace. Body flush against her back, Nat pressed a kiss to the side of her neck.

"Just how long *has* it been?" Capturing Emily's nipples between her fingertips, Nat twisted until she elicited a high-pitched cry. "Months? Years?"

"Years," Emily whispered. "Mistress."

"Almost like being a virgin again." Nat nipped at her earlobe, dropping a hand to comb through the trimmed hairs between Emily's thighs. "How exciting for me."

It took all of her willpower not to spread her legs for Nat. "Yes, mistress."

"Are you frightened?"

Good question. The answer was yes, but she wasn't sure she wanted to admit her fear. It had more to do with her pathetic insecurities than the prospect of being fucked, anyway. "I...the anticipation is killing me, mistress."

Nat grabbed Emily's pussy, gripping her lightly. "Me, too." Then she released her and opened the bathroom door. "Come along."

Emily followed Nat down the hallway to a closed door. Nat caught her hand, pushed open the door, and strode inside an attractively decorated bedroom. The décor was light and casual—nothing like the torture chamber she had envisioned in her most paranoid fantasies of what paying for kinky sex might mean. The familiarity of the bedroom immediately put her at ease.

Until she spotted a table full of sex toys in the corner.

Nat tugged her closer to the bed. "Kneel," she said, pointing at the rug beside it.

Emily obeyed, trying not to let her eyes stray to the mind-boggling assortment of dildos, paddles, and other gear she'd glimpsed on the way in. Just what was Nat planning to do to her? She'd asked for some strap-on play and spanking, but the dizzying array of toys suggested a far more extensive encounter than she'd paid for. Curiosity piqued, she clenched her fists and waited to see what would happen next.

Nat lifted her right foot to rest on the edge of the mattress, nearly bumping Emily's chin with her slick, swollen folds. She glanced up into Nat's face, seeking permission. Rather than speak, Nat placed her hand on the back of Emily's head and pulled her in roughly.

"Lick me, slut," Nat growled.

Emily went to work with an enthusiastic moan. She loved performing oral sex, and she was thrilled to be able to make up for lost time. Nat tasted so light and delicious, and despite what seemed like a herculean effort not to react, she was exquisitely responsive. Her entire body quaked every time Emily circled her clit with her tongue.

Nat moved her hand to Emily's throat and gripped her gently. "Can't get enough of that, can you?"

Shaking her head, Emily sucked Nat's clit into her mouth, making her shudder. She brought her hands to Nat's firm thighs, hanging on, but Nat batted her away.

"Keep your hands behind your back."

Emily did as Nat commanded, never faltering in her ministrations. She alternated between long, hard licks up Nat's length and gentle, insistent suction on her distended clit. The trembling of Nat's thighs intensified with every pass, assuring her that she was most definitely pleasing her mistress. Somehow, that meant everything.

"Fuck." Nat groaned. "That's my good girl." She tangled her fingers in Emily's hair, forcing her mouth lower. "Put your tongue inside me."

Angling her head, Emily stiffened her tongue and pushed it into Nat's opening. Immediately, Nat cried out, reached for her clit, and rubbed hard until she contracted in pleasure. This orgasm was much more unrestrained—and louder—than the first one in the front hallway. Eyes closed, Emily couldn't suppress a grin at the heady sensation of making her intense, confident mistress come apart at the seams. She'd never felt so powerful.

Abruptly, Nat grasped Emily's chin and lowered her foot to the ground. Then she stepped away, chest heaving. "I'll be right back. You…stay right there. And behave."

"Yes, mistress." She met Nat's eyes and swiped her upper lip with her tongue, smiling at the flavor that lingered there. "Thank you. Again."

"Fuck," Nat breathed, exhaling in a rush. She ran her gaze over Emily's body, then shook her head, smoothing a hand over her shaved head. "My pleasure."

Emily hid her smile until Nat left the room. Once the bedroom door closed, she brought her hand to her chest, overcome by a rush of pure happiness. How incredibly *fun* that had been. How sinfully *hot*. This was exactly what she needed. When she served Nat, nothing else existed. Not the demands of her job or the terrible pressure of raising her younger sister. There was just her body, and Nat's, and the pleasure of letting go.

Exhaling, she glanced over her shoulder, trying to get a better look at the table full of sexual implements. She itched to investigate while Nat was out of the room. Tonight's fantasy included strap-on sex, yet another new experience. She couldn't help wondering what the dildo would look like. How big it would be. Would she really enjoy it?

Even having designed this encounter, Emily felt her anxiety rise as she wondered what would happen next. She'd answered questions and outlined erotic acts and dialogue she wanted to enjoy, but it was up to the agency—and the escort—to bring those elements together to create a uniquely tailored fantasy. That meant that although she knew *what* would happen, generally, she had no idea *when*. Strictly regimented by nature, Emily couldn't help feeling unsettled about the uncertainty of the evening.

Taking a peek at the toys would at least remove some of her hesitation surrounding the rest of the night. She'd be quick. Nat would never know.

And if she got caught…well, she was pretty sure she could handle her punishment. With pleasure.

CHAPTER THREE

Nat Swayne fled the bedroom on rubbery legs. Her first instinct after an orgasm like she'd just had was to collapse on the bed and recover. Since that wasn't an option, a speedy escape would have to do. She'd actually already planned on leaving the room at this point in the encounter, hoping to give Emily some time to stew in anticipation—and perhaps even disobey the order to stay put. As it turned out, she was the one who needed a moment of respite.

She had just done something completely unplanned, something so far outside her norm that she didn't know how to feel about it. She'd asked Emily Parker to penetrate her. Sure, it was only her tongue, and yeah, Emily had been on her knees in submission at the time—but still. She didn't demand that from clients. Ever.

Penetration was something she occasionally enjoyed, but only when she was alone. There was a time when she'd had sex with men for money, and that act was rarely negotiable. She'd never liked how it made her feel. These days, she could choose her clients—women only—and set her own limits, so she no longer did anything that made her feel vulnerable. Being penetrated was an intimacy she had chosen to reserve for someone she genuinely trusted, should that woman ever come along. Despite her admittedly rough past, Nat still held out hope that she would appear.

A half hour with a client wasn't nearly enough time to build trust, so her impulsive command to Emily baffled her. As good as this particular client was with her mouth, as perfectly cute and sweet as she seemed, Nat didn't understand why she had so easily lowered her defenses.

On paper, Emily Parker was her dream client. Her sexual turn-ons almost perfectly complemented Nat's—where she liked taking charge, Emily clearly yearned to have her own sense of control stripped away. Reviewing Emily's file had actually excited her, which didn't happen often. The photograph that Janis had taken during their initial appointment revealed a very pretty girl-next-door—blond-haired, brown-eyed, with light freckles spattered across her nose. Nat would notice her across a room, but never approach someone like her.

Emily Parker appeared to be a preschool teacher, or a cupcake decorator in a chic bakery, or something similarly innocent and good-natured. In other words, she appeared to be Nat's polar opposite. While Nat found that wildly attractive and infinitely exciting, she was fairly certain that a woman like Emily wouldn't be interested in someone like her—at least not for more than a one-night stand. And as ironic as most people seemed to find it, she wasn't really into casual sex.

Hoping to walk off her strange lapse, Nat headed for the kitchen. She craved a beer, but would have to settle for water. Drinking was strictly forbidden during work, not that she was much of a drinker, anyway. She'd engaged in her fair share of stupidity as a teenager, but at nearly thirty, she'd outgrown the easy escape of sex and substances.

She pulled two bottles of water out of the refrigerator that Janis kept fully stocked. This condo was one of a few that the Xtreme Encounters agency leased for all-night appointments, and it was a nice place, if a bit more posh than Nat would choose for herself. Her clients seemed to love it, though.

On her way out of the kitchen, she glanced at the counter where she'd left Emily's file. She reached to pick it up, then stopped. Having already memorized its slim contents—the questionnaire, the health-screening results, the adorable snapshot—she knew it didn't contain any answers. Nothing in there would tell her why Emily Parker affected her so powerfully.

Asking for penetration hadn't been her first lapse. The first was in the car, when Emily had asked her name. She never gave her real name to clients. Never, until tonight. It had just fallen out of her mouth, as though her brain were insisting that Emily should know something real about her. She'd surprised herself with the disclosure. Perhaps she'd done it because Emily seemed so nervous. Maybe she'd been trying to comfort a woman who clearly didn't have a lot of experience with this type of thing. Whatever the reason, revealing something so personal was out of character.

Two extensions of unearned and instinctive trust to a perfect stranger in one night. Nat snorted. She almost felt like a kid again.

Forcing away her slight unease, Nat walked back to the bedroom. There was nothing wrong with telling Emily her name, much less demanding that Emily put her tongue to good use. This was a woman she actually wanted to fuck. She might as well go with her gut and enjoy their evening together. This situation didn't often arise in her line of work, so she damn sure didn't plan to let her emotional baggage ruin her good time.

Before entering the room, she quietly placed her hand on the knob and put on her game face. It was possible that Emily was still kneeling on the floor where she had placed her. But if she wasn't, Nat needed to react swiftly and with confidence. The scene depended upon it. Taking a breath, she threw open the door and stepped inside.

Emily hadn't disappointed—she wasn't where Nat had left her. She visibly startled when Nat entered the room, jumping away from the table of toys she had been perusing. Immediately her gaze went to the place where she was supposed to be, then she looked back at Nat, eyes widening. Her genuine surprise and confusion was so cute that Nat wanted to laugh out loud. Moments like these made her glad she'd cultivated some respectable acting skills.

Without smiling, Nat strode across the room and seized Emily's upper arm in a tight grip. She paid close attention to Emily's breathing and her body language as she squeezed, gauging her desired pain level. Emily's fantasy contained elements of BDSM, including spanking, light slapping, and verbal humiliation, but Nat didn't sense that she wanted to be *hurt*. Nat had worked for clients who got off on real pain, even the drawing of blood, but Emily seemed like a woman who wanted to skirt the edge of actual pain and danger, yet still feel safe. Nat was all too happy to oblige—that was her favorite way to play.

Emily's lips parted and a tiny gasp escaped, making Nat shiver. The sound triggered clenching pleasure between her legs, and she had to grit her teeth not to react out loud. "Where are you supposed to be?"

Emily opened then closed her mouth, clearly at a loss for words.

Nat slapped her sharply on the bottom and Emily yelped. She repeated, "Where are you supposed to be?"

"Over there, mistress." Emily gestured without meeting her gaze. "On the ground."

"Like an obedient slut, isn't that right?" Turning them to face the table, Nat pressed against Emily's back and nipped at her shoulder. She pushed her hips into Emily's bare bottom, indulging in a brief moment of fantasy about strapping on her cock later. "What were you looking at, slut? Tell me."

Emily shivered and opened her mouth, but no words emerged. Energized by her hesitation, Nat moved forward slightly, pinning her to the table. Emily gripped the edge as she was thrown off-balance. "Nothing, mistress."

"Nothing?" Deciding to toy with Emily a bit, Nat trailed a string of gentle kisses across the back of her neck. She eased away, allowing Emily to push off from the table. "Really, darling?" Not waiting for a response, she placed her hand on Emily's hip, slid it across her belly, then moved down to cradle between her thighs. "Nothing?" When Emily bit her lip and leaned back slightly, Nat kissed her throat, then tightened her grip on Emily's mound roughly. "You must think I'm stupid."

"No, mistress—"

Nat used the narrow space between Emily's hips and the table to deliver a quick slap to her pussy. Hips jerking, Emily cried out in surprise. The noise lanced through Nat, filling her with heady power. She brought her lips to Emily's ear. "Standing in front of a table full of sex toys and you expect me to believe you were looking at *nothing*? How could that be? Who would believe such a silly lie?"

Emily shook her head, but before she could offer an explanation, Nat pushed her against the table again and grabbed her hands, dragging them forward to trap them against the wooden surface. Bringing her mouth to Emily's ear, Nat murmured, "I'm not stupid. Do you understand?"

"Yes, mistress." Emily's bare whisper contained a trace of fear, but her excitement was more than obvious. The scent of her arousal permeated the scant space between them, and Nat could feel slick wetness painting her skin where their lower bodies touched. Emily shifted, grinding her ass into Nat's hips. "You're right, mistress. I'm sorry."

"You're sorry a lot, aren't you?" Enjoying the way Emily squirmed against her, Nat waited a moment before reluctantly releasing her right hand. "Show me what you were looking at."

Emily hesitated before pointing at a peach-colored dildo. "That, mistress."

It wasn't the biggest cock on the table, but not the smallest, either. Interesting. Nat knew from Emily's questionnaire that tonight would be her first experience with strap-on play. She appreciated the bold choice. "Very nice." Tracing a fingernail down the length of Emily's arm, she said, "Did you look at anything else?"

Emily nodded.

"Tell me," Nat demanded.

Emily's hand shook as she picked up a leather paddle. "This, mistress."

Nat didn't bother to suppress her grin this time. "Is that why you disobeyed me? You wanted to be punished?"

Biting her lip, Emily turned her head to briefly meet Nat's gaze. "No, mistress."

"But you know I need to correct you now. Don't you?"

Emily exhaled. "Of course, mistress."

Nat stepped away from the table. "Come on, then." She walked to the bed and sat on the edge of the mattress, then patted her thighs. "Lie across my lap."

Emily's face reddened. Precious, Nat thought, considering that she was the one who had requested an over-the-knee spanking. She leered when Emily folded her arms over her bare breasts, so innocently demure.

Earlier Emily had needed reassurance, but now she seemed to need an unwavering show of strength. "I'm *not* asking." She waited a beat. "The longer you wait, girl…" Since Emily's imagination would fill in the blanks better than she ever could, Nat left the threat unfinished.

Emily took a tentative step forward, playing with her fingers nervously. Hesitating, she took a deep breath. Nat could practically hear her internal pep talk. After a moment, Emily threw back her shoulders, exhaled, then crawled onto the bed and across Nat's lap.

"Goddamn," Nat murmured, taking a moment to survey the sensual, feminine landscape of Emily's body. Her bottom was deliciously round, perfect for spanking. Nat rubbed light patterns over one cheek, then the other, drawing out the anticipation of the first blow. "You are a sweet little thing, aren't you?"

Emily's breathing hitched. "Yes, mistress."

"I'd use that paddle you were eyeing, except I want you to feel my hand warming your ass. I'm not going to lie—I plan on enjoying every second of this." Nat used her free hand to grip the back of Emily's neck and hold her against the mattress. The heat from Emily's flushed skin scorched her fingers and unleashed a surge of primal desire. Deciding to take a chance and ad-lib slightly, she issued a command from her own BDSM repertoire. "Count off each blow."

"Okay, mistress." Now Emily's voice was a bare whisper.

Delighted by the way Emily trembled under her caress, Nat drew back and delivered a firm smack with a cupped hand. The blow was meant to be felt, but not cause real pain. She would start out slow and, depending upon how Emily reacted, increase the intensity by degrees.

Emily whimpered. "One."

"Good girl." Nat rubbed the spot she'd just slapped, then drew back to smack the other cheek. She waited for Emily's breathless "Two" before saying, "You have a lovely bottom."

"Thank you, mistress." Wiggling, Emily spread her legs slightly, allowing Nat to confirm that she wasn't the only one enjoying this.

Pleased that Emily was beginning to relax, Nat immediately went back to the first cheek with another sharp slap. Emily flinched, and before she could call off the number, Nat spanked her again.

"Three. Four." The words came out clipped and tense, but Emily arched her back, offering up her ass for more. Clearly she was loving what Nat was giving her.

God, Nat wanted to fuck her. So innocently pretty, such a good girl, but so responsive to rough play. She wasn't sure it was right to accept money for tonight when it was honestly fulfilling both their fantasies.

Upping the ante with blow number five, Nat delivered a hard, stinging slap to tender skin that was already beginning to turn pink. Gasping, Emily tried to roll her hips away on instinct, but Nat kept her in place with the hand on her neck. "Count," she reminded Emily in a stern voice.

"Five." The quaver in Emily's voice hinted at tears. She remained silent and stoic, resting obediently over Nat's lap, but it was clear that the last smack had been intense.

Time to work on heightening Emily's arousal. The more turned on she was, the easier it would be to receive physical punishment. Nat slipped her hand between Emily's thighs, dragging two fingers up over her drenched folds. "You're wet." She brought her hand to Emily's mouth. "Taste."

Emily took Nat's fingers between her lips, laving them with the warm tongue that Nat so vividly remembered inside her. When Nat withdrew, Emily said, "Thank you, mistress."

Nat returned to Emily's pussy without answering. She spread her swollen labia open, traced the intricate contours of her sex, then teased her thoroughly without venturing inside or lingering on her impressively erect clit. Emily had asked to have her orgasm withheld, a form of torture Nat personally couldn't stand but took perverse delight in delivering.

"Why the fuck are you so wet?" Gently, Nat captured Emily's labia and gave the slick flesh a light tug. "Do you like being punished?"

Emily hesitated. "No...no, mistress."

Nat released her, pulling back to rain down four hard slaps on Emily's bottom, alternating from cheek to cheek. "You're lying. Aren't you?"

Coming up on her elbows, Emily glanced back over her shoulder and met Nat's eyes. Dark and needy, Emily's shone with unshed tears. "Six, seven, eight, nine."

"Are you being smart again?" Nat hardened her tone even as she rubbed Emily's bottom to soothe the pain.

"No, mistress. I'm counting."

She couldn't let herself grin, even if she did appreciate Emily Parker's sass. Staying in character, Nat narrowed her eyes and rumbled, "Spread your fucking legs, slut."

True to her own submissive role, Emily lowered her head to rest against the mattress again before slowly easing her thighs apart. "Yes, mistress."

"Count these." Without preamble, Nat pushed two fingers into Emily's snug opening. She stopped when she was buried as deep as she could go, reveling in Emily's surprised moan. When it became clear that Emily wasn't going to do as she'd asked, Nat said, "That was *one*." She pulled out and thrust back inside, harder this time. "And *two*."

"Two," Emily echoed. "Mistress."

"Clever girl," Nat murmured, then pressed into her again.

"Three." Emily brought her hands up to cover her face as Nat continued to fuck her. "Four, five, six, seven...eight...n-nine, ten."

By the end of the series of deep, deliberate strokes, Emily was whimpering with pleasure. Nat pulled out and unleashed a flurry of slaps across both buttocks. Crying out, Emily brought her hands down and tried to protect her sensitive flesh. Nat reacted without hesitation, capturing Emily's wrists in her free hand and holding them against her waist. She followed up with only two more smacks, then paused to make sure Emily was still with her.

"Do you like being punished?" Nat repeated.

Emily struggled within her grasp before sagging in defeat. "Yes, mistress."

"Bad girl." Nat slapped her lightly, low on her bottom, her fingers making wet contact with Emily's labia. Emily jerked in surprise. "What kind of woman enjoys being taken over a stranger's knee and spanked like this?" Nat tapped her pussy again, hard enough to startle but not to cause real pain. Her fingers came away coated in Emily's slick juices. Nat let go of Emily's wrists so she could spread her open with both hands, exposing engorged pink flesh and thrillingly abundant wetness. "You deserve every last thing I'm going to do to you tonight."

"I know, mistress." Thighs quaking, Emily pressed her hips down on Nat's lap as though seeking friction.

"Oh, do you want to come?" Nat spanked her hard once, then followed up with multiple lighter slaps. "Is that what your body is telling me? What happened to the girl who couldn't take off her clothes for me? Who I had to force into her car against her will?" She slipped her hand between Emily's thighs, pushing her thumb inside her opening and gliding her fingers up to press against her hard clit. "Where did that good girl go?"

Emily bucked against her hand, pumping her hips as though hoping to encourage Nat to fuck her again. Then she stilled. "I don't know, mistress." The vulnerability in her words threatened to loosen Nat's control on her character. Usually it wasn't hard to stay in a scene. With Emily, Nat couldn't stop worrying about how she was feeling, if she was okay. It was less like being with a client and more like caring deeply for a lover.

Not allowing herself to dwell on thoughts that could upset her professionalism, Nat soldiered on. She rubbed the pads of her fingers over Emily's slippery clit, circling the tip of her thumb inside her opening. "Fuck my hand. Fuck my hand like you want me to fuck you."

She could *feel* Emily's embarrassment as she began rocking her hips. At first her movements were self-conscious, but soon enough Emily jerked against Nat with unabashed enthusiasm, clearly building toward climax. Nat slapped her ass hard with her other hand, drawing out a throaty moan.

"Don't you dare come." Nat gave her an extra-hard smack when she stopped abruptly. "Don't you dare stop, either. Show me what a nasty, horny slut you are."

Emily pushed herself up on her elbows again, riding Nat's hand in measured rhythm. Nat angled her thumb to penetrate Emily deeper and wiggled her fingertips in lazy patterns over Emily's labia and clit. Keening, Emily pumped her hips madly before freezing mid-thrust, her entire body trembling.

Nat delivered a swift, heavy smack that made Emily choke out a gasp. "I told you not to stop."

"Yes, mistress." Emily remained tense. "I know, mistress, but…if I keep doing that, I'll come, and you told me not to do that, either…" She hung her head. "I don't want to disobey you. I swear."

Nat believed her completely. She pulled her hand from Emily's pussy and, unable to resist, licked her fingers clean. Emily tasted delicious in a way that didn't surprise her in the least. She couldn't wait to sample her flavor straight from the source. Nat gave her one more swat on the behind. "Stand up."

Emily rushed to obey, nearly losing her balance as she struggled to her feet. She stood in front of Nat with her eyes lowered to the ground, her face nearly as pink as her ass. When she laced her fingers in front of her trimmed thatch of curls, the delightful show of vulnerability stirred Nat's darkest lust.

"Did you see the anal toys on that table?"

Blinking rapidly, Emily shot to attention. "Yes, mistress."

"Choose one and bring it to me. Don't forget the bottle of lube."

"I…won't, mistress." Emily swallowed, then turned to approach the table with obvious trepidation.

Even before learning that Emily had no prior experience with anal penetration, Nat had decided to offer her a range of options. Unless she knew that a new client was particularly adventurous, she preferred to allow them the opportunity to determine their own limits for the first encounter. That not only made her client more comfortable, but often the choice revealed vital information she could use to her advantage.

As Emily studied the selection of toys, Nat tilted her head and admired the red handprints she'd left on her luscious bottom. She was a sucker for a nice ass, and Emily's was perfection. She couldn't wait to run her tongue over every dip and curve, to make Emily squirm. Given the chance, Nat would worship her ass with a level of devotion she suspected Emily couldn't conceive of. She'd happily do it for free.

Emily turned and caught her staring. She hid her smile when Nat hardened her expression, then quickly lowered her gaze to the floor.

Clearing her throat, Nat said, "Bring it here." Emily crossed the room and handed her the bottle of lube and a slim purple plug—once again, not the biggest on the table, but not the smallest. "Nice choice."

"Thank you, mistress."

"Back on my lap," Nat said, patting her thighs.

Emily crawled into place without hesitation. She folded her arms on the mattress and rested her head upon them, then took a deep breath.

"This will be easier if you relax," Nat reminded her, and waited for her to exhale. She uncapped the bottle of lube. "Spread yourself open for me."

Emily obeyed. Though she couldn't see her face, Nat imagined she was closing her eyes as she gripped her buttocks and exposed her puckered opening to the cool air. Pouring a generous amount of lube onto her fingers, Nat rubbed them together to warm the thick liquid, then carefully stroked the tight ring of muscle. She probed at her cautiously, thrilled to find her open and receptive to the gentle invasion of her fingertip to the first knuckle.

She used her free hand to stroke Emily's blond hair. "You're doing so well, darling."

"Thank you."

Deciding not to reprimand Emily for forgetting to use her title, Nat slid in deeper. Emily groaned and rocked back onto her finger, taking her in all the way. Chuckling, Nat withdrew then pressed back inside. "You sure you've never done this before?"

"Yes, mistress."

"So you're just a natural at taking it in the ass?" Nat tightened her fingers in Emily's hair and tugged. Time to unleash some of the harder language Emily had requested to see how it would be received. "Look at you, cunt dripping, fucking my finger like a goddamn anal whore." Despite her rough language, she kept her thrusts slow and gentle, allowing Emily to set the pace with her counter-motion. "Nasty little bitch."

Emily moaned loudly, unrelenting in her wanton movements. "Yes, mistress."

"Are you ready for something bigger?" Nat withdrew her finger to the tip, released Emily's hair to squeeze more lube into her hand, then pressed back in with two fingers. She moved torturously slow, pleased that Emily was still relaxed. "Sure you are, darling. Ask for something bigger."

"May I...may I have something bigger, mistress?"

"Of course you may, you fucking slut." Nat removed her fingers, squirting still more lube on the slim plug Emily had chosen. "And you'll keep it there until I make you come."

Emily's breathing stuttered as Nat swirled the lubricated tip of the toy around her anus. "Yes, mistress," she whispered.

Nat bit her lip as she pushed the toy inside. She darted her gaze to Emily's shoulders, her hands, the back of her head, trying to monitor her reaction to the penetration. Anal sex could quickly turn unpleasant, especially for the uninitiated, and she wanted this to be a positive, pleasurable experience from start to finish. "Does that feel good? The truth."

"So good, mistress."

Emboldened by the naked desire in Emily's throaty voice, Nat drove the plug in as deep as it could go. "You took that like a naughty girl, didn't you?" She brushed Emily's hands away from her bottom, then gave each cheek a firm swat. Emily cried out in surprise, no doubt feeling every inch of the toy. "Stand up."

Emily stumbled as she got to her feet. She stood stiffly, clearly trying to acclimate to the unfamiliar sensation of the silicone plug inside her. Her face was flushed, her hair tousled and wild. Nat recognized the desperate, clouded look in her eyes—the fog of sex that had settled over her. Emily Parker needed to come, and she needed to come *now*.

Nat's nostrils flared at the heady power of being the one who could grant Emily the release she so clearly craved. She stood and pointed at the bed. "Lie on your back." As Emily rushed to comply, Nat walked to the table to retrieve a set of fur-lined wrist cuffs. "And raise your hands."

When she turned around with the restraints in hand, the sight of Emily spread out on the bed—naked and so very unguarded, brown eyes dewy with trust—struck her dumb. And she suddenly, uncharacteristically, became nervous. Her breath caught in her throat, her heart began to race, and for the first time in her professional life, she faltered and nearly broke character.

Goddamn. Was this...*performance anxiety?*

She wanted to please Emily. Like, *really* wanted to in a way that went beyond taking pride in her work. She wanted to make Emily's whole body shake with pleasure, to give her the best sex of her life. She *needed* to feel as though she'd earned the money she no longer even wanted to accept. The night might have started as a simple business transaction, but she couldn't deny that it had turned at least a little personal. She wanted to fuck this woman, and she wanted Emily to always remember how it felt.

Emily fidgeted, breaking Nat out of her stupor. Straightening, she put on her game face and strode to the bed, raising the cuffs in the air so Emily could see. She refused to come across as anything other than a compassionate but firm professional. Emily hadn't paid for the privilege of having a sex worker develop an adolescent crush on her, and letting her silly infatuation be known would certainly put a damper on an evening Emily had spent a lot of money to enjoy.

Sitting on the edge of the bed, Nat took Emily's wrist and fitted it inside a cuff. Rather than avoid Emily's gaze, she stared directly into her eyes. She projected powerful, unrelenting strength, just as Emily's fantasy required. Predictably, to her relief, Emily submissively shifted her attention to her wrists as Nat tied them to the corners of the headboard.

Once she had Emily secured, Nat grasped her chin tightly. "Not going anywhere now, are you?"

"No, mistress," Emily whispered. She gave one wrist a subtle shake, as though testing her bonds.

Nat laughed, releasing Emily's chin. She flicked her hand across the tip of Emily's breast, slapping a rock-hard nipple. Moaning, Emily arched her back and tugged harder against the cuffs. "Try to get away." Nat slapped her other breast, drawing out a breathless, excited cry that made her clit throb. "Do it, slut. Try to get away from me. Before I really punish you." She slapped her twice more, once on each breast.

Emily began to struggle against her restraints, nostrils flaring and legs kicking. In one of her more personal answers on the agency's questionnaire, Emily had revealed that her fantasies were driven by a deep need to have control taken away in a situation where she felt safe. Their safe word—*unicorn*—ensured her security. Nat's job was to make Emily feel powerless in a way that fulfilled her most secret desires. Asking her to try to escape was the perfect way to drive home the fact that she was at Nat's mercy. From the way Emily's chest began heaving and her movement became erratic, Nat could see that she'd gotten the message.

Now it was time to stop her panic. Grabbing Emily's shoulders, Nat pinned her against the bed and stopped her upper body's struggle. Emily continued to kick her legs until Nat shifted, trapping Emily under the weight of her naked, painfully aroused body. Ignoring her whimper of defeat, Nat slipped her thigh between Emily's and grinned at the feeling of slick juices coating her skin.

"You're not going anywhere," Nat murmured. Seeing real anxiety in Emily's eyes, she bent to kiss one corner of her mouth, then the other. "You look so frightened, but I'm willing to bet that if I uncuffed you right now, dressed you, and offered you a ride home…" She rocked her hips into Emily's, and Emily mirrored her movement. "Well, what would you say?"

Emily drew her lips into a thin line. Nat sensed her hesitation and thrust against her again. Exhaling, Emily whispered, "I would say no, thank you. Mistress."

"Because you want to be fucked?"

Emily turned her head to the side and closed her eyes. Nat stared, fascinated, at the play of emotion across her beautiful face. "Yes, mistress."

"Say it."

"I want to be fucked."

Taking Emily's chin in her hand, Nat returned her head to its original position. Then she slapped her cheek, just hard enough to startle Emily into opening her eyes. "Look at me," Nat said. "Look at me and say it again."

Nat regretted the command as soon as she uttered it, because when Emily stared up at her—*into* her, more like—the intensity in her eyes threatened to derail Nat completely. Beneath her, Emily seemed to relax. "I want you to fuck me, mistress."

It took Nat the span of a couple of breaths to switch her brain back on. She blinked, then released Emily's chin, caressing the side of her face instead. Instinct screamed at her to kiss Emily, because she had never wanted someone this badly without giving in to the urge to connect in that most intimate way. She rarely kissed clients—yet she'd already succumbed once tonight. Earlier it had been to reassure Emily, but now there was no reason to go back for more except to satisfy her own desire.

"Mistress," Emily whispered. Her eyes burned with the same hunger that gnawed at Nat's belly.

Nat lowered her head and pressed her lips to Emily's. The breathy moan that met her, and the warm, wet bliss of Emily's tongue coming out to greet her, chased away any thought of holding back. Nat moved her hands to Emily's hair, stroking reverently as she luxuriated in the decadent pleasure of kissing a sweet, beautiful woman.

They broke the kiss mutually some time later, both of them gasping, Nat struck speechless at the sheer perfection of their make-out session. Her thigh had worked its way between Emily's legs, and she could feel the slippery heat of her sex pressed against her skin. Emily's hips jerked, her entire body tensing in a way that Nat now realized meant she was trying to hold back an impending climax.

The desire to further stave off Emily's orgasm propelled Nat into action. She rolled off Emily and got out of bed, once again weak in the knees. If she managed to survive this appointment without making a total fool of herself, she'd consider herself lucky. Emily Parker was something special, no doubt.

Exhaling, Nat rasped, "I'll be right back. You stay here and think about what I'm going to do to you when I return."

In a similarly breathless voice, Emily said, "I will, mistress."

Nat shivered. Time to go wash her hands and take a quick walk around the penthouse. Whatever it took to get her head on straight, because when she came back, she planned on rocking Emily Parker's world.

CHAPTER FOUR

A s soon as Nat walked out of the bedroom, Emily slammed her eyes shut. She was in a state of sensory overload, and adding visual stimulation to the mix was just too much. Her skin tingled in all the places Nat had spanked and slapped, and her pussy literally throbbed, open and dripping and so mournfully, terribly empty. Her wrists burned from struggling against the cuffs, and the sensation of the plug inside her ass made her feel crazy, frantic for an orgasm. She was nothing but pure sensation, intellect stripped away for the night—just as she'd wanted.

And that kiss Nat had just given her? She didn't even know how that made her feel. Warm all over. Lonely. Infatuated.

Emily took a deep breath, then exhaled. So far, tonight had exceeded all her wildest hopes. Not only was she enjoying every detail of her most secret fantasy, but Nat had made her feel things she never thought possible. She'd kept her expectations for her escort low on purpose, unsure what she would get. But this woman, so sensuously masculine, so strong, was exactly what she'd desired. To top it all off, no matter how rough she became, no matter how convincingly she delivered the crude dialogue Emily had asked to hear, Nat made her feel safe.

And that was crazy, because *nothing* had made her feel safe in a very, very long time—longer than she could remember. She didn't know whether to laugh or cry that it had apparently taken meeting a hooker to discover this type of intimacy and connection.

The bedroom door opened, startling her into awareness. She lifted her head and looked at Nat, who paused in the doorway and stared at her with smoldering eyes. She was magnificent: feminine curves, lean muscle, and darkly handsome features that hid the breathtaking vulnerability Emily had glimpsed more than once. She was fascinating, sexy, mysterious—and worth every penny.

Nat shut the door and walked to the table of toys, turning her back to Emily as she stepped into a leather harness. With Nat's attention focused on strapping on the dildo she had chosen, Emily took advantage of the opportunity to stare. Nat's well-defined ass was a thing of beauty. She yearned to sink her teeth into one of her firm cheeks, then taste her pussy again.

"What are you smiling about?" Nat turned, giving Emily her first glimpse of the peach-colored dildo jutting out from between her firm thighs.

Emily's inner muscles clenched at the sight, unleashing shock waves deep inside her ass. What had she been thinking, choosing one so big? But she knew exactly what she'd thought—what she *still* thought. Tonight was a once-in-a-lifetime experience, so she ought to make it count.

Nat sat down on the edge of the bed, tweaking Emily's nipple hard enough to elicit a tiny shock of pain. Her pussy clenched harder this time, threatening to trigger the orgasm she'd been fighting off for what felt like hours now. Without hesitating, Nat tweaked the other one. "I asked you a question. Answer it."

Emily blinked, trying hard to recall what Nat had asked. "I... don't remember, mistress."

"You don't remember what you were smiling about?"

Oh. Well, technically she didn't remember anything right now. Her brain had all but short-circuited. "No, mistress."

"Maybe you were thinking about taking my cock?"

Probably. "Yes, mistress."

Nat shifted farther onto the bed to sit near Emily's legs, which were crossed at the ankles. "Let me see your cunt."

The word—*cunt*—hit Emily in the stomach like a soft punch. She had asked for Nat to use it. And it did turn her on—but it also embarrassed her. Which had been the point of wanting it, she supposed. Nat slapped the inside of her thigh, snapping her out of her self-analysis. She needed to stop thinking and just start reacting.

She spread her legs, shuddering when Nat eased back, tilted her head, and studied her obscenely wet sex with interest. "So pretty," Nat murmured, running her fingers over her labia. "Such a pretty, pink, *wet* cunt." She checked Emily's face as she said the words, smiling at whatever she saw there. "Remember, slut, that you are *not* allowed to come. No matter what I do. No matter how badly you want to."

The words elicited another shudder. That was an extremely tall order. All it would take was the slightest bit of stimulation and she would orgasm. She knew her body well enough to realize that holding off her climax would be impossible. But she also knew she couldn't tell Nat "no" again.

"I understand, mistress. I'll…try my best."

Nat removed her hand from Emily's pussy and dragged her wet fingers across Emily's mouth. "You'll do better than that, my darling. Or I'll make you sorry."

Emily would have more faith in her ability to obey if Nat would only stop being so damn *hot*—and intimidating. Despite her doubts, she said, "Yes, mistress."

"Excellent." Nat crawled between her thighs, lying on her belly. She used her hands to press Emily's knees apart, then stroked her thumbs along sensitive, exposed folds. "You have such a tight little cunt…I need to prepare you for my big, hard cock." She lowered her face and planted a gentle kiss on her labia. "You're going to taste so fucking nice, aren't you?"

"Oh, God," Emily whispered at the touch of Nat's tongue against her clit. It was too much already—she would never be able to withstand an oral assault.

Nat didn't say anything, just pressed in farther and ran her tongue up and down the length of her sex. When Nat stopped to suck gently on her distended clit, the pleasure literally brought tears to Emily's eyes.

"Oh." Emily gasped. "Oh, please stop." She cried out in relief when Nat released her clit, then keened at the sting of a soft hand slapping her aroused sex.

"You don't tell me to stop." Nat lowered her face, lapping at her in defiance. "You don't *ever* tell me stop, do you understand? Your pussy is *mine*." With one last suck of her clit, Nat trailed her tongue down to Emily's opening, then pushed inside. Her other hand found the base of the anal plug, wiggling it gently.

The combined stimulus was almost too much. Hips bucking in pleasure, Emily fought not to give in to her wrenching need. Nat was testing her and she so badly wanted not to fail. Surely Nat would relent soon. She had to realize that everyone had her limit, and Emily was teetering right at the edge of hers. "Yes, mistress." Emily let out a sob of relief when Nat pulled back, then wailed in despair as her hot tongue again circled her clit. "Oh, God, mistress. I...I can't—"

"But you must." Nat grinned up at her, looking so handsome Emily had to curl her toes to forcibly chase away her climax. She slithered her tongue through Emily's wetness, paused long enough to raise an eyebrow, then licked her again. "You *must* be strong. Don't come. Don't let me do this to you."

Emily yanked against the restraints as Nat continued to lick and suck without mercy. She wouldn't be able to stop herself if Nat kept going like this, and there was nothing she could do about that. The harder she struggled, the stronger Nat's grip on her hips became, the more unrelenting her tongue. Her thighs quaked uncontrollably as she fought to twist out of Nat's steel hold.

"No, oh fuck, no, no, no," Emily moaned. She wished her hands were free, that she could use them to grab onto Nat's head and force her mouth away. The sight of Nat kissing her so intimately was just too much, *too much*, so she slammed her eyes closed because it was the only thing she could do. "No, no, no," she whispered. "You need to...or I'll...*fuck*, mistress, *stop*. Please. *Please.*"

And then Nat's fingers were inside her, stretching her open, and she knew Nat wouldn't stop. She was going to force her to come— force her to disobey, to fail. Emily's eyes stung, tears burning their way to the front. Nat's hot, wet mouth was the single most exquisite thing she'd ever felt. Sweat dripped between her breasts, down her neck, as Nat stole the last bit of her control. Orgasm was inevitable. With a hoarse cry, Emily surrendered. Her hips jerked harshly against Nat's face, her body's betrayal triggering a mixture of shame and elation that shattered her. She'd never known this kind of pleasure existed, that another person could make her feel like she was dying—and loving every second of it. She was only dimly aware of how expertly Nat's fingers were stroking her, or how loving her mouth seemed as it explored every inch of her pulsating flesh.

When Emily came down from her peak, she tried to pull away from Nat, who clung to her insistently and continued to feast. Now it really was too much—*just too goddamn much*—and she knew that she could utter one word and end the exquisite torment, but she couldn't bring herself to do it. She didn't want this to end.

Finally Nat released her, leaving her with one last, lingering lick. Emily's stomach muscles twitched and she shuddered as the tension finally eased. Hot tears snaked over her temples and disappeared into her sweat-soaked hair. Her entire body buzzed with the rush of long-absent endorphins.

Thoroughly wrecked, she didn't have the presence of mind to wonder what would happen next until Nat climbed on top of her body and settled between her still-spread thighs. The hard length of the dildo slid against her oversensitive folds, nudging her back into awareness. Nat grabbed hold of her cuffed wrists, still tethered to the bed, and held them against the mattress.

"You are a *very*, *very* naughty girl." Nat shifted her hips, dragging the dildo through Emily's wetness. Then she released one of Emily's wrists, reached between their bodies, and guided the bulbous head to her opening. "I told you not to come."

"I'm sorry," Emily whispered, then cried out as Nat thrust inside her—slowly at first, driving the cock home in one torturous motion. Breathless, Emily arched beneath her and whimpered, "Mistress."

"How should I punish you?" Nat seized Emily's wrist again, pinning her to the bed. She rocked her hips, withdrawing the cock, then forcing it in deeper. "Like this? Fucking you? Should I make you beg me to stop?" Her thrusts increased in strength and tempo, bringing fresh tears to Emily's eyes. "I could fuck you like this all night."

Oh, it was wonderful. Being filled by Nat, taken, used like the horny slut she often fantasized playacting—miles away from the responsible adult she'd had to be for most of her life. Wishing she could wrap her arms around Nat's back, Emily had to content herself with pressing her lips to Nat's shoulder instead. "Yes, mistress. *Fuck*, mistress."

And then Nat stopped moving. Emily cried out in alarm, rocking against her in a futile attempt to keep their rhythm going. Nat simply held her down more firmly. Exhausted, she gave up, accepting that she was at Nat's mercy.

Nat brought her mouth to Emily's ear. "But you *like* being fucked, don't you? The way you're squirming beneath me, this seems less like discipline and more like giving you *exactly* what you want."

Emily's heart thundered at the implication of Nat's words. Was she going to *stop*? Not knowing how to respond, Emily stayed quiet. She didn't want to say the wrong thing, to lose this contact. The thought of having Nat pull out and leave made her want to burst into tears.

Lifting her head, Nat took deep, slow breaths and allowed the silence to stretch out between them. She seemed to search Emily's eyes as Emily searched hers, and Emily's chest swelled, because this was the closest she had felt to another human being, ever. The realization stunned her into silence.

"Should I stop?" Nat murmured.

Emily shook her head, trying not to look as panicked as the question made her feel. She never wanted this closeness to end. "Please, no."

Nat raised an eyebrow.

"No, mistress." She corrected herself in a whisper.

"Why?"

Emily bit her lip hard, fighting back her emotion. Trying to explain how Nat was giving her something so much bigger than physical pleasure would make her sound crazy. Or pathetic. Struggling to articulate, she said, "Because...I don't want you to, mistress."

"Because you like this?" Pulling back with her hips, Nat retreated, then slowly filled her up again. "You like that?" When Emily nodded, Nat murmured, "Then say it."

"I like it, mistress, when you fuck me."

Nat stilled. "With my cock."

With no pride left, Emily said, "I like it when you fuck me with your cock."

"So ask me for it."

Earlier Nat had said she'd make her beg. Clearly she knew what she was doing. Lowering her gaze, Emily said, "Fuck me, mistress. Please, *please* fuck me." More than being fucked, she needed this close human connection, the heavy weight of Nat's body on hers. If she had to grovel to prolong this moment, she would do so gladly. "Don't stop. I don't want you to stop."

Nat's expression softened, and Emily sensed that Nat had recognized the sincere desperation in her words. Rather than be embarrassed, she felt dizzy with relief. All at once, she was sure of at least one thing—Nat wouldn't stop. Over the course of the evening, she had developed a deep trust that this handsome stranger always did the right thing. And now Nat knew that stopping wasn't the right thing, right now.

As though reading her mind, Nat released her grip on Emily's wrists and undid one cuff, then the other. Surprised by the sudden turn of events, Emily didn't dare move, unsure what Nat expected from her. Nat slipped an arm beneath her shoulders, pulled her closer, and said, "Put your hands on me."

Finally given permission to do the very thing she'd been burning to do, Emily wasted no time. She wrapped her arms around Nat's strong back and clutched her shoulders, hanging on tight. Her hands acted as an anchor, keeping her tethered safely in the moment. The fear of losing this feeling vanished, replaced by the unbelievable joy of savoring every second of it.

Nat kissed her gently, then whispered, "I'm not going to stop. Not until we both come."

The quiet promise made Emily's pussy contract, sending waves of pleasure deep into her womb. The small toy buried in her ass only intensified the sensations. Whether Nat began to move or not, Emily knew she wouldn't last long. Aware she was probably pushing her luck, Emily lifted her head and sought another kiss.

Nat returned the kiss immediately, gathering Emily in her arms and rocking her hips to work the thick toy against ever-increasing resistance. Emily slid one hand from Nat's sweat-slicked back to cradle her head, no longer worried about playing her part. They had obviously deviated from the script, but she didn't care. She was acting from her gut now.

Nat broke their kiss. "You feel so good," she rasped. Her hips sped up, each and every hard thrust pushing Emily closer to the edge. "I'm going to come inside you, sweet Emily. Sweet, sweet girl."

The desire in Nat's voice brought Emily to sudden, screaming climax. The internal contractions, the embarrassing rush of hot juices, the way her entire body quaked—the strength of all those things surprised her, even though she'd known orgasm was coming. But what shocked her the most were the *noises* she made: uninhibited, full-throated, and distinctly feminine. She'd never heard anything like it from her own mouth. It was as though she was truly someone else tonight.

Nat came up on her hands, biceps flexing, and pumped twice more into her, then stiffened and groaned her own release. Vision blurring, Emily stroked her hand over Nat's shaved hair and enjoyed the sight of pure satisfaction playing across her face. If she'd felt a connection with Nat before, it was nothing compared to now. Seeing Nat unguarded and lost in pleasure felt so uniquely special, it left her breathless.

As Nat's body relaxed, a grim reality swept over Emily. Nat felt nothing uniquely special about this encounter. It was just another business transaction. She was just another client. And even if tonight had seemed somehow transformative, allowing her a glimpse of what it meant to truly surrender, none of this was real. Nat was a prostitute, not her lover. The single most intimate experience of her life, and she'd had to pay for it.

Emily's throat tightened as she choked back a sob. Her stomach churned at the thought of breaking down in front of Nat, but as hard as she tried to hold back the tears, the night had shattered her normally iron hold on her control. Turning her head to the side, she closed her eyes and tried not to let Nat see just how weak she really was.

"Hey." Nat's husky voice, tinged with worry, unleashed a renewed flood of tears. She ran her hand across Emily's cheek, coaxing her to face forward. "Emily, hey. Don't cry."

Emily shook her head and tried to laugh but it came out all wrong, and she just sounded so pathetically sad. Fresh humiliation washed over her, and this time there was nothing arousing about it. "I'm sorry." In a desperate attempt to swing the evening back toward normal, she opened her eyes and whispered, "I'm so sorry, mistress."

Nat blinked. "Unicorn."

CHAPTER FIVE

The confusion on Emily's face mirrored what Nat was feeling inside. She'd never used the safe word with a client before. Ever. Not only had she never stopped a scene, but she'd only ever had one woman make that choice with her. Usually Nat did an excellent job of staying safely within individual limits, which allowed the safe word to remain a mere formality. The idea of breaking scene had rarely crossed her mind in the past, and she'd never even come close to succumbing to the notion. To say she was shocked didn't begin to describe her state of mind—especially because she'd chosen to disrupt her client's fantasy when Emily had been making a valiant effort to stay in character.

But Emily was different. That was the only way to explain why she kept upsetting years of routine for this woman. This wasn't the first time she had reduced a woman to tears, but watching a stranger's emotional release had never before elicited such an intense answering reaction. When she saw real sadness in Emily's eyes—and not just the usual post-euphoric explosion of emotion—Nat's immediate impulse was to protect her. To comfort her. Maybe even make her smile.

Unfortunately, she didn't really know anything about Emily Parker beyond the fact that she was achingly pretty, with a delightful penchant for kink. Also that she'd just given Nat the best sex of her life. It wasn't much to go on as far as figuring out the perfect thing to say, but it was enough to intimidate the hell out of her.

Emily's lower lip quivered. "I'm so sorry. I didn't mean to ruin everything."

Instinct took over. Nat used her thumbs to wipe away the tears that rolled down Emily's face, then pressed a soft kiss on her forehead. "You didn't ruin anything." Though she didn't think the tears were a response to physical pain, she had to check. "Did I hurt you?"

Wide-eyed, Emily shook her head. "Oh, no. Not at all. It was..." She smiled shyly. "Incredible. Thank you."

"Yes, it was." Relieved to be able to drop the stern mistress stuff, she gave Emily a playful eyebrow waggle. "*Incredibly* incredible." Emily tightened her expression in an obvious effort not to dissolve. Alarmed, Nat cradled her face tenderly. "Hey, that wasn't supposed to make you sad. The opposite, actually."

"I know, and I appreciate that." Emily fidgeted, making Nat uncomfortably aware that their lower halves were still intimately entwined. "I'm just a little embarrassed right now. I'm never this emotional."

"Let me just—" Nat lifted herself up slightly, nodding between them. "I'm going to pull out now, okay?"

Emily nodded, twin tears sliding down her cheeks. "Okay."

She withdrew as gently as she could, wincing along with Emily. "Sorry."

"You're fine." Chuckling, Emily shook her head and swiped at the wetness on her cheeks. "Ignore the crying. It's nothing, really. Endorphins."

Nat rolled off to the side and studied Emily's profile. As a little girl growing up, she had never aspired to be a sex worker. She honestly didn't aspire to remain one much longer. However, the one thing this vocation had provided her was a terrific insight into human nature. Emily was clearly a woman who thrived on being seen as put together and in control. Her sudden, calm competence seemed like a well-practiced mask, making Nat suspect that she didn't often confide in strangers.

That meant Nat had to tread lightly, approach her like a skittish animal. Putting aside the subject of Emily's breakdown, she said, "Do you want me to get the other toy out?"

Emily blushed. "Yes, please."

No longer in the heat of the moment, Nat battled an uncharacteristic twinge of shyness as she reached between Emily's legs and grasped the base of the slim plug. "You need to help me with this one." When Emily's brown eyes found hers, she struggled not to join in her red-cheeked modesty. She hadn't felt this awkward with a woman since she was a teenager. "Just...push."

Emily did so with a self-conscious giggle, covering her eyes with the back of her hand as Nat extracted and then tossed the toy over the side of the bed. "Not something I've heard after sex before."

"Here's to new experiences," Nat said lightly. She propped herself on her elbow, winking when Emily finally uncovered her face. "Did you enjoy it?"

For a woman who'd just been taken over the knee and spanked, then tied to a bed and forced to orgasm before getting fucked with a strap-on, Emily managed to look positively prim as she replied, "Very much."

Emily's innocence stirred her predatory lust, making it difficult not to reach for her again. The only thing that kept her from doing so was the knowledge that Emily was likely still troubled. Gentling her voice, Nat murmured, "I wasn't kidding. I had a really, *really* nice time just now." When Emily averted her gaze, Nat caught a lock of blond hair between her fingers and tested its softness. The caress instantly drew Emily's attention back to her. "And no, I don't say that to all my clients."

Emily bit her lip, only partially able to hold back the smile that threatened to appear. "Just the ones who burst into tears afterwards?"

"Not even them." Since beginning to choose her own clients, she had taken true pleasure from only a handful of appointments, but she always remained professionally detached. She doubted that Emily realized just how much she was putting herself out there. "You'd be the first, actually."

A fresh tear tracked down Emily's cheek into her hair. "God," she mumbled, then swiped at her face and sat abruptly. "This is mortifying. I must seem so pathetic, so…" She exhaled, bringing her knees up so she could hide her face in them. "Weak."

"Weak? No way." Nat sat as well, trying to decide whether Emily wanted contact or space. Yearning to offer the former, she decided to take the chance that Emily would accept her touch. With an easy familiarity she hadn't yet earned, Nat wrapped her arm around Emily's waist. "No one who does what you just did is weak. You not only owned your sexual fantasy, you also found the courage to make it a reality. That takes guts."

Emily snorted. "No, it takes money." She lifted her face from her knees and offered Nat an apologetic look. "Don't get me wrong. Tonight was…" Satisfaction ghosted over her face. "Magical. But it didn't take guts—just two months' salary."

Guilt swept through Nat at the thought of accepting money for sex she absolutely would have had for free. Knowing it wasn't the right time to broach that subject, she said, "Never mind the economics involved in bringing us together tonight. Submitting to me, trusting me to introduce brand-new experiences, required courage. Letting your secret, kinky self out to play? Also very brave. So no, you're not weak. And this did take guts." She ducked her head, pleased when Emily finally cracked a tiny smile. "Deal with it."

"Yes, mistress." Emily's eyes twinkled playfully.

Only five minutes outside her third orgasm of the night and Emily Parker had her locked and loaded with just one look. Unbalanced, Nat dropped her gaze to her lap. The sight of the harness and dildo still strapped to her hips startled her. Mumbling an apology, she worked to free herself as Emily watched with obvious interest.

"You're very talented with that." Emily stretched out her legs and leaned away, giving her room to maneuver. "I liked it a lot."

"I know you did." Nat dropped her rig over the edge of the bed, thrilled by the way Emily flushed at her words. Unable to help herself, she kissed Emily's warm cheek. "So did I."

Emily turned slightly so their lips nearly brushed. "I was nervous about tonight, but you made it so easy. You've made me feel safe."

"Good."

"Honestly, you have no idea how much I needed this. I *really* needed it. So thank you, Nat. Truly. You were perfect."

"You, too. A dream client." She dragged her gaze up Emily's body, ending at her sorrowful eyes. "So why are you so sad?"

Emily's chin trembled. "I'm not."

Raising an eyebrow, Nat scooted down and propped herself on her elbow. Then she brushed her lips over Emily's thigh, hopeful that her affection was still welcome. "We don't have to talk about it, but if you want to tell me, I'll listen." She paused. "I know what sadness looks like, Emily. I hate seeing it on you."

Emily pressed the heels of her hands to her eyes, sighed, then slid down to lie beside Nat. She rested on her back and stared at the ceiling, adjusting the sheets to cover her bare breasts. "Is this typical? Do you often end up playing therapist to your clients?"

"Occasionally." Nat edged closer to Emily, but didn't touch her. She didn't want to do anything to spook her out of bed. "Look, you don't know me. I get that. But even if we've only spent a couple of hours together, I do care about you—really, truly—and if I can do anything to help, I'd like that very much."

Emily laughed again, nervously. "Dark, handsome, dangerously sexy—yet also kind, compassionate, and scarily insightful. You must have women falling all over you."

"I haven't had a relationship in a long time." Once again, Nat was surprised by the ease with which she revealed her personal life to Emily. "The only women I see are clients."

"Well, then I'm sure you're incredibly popular with your clients."

Nat lifted a shoulder, both pleased and embarrassed by Emily's words. According to Janis, she was the agency's most requested escort. These days she took far more pride in her developing culinary skills and the new career she hoped to pursue with them, but she still reveled in the fact that she knew how to please a woman. "I do all right."

"I'll say." Emily's lower lip quivered. Her throat tensed as she gave Nat a self-derisive smile. "That was the best sex I've ever had. *Ever*. And I've never felt closer to anyone than I just did to you. How pathetic is that?"

Uncertain how best to react to that stunning confession, Nat simply trailed her fingers down Emily's arm. "I can't say I'm sorry to hear that, but I hate that it's upset you."

Emily hesitated, inhaled, and then suddenly words began pouring out. "I don't date—no time for a relationship. There are too many other things on my plate. The sex I have had has been mostly awkward, very vanilla, and not even in the same universe as what we just did. Tonight was a crazy, extravagant gift to myself—and let me tell you, it was worth every cent. *So* worth it." Another errant tear escaped, dripping onto the sheets. "But this wasn't real. It was make-believe. So even though I loved every second of it, fucking you has somehow made me feel even lonelier than before. And that wasn't what I expected." She forced an unconvincing smile. "I'm okay, though. Honestly."

Nat didn't believe that for a second. "How do you feel about cuddling?"

Emily shrugged, her smile fading. "Not sure. But I wouldn't mind trying it."

It was hard to imagine how physical contact could be so foreign to a woman like Emily. Certainly it wasn't for lack of interested suitors. Counting herself lucky to have somehow breached Emily's obvious defenses, Nat opened her arms. "Another first?"

Emily moved into her embrace, all warm curves and soft skin. Without looking at Nat's face, she easily settled against her with the comfort of a longtime lover. Nat buried her nose in Emily's hair and kissed the crown of her head. Careful to keep her hands away from Emily's most sensitive areas, Nat caressed her sides and her hips, putting just as much thought into holding Emily as she had into crafting their scene.

Emily exhaled deeply, her tense muscles finally starting to relax. "Honestly, I have tried cuddling a couple times. It wasn't like this. I couldn't relax with her—this girl I dated briefly in college. I remember wondering when it would end so I could leave. The sex was pretty good, but as soon as it was done, so was I."

Nat chuckled into her hair. "She wasn't the right one for you."

"Maybe I was the one who wasn't right."

Giving Emily's hip a gentle pinch, Nat murmured, "Stop." Emily shifted a little, but Nat tugged her closer and held her tight. From the way Emily practically melted against her, it was clear that she still enjoyed her dominance. Good. "Cuddling is very intimate. I can't enjoy it with someone I don't trust. You probably can't, either. You couldn't relax because you didn't trust her. That means she wasn't the right one for you."

Emily was quiet for a few moments, then pulled away, eyebrow cocked. "Oh my God. Are you one of those sappy, romantic types?"

"Deep down, yes. For the right woman." Skirting the issue of her very real attraction, Nat steered the conversation back to Emily. "There's nothing wrong with you. One day you'll meet someone you trust. Someone you want to cuddle." Unable to help noticing how naturally Emily fit into her arms, she trailed off. She wanted to lift Emily's spirits, not freak her out with unprofessional stirrings.

"This does feel really nice," Emily whispered, snuggling closer.

Nat closed her eyes. "So what do you have on your plate?"

"Excuse me?"

"You said you don't date because you have too many other things on your plate. What kinds of things?" As much as she hated to admit it, Nat was hungry for details. So far Emily hadn't presented herself as ideal girlfriend material, but Nat still needed to know everything. She couldn't help it.

"My job, for one," Emily said. "I'm an accountant at a large corporate firm."

"That would be the place where I kidnapped you tonight."

Emily swallowed audibly. "Yes."

"So you're a workaholic."

"Sometimes." Emily hesitated. "Raising my sister is what mostly keeps me busy."

That was interesting. Nat opened her eyes. "How old is your sister?"

"Eighteen. I've had custody of her since she was twelve."

Recalling Emily's biographical information, Nat did the math. "You're twenty-five now, so you've been raising her since you were, what, eighteen or nineteen?"

"Almost nineteen."

Nat whistled. "Forced to grow up fast." She knew what that was like.

"Our parents died shortly before I turned eighteen. It took a while before I could demonstrate that I was able to take care of Colleen. She was in foster care for over a year while I fought to get her back." Emily's voice wavered. "Unfortunately."

"I'm sorry." Wanting to offer her very real empathy for the tragedy of a lost childhood, Nat ignored the twinge in her gut that warned her not to get too personal. It was a little late for that, anyway. "I had to grow up fast, too. My mother left my father when I was just a couple months old. Apparently I ruined their lives and their relationship...or at least that's what my father always told me. My mother died when I was two years old—beaten to death by her new boyfriend." Emily's soft lips brushed over her shoulder, sending a shiver through Nat's body. "My father raised me after that. He never forgave me for her leaving him—or let me forget that I was a burden he wouldn't have chosen to bear alone. I moved out of his house at sixteen."

Emily sighed, pressing her hand to the center of Nat's chest. "Sounds like neither of us won the parent lottery. Mine were addicts for almost my entire life. Mom did clean up for a bit when she was pregnant with my sister, but after Colleen was born it got so much worse." She snorted quietly. "I remember being eight years old, making sure the baby got fed while they were passed out on the floor. I may have only gotten custody of Colleen six years ago, but I've been taking care of her for our entire lives."

Nat could hear the love in Emily's voice when she spoke about her sister, along with her pain. It tugged at her heart, as did the thought of the childhood Emily's parents had stolen from her. "You're right, that is a *lot* to have on your plate. No doubt."

"Yes." Emily ran her fingernail between Nat's breasts. "Don't get me wrong, I love having my sister. I'm not sure I'll know what to do with myself when she goes away to college in a few months."

"Maybe take up cuddling?"

She could feel Emily smile against her shoulder. "Maybe."

By now Nat wasn't surprised by the pang of longing she felt at the thought of being the one to introduce Emily to the pleasures of real intimacy. Emboldened by how comfortably they fit together, she whispered, "If I tell you something, will you believe me?"

Emily's mouth twitched. "I'll try."

"That was the best sex I've ever had, too."

CHAPTER SIX

Emily went still, listening to the thump of Nat's heartbeat beneath her ear. She wasn't certain how to respond to Nat's words, because even though she'd promised to try to believe her, and even though Nat sounded wholly sincere, Emily simply couldn't fathom that what she'd just said was true. Nat had obviously fucked a lot of people. Even if most of the sex had been bad or unpleasant, surely one or two experiences had surpassed what they'd just shared. Granted, Emily had found the sex transcendent, but she'd assumed it was partially due to her inexperience.

"Do you believe me?" Nat murmured.

Emily weighed what to say. She didn't want to call Nat a liar, especially because she was sure Nat just wanted to make her feel good. "I wish I could, honestly, but…it is a bit hard to believe."

"Why? Didn't you think it was mind-blowing?"

"Well, yes." Taking a deep breath, Emily raised up so Nat could see her face. "But surely you've had plenty of great sex. And I'm… not very experienced. So I sort of assumed—"

"What? That I was faking it?"

Emily's face burned with embarrassment. Was Nat teasing her? "Well, you're obviously good at your job. I'm sure every woman you fuck walks away convinced that she was the best you've ever had. Because that's what you do, right? Make lonely women— women like me—forget how sad their lives are, for just one night. Isn't that right?"

Nat frowned. "I'm being honest with you. And just so you know, I don't make it a habit to lie to my clients. There are plenty of other ways to make a woman feel good."

Emily sighed. She hadn't wanted to offend Nat, and now it seemed she had. "I apologize. My skepticism has much more to do with me than with you, I promise."

"I get it." Nat softened, rubbing her thumb over Emily's lower lip. "For the record, I don't tell every woman I fuck that we've just had the best sex of my life. Most of the time I don't even tell them my real name. But I told you."

Perplexed, Emily went back to the moment when she'd asked. Nat had offered her name without hesitation, only minutes after they'd met. Long before Emily could have done anything to inspire that level of trust. "Why? What makes me so special?"

Nat grasped her upper arms, tugging her closer to kiss the tip of her nose. "I don't know." Moving a hand up to touch Emily's throat, Nat held her in place so that they stayed face to face. "Something."

Blushing, Emily tore her gaze from Nat's. She stared at the ink on Nat's arm, admiring the bold lines etched over well-defined muscle. Despite her lingering shyness, her libido stirred. Too unsettled to initiate another go, she rested her head on Nat's chest and exhaled heavily. During sex, not being in control had been a heady aphrodisiac. Now it made her sick to her stomach. Confused by her emotions—and by Nat's—Emily closed her eyes and fought the instinct to leap out of bed and run away.

"I'm sorry if I've upset you." Nat tensed beneath her, allowing her hands to fall to her sides. "I didn't tell you that to make you uncomfortable. I just wanted you to know that you aren't the only one who felt that way…about the sex. But it was unprofessional to say anything. It won't happen again."

She should just accept Nat's apology, thank her for the lovely evening, and leave. It was better than staying here in this awkward moment, flayed open and exposed. But the self-recrimination in Nat's voice stopped her. She thought Emily was upset by her attraction, when in reality it frightened and excited her equally.

Emily opened her eyes. "You enjoyed my fantasy?"

Nat relaxed slightly. "You might as well have written it with me in mind. It was *perfect*."

Shivering, Emily drew a circle around Nat's navel with her fingertip. "I'm glad you had a good time. Makes me feel slightly better about the whole paying-for-sex thing."

"Makes me feel worse," Nat said lightly. "In fact, I would be happy to refund you my cut of your fee. It hardly seems right to accept it, considering."

Emily raised her head and met Nat's cautious gaze. "I can't let you do that. But thank you." Despite her initial skepticism, she was beginning to believe that tonight had been mutually satisfying. Unsure what that meant, she remained guarded even as a tiny bubble of excitement rose in her belly. "And I believe you."

"Good." Nat brushed a lock of hair away from Emily's face. "You really are beautiful."

Emily knew better than to question Nat's sincerity this time. "Thank you." Again her gaze flitted to Nat's tattoo, then to her handsome face. "I have to admit, I never imagined Janis had my dream butch in her employ. But here you are, in the flesh." It was embarrassing to admit the depth of her attraction to Nat, but what the hell. Unless Nat was an excellent liar, she seemed to reciprocate her interest. "You happen to be *exactly* my type."

"Lucky me." Nat's eyes darkened. "You know, we have at least an hour and a half left on the clock."

Emily's heart rate picked up at the seduction in Nat's deep voice. "Oh, yeah?"

"And I happen to know that this penthouse won't be used again until tomorrow evening, anyway. So, technically, we have all night."

Despite the strength of her orgasm and the overwhelming emotion it had conjured, Emily was suddenly more than ready for round two. As expensive as this appointment was, it would be foolish not to take advantage of every second of their time together. "What are you suggesting?"

Nat reached between their bodies and stroked Emily's nipple, then cupped her breast. "I'm suggesting you come up here and sit on my face. To start."

That knocked the wind out of Emily. She couldn't imagine anything more delightfully hedonistic. "I've never done that before, either."

"Even better." Nat winked. "Think it's something you might like?"

"Silly question." Emily moved to climb up Nat's body, but stopped short. She had one thing she needed Nat to know before they'd moved beyond words. "Nat?"

"Yes, my sweet girl?"

"I like cuddling with you. A lot."

Nat's eyes sparkled. "See? Told you there was nothing wrong with you." She lifted her head and captured Emily's mouth in a deep, passionate kiss. Breaking away with a gasp, Nat gripped Emily's hips and growled. "Now get up here and let me taste you again."

Forgetting her worries, Emily said, "Yes, mistress."

CHAPTER SEVEN

Nat opened her eyes and blinked at the sun-striped ceiling, disoriented for only an instant before she remembered where she was. The penthouse. She turned her head, breath quickening at the sight of blond hair fanned over the pillow beside her. She was in the penthouse, with Emily Parker.

Still asleep, Emily somehow looked even more gorgeous than she had the night before. Nat knew the hours they'd spent pleasuring each other had everything to do with her changed perception. Emily was no longer merely an attractive client. She was her lover. They'd fucked long past the end of Emily's appointment, stopping only when the need for sleep outweighed their desire to keep going. And now, after a few hours' rest, Nat burned to make love to her again.

But she didn't reach for Emily. Even as her fingers tingled with the urge to stroke over smooth, creamy skin, she kept still, taking stock of her feelings.

She wanted to see Emily again after this morning. She had no interest in denying that to herself; after more than ten years of selling her body and mostly avoiding relationships, she was ready to try something new. That's why she'd spent the past five years perfecting her culinary skills in the hope of one day becoming a chef. She couldn't see herself living this life much longer, now that she wasn't a kid without options. A girlfriend had never seemed like a possibility before, but the thought of getting to know Emily better had her imagining all sorts of things she'd never dared dream for herself.

Emily stirred. Then she slowly opened her eyes, immediately dissolving into a sheepish smile. "Good morning."

"Morning." Nat gave her a chaste kiss on the cheek. "How did you sleep?"

"Like a woman fully satisfied." Emily ran a hand through her tousled hair, then adjusted the comforter over her chest as though trying to preserve her modesty. "You?"

"The same." Nat grinned. "Sore?"

Emily shifted, crinkling her nose even as amused discomfort flashed across her face. "Oh, yes."

"I'm not surprised." Last night Emily had admitted that she hadn't been touched in years. Their marathon session of energetic fucking would have taken its toll on anyone, let alone a born-again virgin. Hell, Nat was grateful she didn't have another appointment this weekend. She needed time to recover, both physically and emotionally. "Worth it?"

"You have no idea."

"I have *some* idea, I think." Nat raised her arms above her head and stretched. "That was a lot of fun."

"To say the least." Emily's gaze tracked the movement of Nat's arms, then flitted lower as the comforter slipped off Nat's breasts. She swallowed. "Thank you for allowing me to spend the night. I know I didn't exactly pay for that."

"It was for selfish reasons." Nat caressed Emily's cheek. "I wasn't ready to let you go."

Emily searched Nat's face, relaxing as palpable confidence swept over her. "And now?"

"Still not ready." Cupping Emily's face, Nat pressed their foreheads together, then kissed her lips softly. "Emily, let me make you come."

Emily drew in a shuddering breath. "I thought you'd never ask."

Thrilled to have permission, Nat threw back the comforter and admired the shape of Emily's body illuminated in the warm glow of morning. She kept getting more gorgeous each time Nat saw her. But that made perfect sense. With familiarity comes true appreciation.

THE NIGHT OFF

"I promise to be gentle," Nat murmured, running her hand between Emily's full breasts on a slow journey down to her center. She licked her lips when Emily parted her thighs, allowing her fingers to glide over her hot, slick labia. "I know you're sore."

Emily gasped at the brush of Nat's thumb over her swollen clit. "I'll live."

"Anything for an orgasm, right?"

The question elicited the same pretty blush Nat had so enjoyed teasing out during their scene last night. Most of their lovemaking after their initial post-coital talk had been very exciting but fairly vanilla. Knowing how much Emily had enjoyed edgier play before, Nat decided to test the waters in the light of day.

Bending, she took Emily's nipple between her teeth and applied firm pressure. Emily whimpered, arched her back, and soaked Nat's hand with a fresh flood of wetness. Nat lifted her head and snickered. "Answer me. You'll suffer a little discomfort—maybe even a little pain—if it means you'll have an orgasm. Is that right, you dirty thing?"

Emily's hips pumped into Nat's hand, but Nat moved with her, keeping her contact light. She didn't want Emily to come until she was damn well ready to let her. When Emily continued to roll her hips instead of answer her question, Nat delivered a feather-soft slap to her sensitive pussy. She knew the impact would be intense despite the gentleness of the contact, but she was certain Emily could handle it.

"That's right, mistress!" Emily blurted, stilling her body with visible effort. "I just want to come, please."

Going on instinct, Nat pulled her hand from between Emily's legs so she could grab her wrists and guide them over her head. She pressed them down softly, relying on Emily's willingness to role-play rather than real force to keep her in place. She kissed the corner of Emily's mouth, then shifted lower to drag her tongue up the length of her throat.

"You like being *forced* to come, don't you? It's even better if you have no say in it. No *control* over it." Keeping one hand on Emily's wrist, she moved the other down her stomach, then lower.

She let her fingers play in Emily's wetness, teasing her labia and flicking lightly at her clit. "Tell me how much you love being at my mercy."

Emily's entire body quivered beneath her touch. "I love being at your mercy, mistress."

"And do you trust me?" Nat locked eyes with Emily, aware of how weighty the question was. With her upbringing, trust didn't come easily for Nat. She assumed the same was true of Emily. And yet she'd felt Emily's trust last night, over and over again.

Emily didn't flinch. "I trust you."

Nat captured her clit between her fingers, holding it carefully but firmly. Emily's reaction was instantaneous. Her back stiffened and her thighs quaked. She snapped her eyes tightly shut, nostrils flaring.

"So if I tell you that I'm not going to allow you to come now, what will you say?"

Emily's eyes flew open. Anguish passed over her face, followed by calm acceptance. She had no control over this situation and she clearly knew it. Her sex seemed to throb harder in Nat's hand, indicating that she wasn't exactly unhappy with the about-face. Taking a tremulous breath, Emily said, "That I understand, mistress. Of course."

Nat released Emily and rolled out of bed. She could see Emily gawping in shock in her peripheral vision and had to suppress a chuckle. Despite her threat, Emily probably hadn't expected her to do that. Strolling around the other side of the bed, she offered her hand. "Let's take a shower."

Emily brightened as Nat pulled her to her feet. "That's a *really* good idea."

Nat gave her a light swat on the rear, mindful of last night's aches and pains. "Don't get too excited. I'll only dirty you up again."

Emily's eyes sparkled. "Oh, I'm counting on that. Mistress."

Leading Emily into the bathroom, Nat bypassed the bathtub for the roomy enclosed shower. She held onto Emily's hand as she turned on the water, loath to release her. The show of possession fit in well with her dominant act, but truthfully, Nat's only motivation was to keep touching her. When the water temperature reached comfortably hot, she tugged Emily into the shower with her and closed the door. Then she grabbed a bottle of shower gel and squirted some into her palm. "Turn around."

Emily presented her back, lowering her head with a satisfied groan as Nat rubbed the soap into her skin. Nat ran her hands briskly but thoroughly over her shoulders, her spine, her ass, then between her thighs to tease her hot, slick pussy.

"You're always ready for me, aren't you?" Nat withdrew her hand, not waiting for an answer. She picked up the bottle of shower gel again, urging Emily to turn and face her. "I can fuck you whenever I want—as long as I want. As *hard* as I want."

Emily's throat jumped. "Yes, mistress."

Nat soaped Emily's breasts, enjoying the myriad of reactions playing across her beautiful face. She could watch Emily Parker take in the world all day, every day, she suspected, and never get tired of it. There was something she recognized in Emily, something that appealed to her deeply. Even though she barely knew her, Nat wanted to make her happy. She wanted to please her.

Luckily, she knew one surefire way to do that.

Nat went back to Emily's pussy, cleaning her with gentle, lingering caresses. Emily's hand shot out and clutched at her arm as she clearly struggled not to orgasm. "Not yet," Nat reminded her. "Not until I say."

Emily hissed in obvious frustration. "Understood, mistress."

Knowing Emily wouldn't be happy with her, Nat drew away once more and grabbed the bottle of soap. She met Emily's predictable whimper with stone-faced apathy. "Wash me now."

Emily gritted her teeth. "*Fine*, mistress."

Nat had been lax about enforcing the rules this morning, but she was pretty sure Emily didn't want a domme who would tolerate her current attitude. So she seized Emily's chin harshly, then gave her bottom a hard, sharp slap. "Excuse me?"

Chastened, Emily lowered her eyes. "Yes, mistress. I'd love to wash you."

"Of course you would." Nat released her chin. When Emily lifted her gaze briefly after gathering some soap, Nat gave her a subtle smile. This morning was different than last night—there was no script. She wanted to be sure that Emily knew they were playing. The nod she received in return was faint but reassuring.

Emily placed her hands on Nat's breasts, rubbing circles over her erect nipples. "I always enjoy touching you, mistress."

Nat set her feet apart, making room for Emily's hand to slide between her legs. She fought not to react to Emily's gentle touch, but couldn't suppress the shiver that shook her frame when slim fingers stroked tentatively lower, near her opening. Emily hadn't penetrated her with anything more than her tongue, and despite Nat's quickly growing feelings, she wasn't ready to let her breach that barrier yet.

Grabbing Emily's wrist, Nat said, "Do you always enjoy licking me, as well?"

Emily ran the tip of her tongue over her top lip, probably unconsciously. "Very much, mistress."

"Then do it." She yanked Emily's hand away from her entrance and guided her onto her knees. The position probably wouldn't be comfortable for Emily, but Nat doubted it would take her long to get off. Emily was uncommonly good at eating pussy. Lifting her foot to rest on a low ledge, she used both hands to spread herself open and offer her aroused sex to Emily. "Show me how you use that sexy little mouth of yours."

With a moan, Emily covered Nat with her lips, licking and sucking with a ferocity that weakened Nat's knees and sent her scrambling for purchase within the shower stall. As much as Emily had seemed to enjoy servicing her last night, it was nothing compared to the experience she was having now. Emily was beyond ravenous, and clearly committed to giving the best head Nat had ever received.

"Oh, fuck." Nat fell back against the shower wall. She stayed on her feet only because Emily caught her and held on firmly, keeping her safe even as her legs dissolved into uselessness. "Oh fuck, you goddamn dirty *slut*, that is so fucking good."

Emily pulled away gasping, but Nat twined her fingers in her hair and forced her back to work. Lifting her eyes, Emily gave her a few good upward swipes of her tongue, obviously enjoying watching Nat watch her. Inflamed, Nat growled in the back of her throat and pushed Emily's face deeper into her folds, bumping against her nose and mouth as she undulated her hips.

"Do you like how I fuck your face?" Nat tightened her hand in Emily's hair and ground against her. "You can't get enough of this pussy, can you?"

Emily shook her head, her answer muffled by Nat's flesh. Nat held her there a moment more, enjoying her enthusiastic suction, then hauled her away. Chest heaving, Emily stared up at her, face shiny with her juices. She swallowed, then rasped, "I can't get enough of your pussy, mistress. May I have some more?"

Heart pounding, Nat urged her forward again. "Stick your tongue inside me, as far as you can. *Just* your tongue." She groaned when Emily angled her head, stiffened her tongue, then pressed into her opening. Trading the hand that held Emily in place, Nat reached for her clit, stroking hard. "Now fuck me with it. Fuck me with your tongue."

Her own words were nearly enough to send her over the edge. *Fuck me.* When was the last time she'd said that and meant it? Somewhere along the way, the idea of being fucked had lost its appeal. And that was okay. It wasn't that she didn't enjoy the sensation of being penetrated—she just couldn't fathom trusting a woman enough to literally let her inside. But she trusted Emily. Improbably, she wanted Emily inside.

Nat stiffened as her orgasm ripped through her body. She contracted around Emily's tongue, soaking her face with a fresh flood of wetness, as Emily murmured contentedly in response. She moved her head back and forth, sliding in and out of Nat's opening with fervor. Nat set her jaw and moved her hips in an unsteady rhythm, riding Emily's face as though she were a living sex toy.

Finally Nat loosened her hand on Emily's hair, the waves of pleasure subsiding. She glanced down to find Emily wearing a coy smile. Feeling so very exposed, Nat called upon the bravado she'd spent years perfecting. "That's my good girl."

Emily swiped the back of her hand across her mouth. "So that was acceptable, mistress?"

"Quite." Nat cleared her throat, then grabbed Emily's arm and pulled her to a standing position. She got the soap, quickly scrubbed between her legs, then gave Emily a thorough cleaning as well. Very thorough. "Let's get you back to bed, shall we?"

Emily bit her lip, moaning softly as Nat circled a fingertip around her anus. "Please, mistress."

Nat turned off the shower and threw open the door of the stall. She'd planned on making Emily come right there, but a new urge had overtaken her. One that required a bed. Nat tugged Emily out of the shower, hastily toweled her dry, then led her back to the bedroom. They had another hour or two before they needed to leave for the cleaning crew. Plenty of time to blow Emily's mind.

"Get on your elbows and knees," Nat said, nudging Emily toward the mattress. "I want your ass high in the air. Make sure your pussy is nice and open for me."

With none of the shyness of their first encounter, Emily quickly assumed her position on the bed. She set her knees far apart and arched her back, showing off her aroused sex with a breathless groan. Hot lust roared through Nat at the sight of Emily so brazen and unguarded, offering her body with enthusiasm. She crawled onto the bed behind Emily, then grabbed her ass with both hands and spread her wide.

Emily whimpered. "Please, mistress."

"Please what?" Nat watched, fascinated, as wetness literally trickled out of Emily. Her need was plain to see, and Nat yearned to slide her tongue through it. "Please do this?" She brought her mouth close to Emily's labia, breathing on her hot flesh. "Or were you hoping for something more?"

Rather than answer, Emily rocked backward on her knees. Expecting the move, Nat retreated, then tightened her grip on Emily's hips to keep her in place.

Emily hissed in frustration when it became clear that she couldn't force Nat to give in. "Shit," she muttered.

Though Nat's first instinct was to give Emily's pretty bottom a light swat, she decided to do something unexpected instead. She pulled apart Emily's buttocks and exposed her anus, which tightened as she moved in, as though anticipating her touch. Nat ran the flat of her tongue across the soft pucker, delighted by the loud, surprised cry she coaxed from Emily's throat.

"Oh my God," Emily whispered.

"Do you like that?" Nat licked her again, then once more. She slid her hand between Emily's thighs, using three fingers to rub large circles over Emily's clit. "Has anyone ever licked you there before?"

"Yes, mistress." Emily trembled. "And no, mistress."

"Should I keep doing it?"

"*Please*, mistress."

Tickled by the urgency in Emily's voice, Nat gave her another gentle lick. She quickened the speed of her fingers on Emily's clit, no longer interested in drawing this out. She needed to hear Emily come—now. Sensing her climax approaching, Nat lapped at Emily's anus with small, precise licks, setting her bucking against Nat's face and hand.

Nat drew away and rasped, "Come for me, darling." Then she went back to work, licking and stroking Emily until she quivered and fell to pieces with a high-pitched cry.

Emily stayed upright on shaking knees as she rode out her climax, until finally she collapsed on the bed with a muffled moan. Nat climbed up her body, trailing kisses along her spine, then settled by her side. She rubbed her hand over Emily's shoulders, waiting for her to recover.

After some time, Emily lifted her head and gave her a dazed smile. "That was a nice surprise."

Nat kissed her on the cheek. "I'm full of them."

"I see that." Emily exhaled, then broke eye contact. "So...I imagine we'll need to leave here soon, huh? Before the next appointment."

This was the moment of truth. Even with as much fun as they'd had over the past twelve hours, Nat wasn't sure whether

Emily would want to keep getting to know each other outside the penthouse. Though they hadn't even spent a whole day together yet, the thought of saying good-bye to Emily forever was painful. Emily might want to become a regular client, but Nat really didn't want to take her money when she was the one who so badly wanted to continue their contact.

Emily tilted her head. "What is it?"

Unable to summon her usual confidence, Nat could only manage an embarrassed shrug. "No, you're right. The cleaning crew will be here in a couple hours."

"But?"

Was it her imagination, or did she detect a glimmer of hope in Emily's eyes? The thought emboldened her. "But," Nat said, smoothing her hand down Emily's spine, "I don't have any plans for the rest of the day, and I was wondering…" She decided that being direct was best. "What I said before, about not being ready to let you go? That's…still the case."

Emily couldn't seem to look away from Nat's face. She seemed caught between happiness, relief, and fear. "Really?"

Backpedaling at Emily's deer-in-headlights expression, Nat said, "If you don't feel the same way, then I'm sorry for making things awkward. I've had such a wonderful time with you. I don't want to make you feel uncomfortable."

"No, that's not it," Emily blurted. "You're not. It's just that I'm…surprised."

"Why?" Before Emily could offer an answer, Nat said, "We have amazing sex together. Who wouldn't want to keep that going as long as possible?"

Emily tilted her head. "I don't know." She hesitated, and Nat watched her make the decision to nod. "My sister is with a friend this weekend. So I don't have plans, either."

"Awesome." Ecstatic, Nat couldn't help but gather Emily into a tight hug. "It'll be fun. We can hang out."

"What did you have in mind?"

She hadn't planned that far ahead. She knew she wanted to spend more time with Emily in bed, but she also craved the chance to get to know her better. As she considered and rejected a handful of possible activities, worrying about the implications of each, a loud growl from Emily's stomach made the decision for her. "How about we start with some food?"

Emily gave her a grateful nod. "Sounds wonderful. I should probably replenish before I expend any more energy. Or lose more fluids."

Nat released Emily and sat up, already running through recipes in her head. "What would you like?"

"I'm easy to please. Wherever you want to go is fine with me."

"Oh..." Inexplicable shyness swept over Nat, nearly changing her mind about cooking their meal. Except she *really* wanted to. "Actually, I thought we could go back to my place. If you don't mind stopping at the grocery store on the way, I'll cook whatever you want."

Emily also sat, not bothering to preserve her modesty this time. "Mind? Having a sexy butch make me breakfast?" Her playful air eased Nat's bashfulness, as did the sight of her full breasts. "As a matter of fact, I nearly picked that as my fantasy for last night."

"Perfect, then." Nat kissed Emily's cheek and rolled out of bed. "Do you like crepes?"

"Will you laugh at me if I tell you I've never had them?"

Aghast, Nat whirled around. "Laugh? There's nothing funny about that."

Emily clambered out of bed, gathering her hair atop her head for a moment before letting it fall back around her shoulders. The action was girlish and unconsciously sexy, and made Nat want to tackle her back onto the mattress and kiss her all over. Only the knowledge that Emily needed food stopped her.

Adorably unaware of just how intoxicating she was, Emily gave a lopsided shrug. "My parents were always broke. We lived off Ramen noodles, macaroni and cheese, peanut butter and jelly... Now Colleen and I mostly make do with frozen meals and takeout. I know it's not terribly healthy, but I rarely have the time or desire to cook. And Colleen is too busy being a teenager to bother."

Nat shook her head. Emily's diet dismayed her, but she loved the thought of cooking her some real food. "Well, I'm making you crepes. I've already seen how much fun it is to introduce you to new things."

Blushing, Emily stepped forward and wrapped her arms around Nat's neck. "Lucky for me you have so many skills."

Nat beamed. Besides sex, cooking was the one other thing she knew she could do well. She wasn't certain whether she was more nervous or excited about sharing that part of herself with Emily. In a way, it would leave her almost as vulnerable as allowing Emily inside her body. Cooking was akin to baring her soul, which is why she'd never been able to do it for anyone other than her best friend Bridget.

But she wanted Emily to see her—to *really* see her—and feeding her was the best way she knew how.

CHAPTER EIGHT

Emily couldn't stop glancing over at Nat during the drive to the grocery store. As much as she wanted to concentrate on the road, it was impossible not to let her gaze stray for occasional reality checks. She couldn't believe the turn their night together had taken. Even though the sex had been fantastic, she had never dreamed that Nat would invite her home afterward. She hoped she understood what was happening between them—she assumed it was casual sex, but something about Nat's affectionate attention told her it could be more. Outside the bedroom, Nat was polite, gentle, and solicitous. She seemed genuinely interested in who Emily was. And if she was trying to hide what seemed like very real infatuation, she was doing a terrible job of it.

Emily was infatuated, too. Nat was her perfect fantasy of masculine femininity. She exuded a definite air of danger, yet Emily sensed that with the right woman, she would be as loyal as a puppy. And she knew how to *fuck*. It all made for a very attractive package, one that Emily couldn't resist, even as her gut told her that trying to make this date last beyond their one special night was flirting with disaster.

There were so many ways this situation could end badly. That Nat might think better of her attraction wasn't her biggest worry, although the thought did sadden her. Scarier than rejection was the possibility that she might actually fall for Nat, and Nat for her. She meant what she'd told Nat—she was too busy for a relationship. She had Colleen to raise, at least for another few months, and after that she had to work and pay for Colleen's college. That left no room in her life for a girlfriend, which suited her fine, most days. Being alone was easier. Relationships were messy, and relying on other people had never gotten her anywhere.

"You're awfully quiet."

Emily startled as Nat's low voice broke through her thoughts. She glanced over, plastering on a grin that she hoped didn't look as anxious as she felt. "Sorry. Just thinking."

Nat rubbed a hand over her head, utterly delicious in all her butch glory. She'd changed into a spare set of clothes she kept at the penthouse, faded blue jeans and an obviously cherished T-shirt that bore the name of a band Emily didn't know. Sexy was an understatement. She was pretty sure that if Nat asked her what was wrong, looking like that, she would have a hell of a time not spilling her guts. Doing so would surely end their date in a hurry. Then again, maybe that would be for the best.

But Nat didn't ask. Instead she said, "So do you like being an accountant?"

Emily relaxed. That was an easy one. "I do. I love numbers. I find them very comforting."

"I'm impressed. I always hated math class, myself." Nat gave her a not-so-subtle once-over, seemingly torn between amusement and desire. "Were you one of those brainy girls in high school?"

"I guess so. I excelled in my classes, if that's what you mean. Math most of all." Aware that she was outing herself as a geek in a very big way, Emily couldn't help but smile at her fond memories of precalculus and geometry. "I loved that numbers would never let me down. They're consistent, understandable, and orderly—everything my life at home wasn't." She rolled her eyes. "God, no wonder I haven't had a date in four years. Listen to me."

Nat reached over the center console and placed a hand on Emily's thigh. "You're adorable."

"Yeah, right."

"Are you kidding me? In high school I was the bad girl...and who do you think this bad girl *always* had crushes on?" Nat brushed her free hand over Emily's breast, teasing her nipple. "The pretty, innocent valedictory types...the good girls. The girls who liked math class and blushed when they caught me staring." She kissed Emily's cheek, whispering, "You're gorgeous when you blush."

Emily inhaled swiftly, nearly missing her turn into the grocery-store parking lot. "And you're incredibly charming." Overwhelmed by Nat's proximity, she quickly pulled into a spot near the front entrance. Because Nat had taken a taxi to her workplace last night, riding together this morning had been a no-brainer. Unfortunately, the arrangement didn't allow her any time to clear her head. "*Dangerously* charming."

"Charming, yes. Dangerous?" Nat shrugged as she unbuckled her seat belt. "I'm harmless."

If only. The strength of the feelings Nat stirred inside her was anything but harmless. Emily liked Nat, a lot, but she had so many things to hold together in her life. If she let any of them slip, she would fail both Colleen and herself. Romance was a distraction—one that would almost inevitably lead to pain. It hardly seemed fair to risk the relative order she'd finally brought to her and Colleen's lives for something that could shatter her if it ended badly.

Of course, none of her fears would convince her to call off their day together. Oh, no. Regardless of what her gut said, she was determined to see where the weekend took them. She was feeling good and having fun in a way she hadn't in years, and she didn't want it to end. Extending their date another day—hell, even two—was a simple matter of embracing joy where she could find it. And it didn't have to be anything more than what it was: a good time.

Emily smiled. "Maybe we have different definitions of 'harmless.' My ass is still aching from that spanking last night."

Quirking her lip, Nat said, "Well, you deserved that. And you seemed to enjoy it...very, very much, if your soaking-wet cunt was any indication."

Emily flinched at the vulgarity, her face warming instantly. Again, as it had last night, the word both aroused and disturbed her. She held her breath when Nat scraped her teeth over her neck, biting gently. The slight pain sent a tiny thrill through her body, and suddenly, embarrassed was the last thing she felt.

Nat pulled back with a soothing lick to her throat. "I mean it. When you blush like that, it takes everything I have not to throw you down and just take you."

Emily's pussy clenched. Gritting her teeth, she said, "We need to go in the store before I beg you to do exactly that."

"Exhibitionist." Nat chuckled. "Come on. I just need to grab a few things. It won't take long." She opened the car door and climbed out like it was nothing. Emily needed a good ten seconds to remember how to use her legs.

She finally got out of the car, rolling her eyes when Nat gave her a shit-eating grin. "Proud, are you? Of teasing the undersexed?" She sniffed, pretending to walk past Nat. "I'm an easy target, I get it."

Nat caught her wrist and tugged her backward, pulling Emily against her chest in a possessive yet tender embrace. Lowering her voice to a murmur, she said, "You won't be undersexed when I'm done with you."

Grinning, Emily glanced around the parking lot to make sure no one was within earshot, then settled into Nat's arms. "Promise?"

"I promise. When you go to work on Monday morning and sit down in your office chair, you'll be thinking about me. Because you'll still be able to *feel* what I'm going to do to you this weekend."

Emily closed her eyes, battling the crush of physical need Nat's words elicited. It was amazing how swiftly her newly reawakened sexual desire wiped away all her fears and doubts about spending the day with Nat. At this point it no longer mattered that she was frightened of all the ways this could turn complicated. She needed to feel Nat inside her again. Even if she was afraid that Monday morning would also bring a pathetic yearning for more, it was too late to do anything about it now. She was hooked.

Nat kissed her ear, squeezed her around the middle, then released her. "Let's hurry and get these groceries. The sooner we eat, the sooner we can go back to bed."

Emily opened her eyes. "Agreed."

❖

They finished their grocery trip in record time, and when they got to Nat's apartment, they were in such a rush Emily barely had a chance to glance around at the décor as she followed Nat inside. The front room contained simple, elegant furniture and four bookshelves that were crammed to bursting. A few photos hung on the wall, but she didn't have time to study them before Nat whisked them into an immaculate kitchen.

"Wow." Emily gazed around in awe as Nat set their grocery bags on the counter. The room looked as though it belonged in a different apartment—a much larger one, possibly a penthouse like they'd just left. Nat had brand-new kitchen appliances of all shapes and sizes lining the wide, stone counters, including some that she didn't recognize. Her double oven was beautiful and expensive-looking—she doubted it had come with the apartment. "This is a pretty incredible setup."

Nat opened the refrigerator, which Emily could see was packed with fresh vegetables and cheeses, and withdrew a carton of eggs. "Thanks. My kitchen is my one real indulgence." She grabbed a blender from beneath the counter, then quickly began pouring and measuring ingredients. "I spend a lot of time in here."

"Can I do anything to help?"

"Sit there and let me admire you while I make you breakfast."

Emily sat on the stool across the counter from Nat. "I can do that."

Nat stopped what she was doing and leaned over the counter, kissing her on the lips. "When's the last time someone took care of you?"

Blushing, Emily said, "I can't remember."

"This weekend, I'm doing just that."

It was against Emily's nature to rely on anyone, for anything. She had always been the caretaker in her house, even when she was little, so not being the one *doing* had a tendency to make her uncomfortable. But she felt no discomfort with Nat. Just as Nat had put her at ease about submitting to a dominant lover, her calm competence in the kitchen allowed Emily to watch, content, as Nat prepared her a meal.

Last night had clearly made an impact. Today she felt almost like a different person. A happier, more relaxed person. Emily folded her hands on the counter and exhaled, enjoying the uncharacteristic peace of a morning free of responsibility.

"You look happy."

Emily laughed. She normally held her emotions close, but apparently Nat had no trouble reading her. "I am. This is a nice morning."

"Good." Nat pulsed the blender. "I'm happy, too."

Nat poured the batter she'd blended into a bowl, covered it with cling wrap, and placed it in the fridge. Then she pulled out a sharp knife and began chopping fresh mushrooms. At the store, she'd told Emily she was making her both a sweet and a savory crepe, and had offered a list of savory items she could incorporate. They'd settled on an egg, caramelized onion, and mushroom crepe, which would be followed by Nat's favorite chocolate hazelnut fruit crepe. Watching Nat move around the kitchen with confidence, Emily sensed she was in for a real treat. The woman knew how to *fuck* and, it seemed, she knew how to *cook*, too.

Emily scanned the room, looking for anything that might give her more insight into who Nat was. A small table with two chairs sat behind them. Hanging over the table, in full view of the kitchen, was a picture of a gorgeous brunette girl with familiar bone structure. She glanced between the photo and Nat's handsome face a couple of times, trying to decide whether the woman in the picture was Nat's mother. And whether it was acceptable to ask.

"That's my mother."

Emily jumped slightly. It was as though Nat was reading her mind. Unnerving, to say the least. "She's beautiful."

Nat lifted her face and gazed at the picture. Emily could see love tinged with sadness in her eyes. "I think so, too."

"You look like her."

Having cut into an onion, Nat's sudden tears might have just been a reaction to the pungent aroma, but Emily didn't think so. It was obvious that this was a difficult topic. "Thank you."

"I'm sorry, I didn't mean to ruin our happy morning." Emily reached over the counter and rubbed away a tear with her thumb. "Let's talk about something else."

Nat shook her head, then shrugged away from Emily and swiped at her eyes with the back of her hand. "It's just this onion. I'm fine."

"Okay." Wishing she knew how to move them past this moment, Emily searched for something to say. Frustrated when she drew a blank, she pulled her hands back and folded them in her lap.

"I didn't even know what she looked like, my mother, until I was sixteen."

Surprised that Nat had chosen to share something so personal, Emily was caught between sympathy and unease. This conversation was a far cry from casual sex. Yet she wanted to know more. "Your father never showed you a picture?"

"No. We never had any around the house. We didn't even talk about her. The first time I remember asking him about my mother, he slapped me so hard I fell down. I was four years old, but I'll never forget it." Nat's hands kept moving as she spoke. She put the onions and mushrooms in a skillet to start caramelizing, then turned to the eggs. "When I got up the courage to ask him what she looked like when I was twelve years old, he told me that all his photos of her had been destroyed in a fire. And that since I was the reason she'd left— the reason she was dead—I didn't deserve to see her, anyway."

"Oh, Nat." Emily swallowed, sick to her stomach at the thought of any child being treated that way. That the child had been Nat— kind, handsome, considerate Nat—was almost unbearably painful. "That's awful. You didn't deserve that."

Nat paused in her preparations and gave Emily a tight smile. "I know. He was a bastard."

Emily glanced back over her shoulder at the vivid image on the wall. "So where did you get her photo? Grandparents?"

"No, my father had been estranged from his family for years. And he never told me anything about my mother's family, of course." Nat paused, and Emily waited patiently for her to reveal more. "One day when I was in high school, I cut class and went home in the middle of the afternoon. My father worked nights—I'm half-convinced just so he wouldn't have to see me—and he was passed out on the couch. He was surrounded by empty beer bottles, and he had these photos scattered across the coffee table. I saw one of a woman that I thought maybe looked a little bit like me, so I picked it up and saw my mother's name written on the back. That's when I realized my father had lied. He had pictures of her, but he was just too spiteful to share them."

Emily tore her attention away from the photo to watch Nat's skillful ballet in the kitchen. Despite the emotion in her voice, she never missed a beat—pouring the crepe batter into a clean skillet, then rolling it around to coat the bottom. "Did you confront him?"

"No, I took the picture and left. I went to my best friend's house and gave it to her. I made her promise to keep it safe, because I knew if my father found it, I'd never see it again. And it meant so much to me, to see it." With her back turned, Nat tensed her shoulders and her voice tightened. "I know it sounds silly, but finally seeing her face…it was the first time I'd ever felt like someone wanted me. Or loved me. Even though my father told me they'd never even wanted a baby, that I was a mistake, I didn't believe it when I finally saw my mother's eyes. They were too kind. And too much like mine."

Emily wiped her own eyes. If Nat weren't so busy multitasking, Emily would have already rushed over to hold her. "I'm sure they both wanted you, sweetheart. Otherwise why would your father have kept you all those years?"

"I don't know. To punish me, maybe." Nat gave her an apologetic frown over her shoulder. "I'm sorry, this is way too much to share on a first date. I don't want to scare you off."

First date. That Nat thought of this breakfast that way implied that she saw this as more than just casual sex. And, terrifyingly, Emily was beginning to forget why that would be a bad thing. To the point where she felt compelled to reassure Nat that it would take a lot more than talking about her asshole father to dissuade her from moving forward with whatever was happening between them.

Emily laughed. "You're talking to a woman who once came home from elementary school to find that the beautiful canopy bed her grandmother had given her had disappeared from her bedroom, sold for drugs. After that, I slept on a mattress on the floor. My parents never replaced that bed, even though they had one of their own. Colleen never had a bed at all. She went straight from the crib to the mattress with me."

Nat flipped the thin crepe over in the skillet, shaking her head. "We had some fucked-up childhoods, didn't we?"

"Mine only made me stronger." That's what she'd been telling herself for years. Even if her childhood made it difficult to trust other people, and to relax, she'd learned self-reliance at a young age. In many ways, she was grateful now. "Sure, I would've loved the chance to just be a kid. But instead I learned to do for myself. I stepped up to take care of Colleen. And I'm proud of that. It's the best thing I've ever done."

"You should be proud. You're an amazing woman, Emily. Truly." Nat leered at her playfully. "In *every* way."

The aroma of the food hit Emily suddenly, making her stomach rumble. "So are you. Whatever you're doing over there smells absolutely delicious."

"Thank you. It's just about ready."

Emily's thoughts strayed back to Nat's story. She couldn't imagine a man who could hold onto misplaced anger for so many years, to the point where he refused to show his only child a picture of her own mother. How heartbreakingly cruel. She stood and walked around the counter, watching as Nat transferred food onto two plates. "So did your father ever realize that you'd taken your mother's photo?"

Nat bent toward the counter, applying some finishing touches to her dishes. "He was waiting for me when I came home that night. Met me at the door with his fist."

"Ouch."

"The school had called to tell him I'd missed my afternoon classes. He obviously put two and two together—missing picture, kid not where she was supposed to be. So he waited for me to get home and ambushed me. He slammed me up against the wall and screamed at me to give it back to him." Nat put her spatula down, finally stepping away from the counter. She stared through the wall, clearly reliving that day. "I told him that it was gone. That it had been destroyed, and he'd never see it again. He had other pictures of her—I'd only taken one—but I wanted to hurt him like he hurt me. When I said that, he punched me, hard, in the chest." Her hand drifted to her right breast, cradling it tenderly. "So I kneed him in the balls."

Emily stepped forward and took Nat's hand. This really was intense first-date material, but knowing that Nat trusted her enough to talk about such a painful memory was heady. Stunned by the gift of Nat's confidence, she wanted to show Nat that she was here and she was listening. "Did he let you go?"

Nat shook her head. "He threw me on the floor and got on top of me. Slapped me, punched me, grabbed handfuls of my flesh and twisted, squeezed, then finally wrapped his hands around my throat. I thought he was going to kill me. Then he just stopped, and I saw fear in his eyes, and I knew—he nearly did. He nearly killed me."

"Is that when you left?" No longer satisfied with simply holding Nat's hand, Emily wrapped her arms around her waist and held on tight.

"Yeah, about ten minutes later. He let me off the floor and told me to pack my shit and get out. That he was done with me. I ran to my bedroom, threw as much as I could into my duffel bag, then went to stay with my best friend." Nat gave her a gentle hug, then released her with a kiss on top of her head. "Savory crepe is ready. Let's go sit at the table and eat. I'll make the sweet one in a bit."

Emily nodded. "I think I'll have a glass of water. How about you?"

"The same, thanks." Nat carried their plates to the table, then returned to take the two glasses of ice water that she had poured. She set them on the table and hurried to pull out Emily's chair.

"Such a gentleman."

Nat's cheeks flushed pink. "Just taking care of you."

Mouth watering, Emily took in the mastery of Nat's dish. The crepes were beautiful, the aroma heavenly. She couldn't remember the last time she'd been served such an incredible meal—if she ever had. "Oh, wow."

"I hope you like it." Nat smoothed her napkin across her lap and searched Emily's face. "Will you think I'm an idiot if I tell you that I'm nervous as hell right now?"

"Why?" Emily cut a neat bite from one end of her crepe, making sure to get equal portions of mushroom, onion, and egg. "This looks amazing. I'm sure it'll taste the same."

"I've never cooked for someone like this before."

"Ever?"

"Well, just for my friend Bridget. But she's known me forever. I'm long past caring about impressing her." Nat twirled her fork between her thumb and index finger, darting her gaze between Emily's first bite and her mouth. "You're only the second person to try my food."

Aware that Nat needed feedback, Emily popped the forkful of warm food into her mouth. Flavor exploded across her palette, drawing forth a low moan from deep in her chest. She closed her eyes in appreciation as she chewed and swallowed, already salivating for more. "Holy shit, Nat!" She sawed off another bite, shoveling it into her mouth with a satisfied murmur. "That's so fucking good."

Nat's entire body relaxed. Grinning, she took a bite of her own crepe, nodding in agreement. "It's not bad, huh?"

"Not bad?" Normally she didn't talk with her mouth full, but she didn't want to stop eating long enough to be polite. "You're really talented, Nat. Like, seriously. I can't remember the last time I ate something so good." She paused to chew, wiggling in pleasure at the sweetness of the caramelized onion. "You could do this professionally. Why *don't* you do this professionally?"

Nat shrugged, uncharacteristically bashful. "I've thought about it. But I don't have any experience, I've never been to culinary school—"

"To hell with that." Pointing at her half-eaten crepe with her fork, Emily said, "You can *cook*." She fell silent, considering. "You probably make more money escorting, huh?"

"No doubt. But I can't sell my body forever. Nor do I *want* to do it forever. I've been saving money for years now, waiting to work up the courage to make a change. The thought of training to be a chef...has crossed my mind." Nat met her gaze shyly. "Thank you for the confidence boost. It means a lot."

"You're very welcome. Thank *you* for an absolutely incredible morning." Emily shook her head, amused. "From the best sex to the best breakfast. Is there anything you can't do?"

"Math."

Emily giggled. "I guess we complement each other well, then."

"That's for damn sure." Nat reclined in her chair, folding her well-defined arms over her chest. She dragged her gaze from Emily's mouth to her breasts. "In bed and out."

Emily warmed under Nat's appraisal. She set down her fork and pushed her plate to the side, folding her hands on the table. "I want you to know, when I asked why you didn't cook professionally, it wasn't because I think escorting isn't just as valid a choice. It totally is. And you *are* unbelievable at what you do."

Nat sobered enough for Emily to notice a subtle shift in her mood. "Honestly, I started selling myself when I was seventeen years old—about five months after I left home—because I was homeless and a high-school dropout and I couldn't imagine any other options. I met a man who offered to help—he'd book the clients, I just had to show up and let them have sex with me. For that I got forty percent of whatever my pimp charged. In the beginning it was really hard. I hated fucking men, and even though my pimp was a relatively nice guy, he was obviously using me. For a while he convinced me that I couldn't make it without him."

Emily battled a twinge of guilt. Nat had fallen into this life because she hadn't known what else to do. People had been using her for impersonal pleasure since she was a kid—even younger than Colleen, she realized with a shudder. "I'm sorry, Nat."

Nat smiled and shook her head. "I left my pimp when I was twenty. He wasn't happy about it—gave me one hell of a beating, actually—but I stood my ground." She pointed to her tattoo, half of which was obscured by her sleeve. "I got this when I stopped fucking men. A symbol of my independence."

"So how did you end up at Xtreme Encounters?"

"I met Janis Copeland at a party only a few months later, and she hired me to work for Xtreme by promising to book me appointments only with women, which was a clientele I hadn't even realized existed. That's when selling sex went from being a nightmare to, honestly, a bit of a dream. I don't always love the sex I have, but it can be fun. Most important, I know my clients appreciate me, that I've helped a lot of women feel less lonely—and more desired—and that's undeniably satisfying." With a shrug, Nat straightened and started gathering their empty plates. "But I'm pushing thirty now. It's probably time to prove I can do more than fuck."

Emily put her hand over Nat's. "Whatever you decide, I'm sure you'll be great."

"Thanks." Nat hesitated a moment, then covered Emily's fingers with her free hand. "You know, I meant what I said before—about wanting to return your money. Whatever it is that we're doing is very mutual. I don't feel right about getting paid for any of it."

Sensing that this was an argument she couldn't win—and didn't particularly want to have—Emily nodded. "Fine."

"Good." Nat exhaled, staring at her with dark, glittering eyes. Emily could see that she was done talking, now that their bellies were full and emotions were running high. In a single, thrilling instant, she was once again the sole focus of Nat's primal need. "I want you again."

Emily's heart thumped. "Then have me."

Nat licked her lips, then stood and carried their plates to the sink. Emily watched from the table, waiting to see what she would do next. Sexual tension hung heavy in the air, and it was only a matter of time before it exploded. But when Nat turned back around, she seemed nervous, almost uncertain.

"Will you excuse me for a few minutes?" Nat braced herself against the sink. "I need to…take care of something."

Emily had a gut feeling that what Nat really needed was a moment to clear her head. And that was fine by her. She felt just as shaken by the intimacy between them as Nat looked. Having never before connected with someone at this level, she didn't quite know how to proceed. She wanted to go back to bed, but she knew it was no longer just sex. Not now that she genuinely cared about Nat.

"I'll clean up." Emily stood and walked to the sink, touching Nat's arm without meeting her eyes. "Take as long as you need."

"You don't have to do that."

Whenever Emily became overwhelmed, she cleaned. It was the easiest way to regain a sense of control over her life. "I want to. Besides, I have a feeling nobody's been taking care of you, either."

"Thank you." Nat caught Emily's wrist as she reached for a dirty plate. "I'll be right back, okay?"

Emily could hear a trace of anxiety in Nat's voice, like she was afraid Emily would run away if Nat let her out of her sight. Summoning her courage, she wrapped her arms around Nat's waist and rested her head on her chest. Nat returned the hug with a grateful sigh.

No, Emily didn't intend to leave. She couldn't. Drawing away, she patted Nat's bottom and edged past her toward the dishes. "I'll be here."

CHAPTER NINE

Nat escaped to her bedroom. She hated to leave Emily alone when all she really wanted was to touch her, but talking about her past had flayed her open and triggered her natural instinct to retreat. As much as she wanted to make love to Emily, she needed to get her head together before she could perform. Sharing her body wasn't an option when she felt this exposed.

She'd never told anyone that story about her mother's photograph. Not even Bridget, who'd been her best friend for eight years now. She had no idea what had possessed her to volunteer so much to a woman she barely knew. Maybe it was Emily's kind eyes, or her beautiful body, or the way her hugs made Nat believe that life was suddenly full of new possibilities. Whatever the reason, Nat trusted her. She shouldn't feel that way about a woman who she sensed could easily break her heart, but there it was.

Nat shut the bedroom door behind her, glad for the brief respite. She closed her eyes and exhaled, trying hard to calm down. She didn't want to be away too long. The longer Emily was alone, the more likely that she would have second thoughts about staying for the rest of the day. Nat had seen flashes of uncertainty in Emily's eyes throughout the morning; she was probably just looking for a reason to bolt.

Nat got it. Emily was scared. So was she, because everything about what was happening between them was scary—the instant connection, the unthinking trust that had sprung up like nothing at all. It was scary but also thrilling. Chemistry like this didn't come along very often, if ever. At least not for her. She didn't want to do anything to fuck it up.

That meant she needed a shot of confidence, and fast.

Nat crossed the room and opened her bottom dresser drawer. Though she didn't often fuck for pleasure, she always had a strap-on harness and dildo ready and waiting. Wearing a cock made her feel powerful and in control, which was exactly what she needed right now. That Emily also enjoyed using toys was serendipitous and just one of many reasons Nat was falling for her already.

She unbuttoned her jeans and shoved them down to her ankles, along with her boxer briefs. She quickly buckled the harness around her hips, then fitted the dildo through the O-ring. Her cock was hard enough for fucking, but with a bendable spine so she could use it to pack. Pleased by the familiar heft of the phallus between her legs, Nat paused a moment to fist its length, already anticipating how good it would feel to bury the thick shaft inside Emily's snug pussy. Aware that Emily was hers for the taking—and waiting—she bent the dildo into place, then tugged her briefs up to conceal it. After a moment of consideration, she found a baggy pair of jeans in her dresser and pulled those on, too.

There. Nat checked her reflection in the mirror, pleased to see that the dildo wasn't obvious beneath her clothing. She wanted the addition to be a surprise—one that Emily wouldn't notice until she felt it pressed against her. Unfortunately, her cock was slightly larger than the one Emily had chosen for herself the night before, but with any luck, Emily would be eager to take it even if she was still a little sore from the first time.

Every bit of Nat's unease vanished when she returned to the kitchen and saw Emily standing at the sink. She washed the last of their breakfast dishes with practiced, efficient hands, humming under her breath with an appealing lilt that made Nat feel warm all over. Immediately her gaze drifted to the tempting sight of Emily's round, spankable ass—it was so supple, so delicious, so hot and tight inside. She had never been this attracted to someone before, and she'd never, ever wanted a woman so badly.

Nat crept across the kitchen and wrapped her arms around Emily's waist from behind. She didn't say anything, just pulled Emily away from the counter so her back was flush against Nat's chest. Emily blindly reached for a towel and dried her hands before relaxing into her embrace. Then she turned her head, searching Nat's eyes before brushing their lips together in a gentle kiss.

"Welcome back," Emily whispered.

Desire surging, Nat turned Emily in her arms then lifted her up. She used one hand to support Emily's ass, splaying the other over her shoulder blades to keep her close. Although she was half-tempted to deposit Emily on the counter and simply fuck her there, she wanted to make this last. Better to go somewhere more comfortable.

She carried Emily out of the kitchen, heading for her bedroom, but changed direction when she spotted the large leather couch in front of the television. It was closer, which meant getting inside Emily faster. Setting Emily on her feet in front of the couch, Nat wasted no time unbuttoning Emily's jeans and shoving them down around her ankles.

Earlier, Emily had changed into clean clothes from an overnight bag she kept in her car, and this was Nat's first glimpse of her spare panties. They were pink and covered in rainbows. But it was the cartoon unicorn emblazoned over the crotch that snapped Nat out of her lust-fueled haze, making her chuckle.

"Unicorn, huh?" Tickled by the idea that these panties might have been the inspiration for their safe word, Nat ran her finger along the elastic waistband. "So darling."

"Right?" Emily caressed her shaved scalp, turning Nat's laughter into a throaty groan. The woman was so soft, so gentle, so *adorable*. Once again, Nat yearned to get Emily dirty, to make her lose control. "If I'd realized how I'd be spending the day, I would've packed sexier underwear, believe me."

"These are very sexy." Nat cupped Emily's mound, rubbing her hot flesh through the thin cotton. She kissed Emily's earlobe, delighted by the way her breathing hitched. "*You* are very sexy." With that, she sat on the couch and beckoned Emily forward. "Come sit on my lap."

Flushing, Emily lowered herself onto the couch. Nat grabbed her hips, encouraging her to straddle the width of her thighs. She pulled Emily down onto her lap and kissed her, then moved her hand back to the crotch of Emily's silly pink panties. She broke the kiss so she could hear Emily's excited whimper as she drew a blunt fingernail along her cotton-covered slit.

"That's my girl," Nat murmured, increasing the pressure of her touch. "You love it when I play with your pussy, don't you?"

Emily moved around in an obvious search for friction. Refusing to give in that easily, Nat tickled her labia through the cotton, then angled lower to graze her opening. Her fingers were damp now, Emily's arousal no match for the thin barrier between them.

"Please don't tease me." Breathless, Emily lowered herself onto Nat's hand. "I can't wait. Not right now."

Nat pulled her fingers away before Emily could find any satisfaction. Her withdrawal wasn't meant to punish, but Emily cried out in disappointment anyway. Swiftly, she grabbed Emily's hips and forced her down onto the hard bulge concealed in her jeans. Emily's protest died with a sharp gasp of realization.

Nat held her in place. "You'd better believe I'm going to tease you—and you're going to love every second of it. You'll also appreciate it, because I need to prepare you to take *this*." She punctuated her words with a thrust of her hips, driving the firm cock up into Emily's sensitive folds. "It's a little bigger than last night, darling, but I promise it'll feel *so* good."

Emily gripped her shoulders, rocking wildly. "Just fuck me, Nat. *Please*."

Nat knew from Emily's tone that she wasn't in the mood to play games. But that didn't mean that she was ready to take out her cock yet. She wanted to draw the moment out, to prepare Emily fully. "Lift up," she said, squeezing Emily's hips. "Let me touch you."

Emily rose up on her knees, bringing her heaving chest level with Nat's face. In the same motion, she yanked her shirt over her head and tossed it behind the couch. Then she unclasped her bra, peeling it away from her shoulders to reveal her bare breasts. Nat flattened her hand on Emily's back to keep her steady and bent to suck an erect nipple into her mouth.

Her skin tasted *so good*—a mixture of this morning's shower gel, light sweat, and the unique flavor of Emily Parker. Nat licked around her pebbled nipple, thrilling at the sensation of the skin tightening beneath her tongue. She snuck her hand back between Emily's thighs and rubbed her sex through her soaked panties, delighted by the tiny grunt of pleasure that she coaxed out with her questing fingertips.

"Nat." The way Emily whispered her name raised gooseflesh on Nat's arms. "*More.*"

"Should I do something about these?" Nat tugged lightly on the crotch of the panties, then traced her fingertip along the elastic edge of one leg, very nearly slipping beneath. "Are they in the way?"

Emily nodded frantically. "Take them off."

But Nat merely pushed the sodden material to the side. She tilted her head, watching her fingers play with the slick pink folds she'd revealed. "No, let's leave them. They're so fucking cute." She lifted her face and made eye contact as she slipped a finger inside Emily, going deep. "You look so darling in them."

Emily threw her arms around Nat's shoulders and shuddered, grinding against her palm. "I don't *feel* 'darling' right now." She rose onto her knees, then sank back onto Nat's finger with a satisfied groan. "And I will fuck *myself* if that's what it takes to get off."

Laughter erupted from Nat's chest. Her amusement seemed to spur Emily on, driving her to piston her hips even faster. Nat watched, enraptured by the fierce determination on Emily's face as she chased her release. Jaw set, eyes blazing, she radiated an intensity Nat hadn't seen from her before.

So this was in-control Emily. *Hot.*

Hot, but only one of them could be in charge. Nat withdrew her finger without warning, eliciting a mournful noise of protest that made her shiver with regret. She licked one of Emily's nipples, then the other, to apologize for leaving her wanting. Then she grabbed two handfuls of Emily's ass, slouched down on the couch, and tugged Emily's hips forward so she could bury her face between her thighs.

"Oh." Emily threatened to tumble backward, but Nat kept her upright in her iron grip. She dragged her tongue up Emily's slit, through her panties, then hooked a finger in the elastic leg and tugged the cloth covering aside. She went back with enthusiasm, pushing her mouth and nose into Emily's pussy, reveling in the wetness that coated her face. "Oh!" Emily cried out again, and placed one hand on top of Nat's head, the other on her shoulder. "*Oh.*"

It wasn't long before Nat saw the wisdom in following Emily's suggestion. "Let's lose the panties," she growled, and without waiting for an answer, she yanked them down roughly, leaving them just above Emily's knees. "Use your hands to spread your pussy open for me."

Emily's throat tensed. She never faltered as she obeyed, using her fingers to hold open her labia and expose her swollen clit and her slippery entrance to Nat's hungry mouth. Keeping the contact light in the beginning, Nat traced Emily's folds with her tongue, paying special attention to her opening. She poked her tongue inside briefly, enough to tantalize, then moved up to suck her clit like it was a tiny cock.

Rocking against her face, Emily released a feral growl that made Nat's clit harden. Her movements became more erratic and aggressive as Nat pushed her closer to release, until she was literally fucking Nat's mouth. When Emily brought one hand up to cradle the back of Nat's head, rubbing her pussy all over Nat's nose, cheeks, and mouth, Nat realized she was nowhere near in charge of this encounter. Not anymore.

But, incredibly, she didn't care. Her tongue was buried inside Emily, and she'd unleashed the animalistic side of a woman who desperately needed to lose control. A woman she cared about. Having Emily use her for pleasure was no less exciting than using Emily. She felt safe, and aroused, and that's all that really mattered.

When she felt certain Emily was right on the edge, Nat swirled a single finger through her wetness and teased at her entrance. Emily gasped, tightening her grip on her head. "*Fuck me.* Now."

Nat dragged her finger away from Emily's pussy, angling upward and pressing deeper until she touched the tight circle of Emily's anus. A deep, vibrating moan rumbled in Emily's chest as Nat gathered as much wetness as she could, then slowly pressed inside. The effect was immediate—Emily locked her legs, arched her back, and convulsed in Nat's mouth with a sharp cry of pleasure.

Ravenous, Nat stayed on task as both Emily's hands flew over her shoulders to brace against the couch. Nat moved her head from side to side, loving the noises Emily made as her climax came to a shivering conclusion. She withdrew her finger from Emily's ass, then surged upward to meet her in a mutual kiss.

Emily sank onto Nat's lap, looping her arms around her shoulders as their tongues met. Nat held her tight, turned on by the thought of Emily's wetness soaking into her jeans. Even more arousing was the way Emily lapped at her tongue, lips, and cheeks, cleaning her juices off Nat's face.

Nat broke their kiss. "Ready for my cock?"

Rather than answer, Emily fumbled with the button on Nat's jeans. Nat didn't move to help her, enjoying the visual of Emily's slim, feminine hands so eager to get into her pants. She cupped Emily's breasts in her palms, massaging them tenderly until Emily finally unzipped her. Excited to see Emily's reaction to her toy, she raised her hips and allowed Emily to shove her jeans down past her knees. Her boxer briefs stayed on.

"You like making me work for it, don't you?" Emily caressed the firm, silicone length through her shorts, tracing its outline.

"I do." Nat grinned, then moaned when Emily wrapped her fingers around the dildo and gave it a firm stroke, pushing the base against her throbbing clit. "But who's the tease now?"

Emily arched an eyebrow. She continued to jerk Nat off through her shorts, then kissed the side of her neck. "You weren't lying. That *is* big."

"I know." Nat shivered at the touch of Emily's tongue on her jawline. "Think you can handle it?"

She felt Emily smile. "Oh, yeah."

"Then take it out."

Emily gave her a coy look. "Is that what you want?"

Taking the hint, Nat said, "*Please* take it out."

Emily reached into the front opening of her shorts and grasped the dildo. She stared at Nat as she withdrew the thick shaft, then slowly lowered her gaze. A thrill ran through Nat at the quickening of Emily's breath.

"Wow." Emily's lip quirked. "Confident, aren't we?"

"Shouldn't I be?" Nat covered Emily's hand that held her cock with her own. She moved their fists along its length, hips pumping at the visual they were creating.

"Good point." Easing closer, Emily kissed Nat on the cheek. "Do you want to put it inside me?"

Nat exhaled in a rush. "Yes."

"Just...go slow."

Softening, Nat whispered, "Of course." She put her hand on Emily's hip, then rubbed the head of the dildo over her labia. "Tell me if you want me to stop. You won't hurt my feelings."

"I don't want you to stop." Positioning herself over the tip, Emily cautiously sank down until she'd taken the first inch or so inside. "Don't you *dare* stop."

"Yes, ma'am." Nat pressed her thumb against Emily's clit, rubbing gentle circles to help her relax. Throwing her head back, Emily rolled her hips and eased the dildo deeper. Utterly transfixed by the fierce concentration etched on Emily's face, Nat surged to the edge of orgasm. "Fuck, you're sexy."

Emily tilted her hips, groaning, and bent for a deep, lingering kiss. By the time Emily pulled away to breathe, she was sitting on Nat's lap, completely filled. Emily bit her lip in obvious pleasure, looking so beautiful Nat's heart ached. "You feel so good inside of me."

At a loss for words, Nat threaded her fingers through Emily's hair and pulled her down for another kiss. She pumped her hips upward, matching Emily's rhythm, and tried like hell not to come right away. Emily felt so good in her arms that she never wanted the moment to end. Their kissing started out ravenous but quickly slowed, growing more passionate as they moved together. Nat's orgasm built, and the only way to delay it would be to make Emily stop so she could calm down—but that wasn't an option. She refused to stop.

She *couldn't* stop.

Nat's climax hit her like a tidal wave, knocking the breath out of her lungs and liquefying her muscles. Breaking their kiss, she clenched her teeth and struggled to keep her eyes open, not wanting to miss one second of Emily's rising pleasure. She changed the motion of her thumb on Emily's clit, stroking up and down, until Emily bucked on her lap and then collapsed into her arms, shuddering her release.

Instinct took over and Nat gathered Emily to her, holding her so close she could feel the rapid thumping of Emily's heart against her breasts. She buried her face in blond hair, afraid to let Emily see her eyes, because if Emily saw her eyes, she would know.

Nat was falling for her. Hard.

Troubled by the heavy silence stretching out between them, Nat murmured, "I think you just topped me."

Emily ran her hand over Nat's head, making her shiver. She started to speak, but her voice came out as a throaty rasp, so she cleared her throat and tried again. "Was it okay?"

"It was phenomenal." Tamping down her high emotion, Nat loosened her hold on Emily and relaxed against the couch cushions. She rubbed her hands along Emily's bare thighs and tried to muster up as much of her trademark swagger as she could. "So I wasn't too big for you?"

Emily's eyes sparkled as she smiled demurely. "Almost." She patted Nat on the chest, then dropped her hand between her legs. Nat lowered her gaze to watch Emily's self-pleasuring, touched by how unselfconscious she seemed to be. Emily sighed, undulating her hips to move on the cock. "I'm sure I'll be sore later, but it's worth it."

Nat brought her hands up to cup Emily's breasts. "You're insatiable."

"For you? Absolutely."

Amazing, the way Emily could make her feel with only a few words. Nat's chest swelled with joy, but she tried not to react too outwardly. Emily made her as nervous and awkward as a teenage boy, and just as deeply infatuated. She *liked* this girl, enough to want to date her—*court* her, even—and that put her in very unfamiliar territory. Dangerous territory, if Emily was as afraid of commitment as she seemed.

Emily's smile faded slightly. "Is everything okay?"

"Yes." Nat forced cheer into her voice. She couldn't get too serious less than twenty-four hours after their first meeting. It wasn't that she was thinking about marrying Emily—*yet*, her traitorous mind supplied—but simply talking about a potential relationship right now, before the weekend was over, would be overly presumptuous. Especially when she suspected that Emily was struggling not to turn around and run the other way.

"You're sure?" Emily softened, caressing Nat's cheek with her fingers. "You can tell me if something is wrong."

Nat knew the offer was genuine, that Emily truly cared about her. She'd felt it in the kitchen, and even more so as they'd climaxed together on the couch. But she'd keep the depth of her feelings to herself for a little while longer. If she could spend the next twenty-four hours just making love to Emily Parker, maybe Nat could convince her that she was worth taking a chance on. Maybe Emily wouldn't run away.

Nat sat up, catching Emily around the waist to keep her in place. "Everything is wonderful. I'm inside a beautiful woman with nothing to do today except make her come until she can't take it anymore." She buried her face between Emily's breasts and inhaled, sighing in pleasure.

Emily chuckled, relaxing in her arms. "Right now I'm nowhere close to telling you to stop."

Nat kissed the inner curve of her left breast, then the right. "Then I'd better get started." She settled her hands on Emily's hips, laving a turgid nipple with her tongue before pulling away. Time to take them back to Nat's comfort zone—and Emily's fantasy. "But first there's something we need to address."

Emily's expression grew cautious. "What?"

"Your attitude. You, my darling, are a *very* naughty girl. One in desperate need of some correction." Nat kissed her on the cheek as she helped ease her off the dildo still buried inside her pussy. Then she stood, pulling Emily off the couch and into her arms. "Let's go to the bedroom. I want you to be comfortable for this."

Trembling, Emily exhaled and relaxed into the embrace. Her hips bumped against the cock, sending an aftershock rocketing through Nat's body. "What are you going to do?"

Nat released Emily, then took her hand and tugged her toward her bedroom. How to choose? There were so many ways she wanted to take Emily, and so little weekend left. She would just have to prioritize.

Knowing that Emily was waiting for an answer, Nat went with the truth. "Nothing you won't love."

Chapter Ten

Late Sunday afternoon, Emily lay naked on her stomach in Nat's bed. Nat's strong hands were rubbing her sore body, giving her a much-needed massage after a weekend filled with intense and frequent sex. Nat had taken her over and over, satisfying so many fantasies Emily had stopped keeping track. She'd been spanked, slapped, restrained, licked, fingered, and fucked in a dizzying variety of positions and role-play scenarios. They'd had sex in nearly every room of the apartment, and even once outside on Nat's balcony in the middle of the night. The exhibitionism had thrilled Emily, just one more revelation in a weekend full of them.

She should've been happy. Satisfied. Instead, she was dreading the inevitable.

Emily needed to leave. Colleen would be home soon and wonder where she was. She had to mentally and physically prepare for work tomorrow. She had laundry to do. E-mails to write. Real life to return to.

As fun as this fantasy weekend had been, it was rapidly winding down. Nat probably had to work tomorrow, too. Surely she needed some time to recover before her next appointment. Emily sighed.

Nat ran her hands up Emily's sides, caressing the swell of her breasts. "Sunday blues?"

Emily picked her head up and glanced over her shoulder at Nat, smiling. It was hard to believe they'd known each other for only two days. She was utterly at ease in Nat's presence, and sometime over the past twelve hours, her guard had dropped considerably. If she didn't feel so relaxed, she was sure she'd be panicking about that. But what she felt now wasn't panic. It was an impending sense of loss. "Yeah. Sundays are rough."

"Especially after a weekend like this." Nat lowered her face, dragging her tongue along Emily's spine until she reached the cleft of her buttocks. She cupped Emily's ass, still tender from the weekend's spankings, and gently smoothed over her sensitive flesh. "Emily, I really—"

Emily's cell phone rang, cutting Nat off and causing Emily to jerk in surprise. Just like that, she knew the weekend was over. That had to be Colleen, wondering where she was. Heart pounding, Emily scrambled out from beneath Nat's lean body to grab the phone from the nightstand where she'd plugged it in. The mellow relaxation Nat had spent all weekend inducing melted away as she answered the call, nervous that Colleen would somehow know what she'd been doing.

"Hey, Colleen."

"Hey, do you know where I left my green sweater? The one with the hood?"

If Colleen suspected anything, she hid it admirably beneath her chipper tone and typical teenaged self-absorption. Emily's death grip on the phone loosened. "Look in the dryer. I didn't have a chance to put that load away."

There was a pregnant pause as Colleen ostensibly walked to the laundry room. Emily glanced back and met Nat's eyes, seeing her own disappointment reflected back at her. Colleen made a triumphant noise. "Found it, thanks."

"Great." Emily craned her neck to glance at the alarm clock. Four o'clock. "I'll be home soon. Want me to bring something for dinner?"

"Sure. Pizza?"

"Our usual?"

"That'd be great, Em. I'm starving." Colleen exhaled loudly. Emily could picture the way she'd flopped onto the couch to produce that sound. "Where are you, anyway? I was hoping we could watch that movie tonight. You know, the one with my future husband."

The thought of spending the rest of her evening zoning out to some inane Hollywood blockbuster starring Colleen's latest actor-crush was downright depressing after the splendor of marathon sex with Nat. But Emily mustered her best lighthearted tone. "Go ahead and fire up the DVD player. I had to run some errands, but I'm nearly done."

"Errands, huh? Did you do *anything* fun this weekend?"

Emily was used to being chided by Colleen for not having a social life. What she wasn't used to was lying. "Don't worry about me. How was your weekend? Did you behave yourself?"

Colleen groaned. She hated that question, but Emily had asked for a reason. Where Emily had always been driven to be perfect and in control, Colleen tended toward the opposite extreme. Now that Colleen had graduated from high school and had one foot out the door toward freedom, Emily was more worried than ever about her constant struggle to rein in her wild tendencies.

"My weekend was great, not-my-mom. I was a very good girl."

Emily frowned. Colleen knew she hated that nickname. She was very aware that she wasn't Colleen's mother, but she was the closest thing either of them had ever had to one. "Don't be like that."

"Well, come on. You're my *sister*. How would you like it if I always asked you whether you've been good?"

Emily was grateful Colleen couldn't see her reaction to that question. "I may be your *sister*, but you're *my* responsibility. I'm not trying to piss you off, just communicate with you. We both know your friends can be a little wild—"

"Em, let's talk about it later. Will you bring me a soda when you come?"

Typical deflection. Emily sighed. "Sure. I'll be there in a bit."

"Okay. Don't do anything I wouldn't do."

Emily's face burned. "Good-bye, Colleen."

"Bye."

Emily made sure the call was disconnected before rolling over to face Nat, who stared at her with a wistful expression.

Nat straightened, clearly making an effort to be stoic. "You have to go."

"Yeah." Emily sat up, setting her cell phone on the nightstand. "I'm sorry. It's just…I've only got a few months left of having her at home. I need to make them count."

"No apologies." Nat offered an easy smile. "I get it. You're a good big sister."

"Well, I try. Even if it annoys Colleen more often than not."

"She's eighteen?" At Emily's nod, Nat chuckled sympathetically. "I'm pretty sure that's normal, then."

"I'm probably a little overbearing sometimes." Emily shrugged. At the beginning of the weekend, it had been unsettling to confide in Nat about her personal life. Now the only unsettling thing was how easy it had become. "I worry about her. I can feel her pulling away and it scares the hell out of me. I'm just not convinced she's ready to take care of herself yet. Not with the way she's been partying this past year—senior in high school, you know, pushing boundaries. So far it seems like normal teenage stuff—she came home drunk one time, smelling like weed another." Exhaling, she voiced her biggest fear. "I don't want her to go down the road our parents did. We're the children of addicts. I keep telling her that drugs and alcohol are nothing to play around with, not for us, but she obviously doesn't take me seriously."

"And now she's going away to college where you won't be there to keep her grounded. Of course you're nervous." Nat gave her calf a reassuring caress. "But there's only so much you can do. At the end of the day, Colleen will make her own choices. I'm sure you've raised her well, being the incredible woman you are, so I'm confident she has everything she needs to thrive."

Nat's words warmed Emily from the inside. She'd never had anyone to confide in. Nobody to reassure her that she was raising a teenager the right way, being little more than a teenager herself. She wasn't sure what felt better—that Nat cared, or that she believed in her.

Emily scooted closer, knowing that Nat would extend her arm to pull her in for a hug. She melted into the embrace with a grateful sigh. After two days, she was more comfortable accepting affection from Nat than she'd ever been from anyone. Even Colleen. It made sense, as she'd spent almost the entire time they'd known each other naked, both physically and emotionally. It was impossible to share what they'd shared and not establish an unspoken bond.

Right now, this easy intimacy didn't panic her nearly as much as it normally would've. She had no idea how she'd feel after she went home. How quickly she would forget how natural everything felt with Nat and remember how terrifying it was to need this companionship from someone who would probably just let her down in the end.

Emily didn't want to forget. She didn't want to leave.

"Thank you," Emily murmured, snuggling into Nat's embrace. "For this weekend. For everything."

Nat hugged her tight. "Thank *you*." She held Emily against her chest for the span of several breaths, seemingly reluctant to let her go. Finally she swallowed, took a deep breath, and said, "May I see you again?"

Here it was, the moment Emily had feared only yesterday. But now that it had come, her heart urged her to say yes while her mind struggled to come up with reasons why she shouldn't. She didn't want to never feel this way again. Being with Nat made her happy— something she hadn't been in a very long time, if ever. So maybe she would get hurt. Perhaps it was worth eventual pain to experience this kind of bliss, even briefly. Besides, walking away now meant guaranteed suffering. She wasn't ready to experience that loss yet.

Still, she didn't know what she had to offer Nat, who deserved the very best. Aware that Nat might interpret her hesitation the wrong way, she said, "I'd like that, but—"

Nat stiffened, easing away so she could meet Emily's gaze. "But?"

A pang of regret tore through Emily's chest at the barely concealed anguish in Nat's eyes. She knew Nat was waiting for rejection—that this sexy, handsome butch hovered on the verge of genuine heartache, over *her*—and she also knew that delivering a rejection would hurt them both. Which made it an extremely foolish thing to do.

Taking a deep breath, Emily tugged Nat back into her arms and kissed her cheek. "But I can't make any promises with my schedule. Like I said, I only have a few months before Colleen leaves. As long as you're cool with just getting together when we can, you know, and keeping it casual…"

Well, that wasn't exactly what she'd wanted to say. But it made sense, she supposed, and gave her an out if she did think better of the whole thing later.

Nat nodded, rubbing her hands over Emily's bare back. "I'll take whatever I can get." She paused, then said, "I really like you, Emily. I'll try not to ask for more than you can give. I just appreciate having the chance to get to know you." Her lips curled into a leer. "And fuck you some more, hopefully."

Emily grinned. There was nothing wrong with having a friend with benefits, right? Having an outlet for her sexual desire would be a dream come true, and having a confidante, well, that really might be worth the risk of being disappointed one day. Emily drew her finger down over Nat's pinup-girl tattoo, raising goose pimples in her wake. "I *can* promise plenty of fucking."

Nat bit her lip. "Do you have time for one more round before you go?"

"No, I don't think so." Emily frowned. Sometimes being responsible sucked. "But if you give me your phone number, I'll call later tonight to wish you sweet dreams."

Nat accepted with a darkly seductive nod that made Emily wonder how she would ever find the strength to actually get out of bed. "Deal."

Emily exhaled shakily. They'd both gotten a hell of a lot more than they'd bargained for this weekend, and Nat had been the brave one as far as taking chances. She owed it to Nat to take one of her own now, no matter how minor. "Hey, Nat?"

Nat held her hand. "Yes, sweet girl?"

"I really like you, too."

CHAPTER ELEVEN

When Emily arrived home an hour later, having crammed a quick shower, a passionate make-out session at Nat's door, and a frantic drive to Colleen's favorite pizza joint into a seemingly impossible amount of time, Colleen greeted her with an annoyed sigh from her spot on the couch. "Took you long enough."

Emily kept her face impassive as she walked across the room and set the pizza box and two bottles of soda on the coffee table. "I told you I had some errands to run."

"Well, I didn't realize you'd be gone so long. Where were you? San Francisco?"

Willing her face not to redden at Colleen's innocent interrogation, Emily glanced around, then sighed. "Did you get us plates and silverware?"

"Just eat with your hands." Colleen flipped open the cardboard box, choosing the closest slice of pizza and taking a healthy bite. "You know, like a normal person."

"How long have you known me, Colleen?" Emily walked into the kitchen, grabbing a plate, utensils, and napkins for both of them. "When have I ever been normal?"

"Good point." Colleen watched her return to the living room, frowning. "Are you okay, Em? You're walking a little funny."

Leave it to Colleen to notice her gait, of all things. Emily couldn't exactly tell her the truth—that a weekend of rough, passionate sex had left her satisfied but undeniably sore—so she took the path of least resistance and lied. "I got up to use the bathroom last night and ran into my dresser in the dark. Not a big deal, but I'm a little sore today."

"Sorry." Colleen chewed pensively, scanning her up and down as she sank onto her end of the couch. "Do you want me to get you some ibuprofen?"

Emily smiled. There was the kind, compassionate girl she knew and loved. "Thanks, but I'm okay. Really."

"All right." Colleen shrugged and reached for a second slice of pizza. "So did you have a chance to read the essay I wrote for that scholarship contest you wanted me to enter? It's due tomorrow. I really want your opinion before I turn it in."

Emily's stomach sank. Damn. She'd forgotten about the essay Colleen had left on the kitchen table on Friday morning. Part of their deal about college was that she would pay for as much as possible as long as Colleen applied for as many scholarships as she could. Colleen's grades had never been stellar, so they'd decided that essay contests were the way to go. Writing came naturally to Colleen, a fact that stirred Emily's pride. She'd always made offering feedback on Colleen's work, fiction or otherwise, her highest priority. That Colleen had a special talent—one she actually seemed interested in developing—meant the world. A talent could save a person, give them something to focus on. Focus was exactly what Colleen needed.

That's why the realization that Colleen's essay was probably still on the kitchen table, sticky note on the front page and all, horrified her. She had intended to read it when she got home Saturday. Instead she'd spent the weekend in bed with an escort, never sparing a thought for Colleen's deadline. So much for being a good big sister.

Colleen snorted. "I'll take that as a 'no.'"

"I'm *so* sorry. I'll read it after I eat. I just...lost track of time this weekend. I meant to read it, yesterday actually—"

"It's okay, Em. Thanks for reading it tonight." Colleen tilted her head, studying her curiously. "What *did* you do this weekend? You left the laundry in the dryer, my essay untouched on the kitchen table…" A slow grin spread across Colleen's face. "Did you discover Internet porn? Get addicted to an online game?"

Colleen could be eerily astute at odd times, but Emily wasn't worried about her guessing how she'd really spent her weekend. She'd never talked about her sexuality with Colleen, no matter how hard her sister tried to nudge her, so as far as Colleen knew, she was a nun. "I may have rewatched too many episodes of *The Golden Girls* on Saturday. And then again this morning."

Colleen groaned. "God, Em, that's pathetic. You need to get out sometime. Go pick up some guy at a bar. Let him put a smile on your face. When's the last time you had an orgasm you didn't give yourself?"

Emily nearly choked on her pizza. "Colleen!"

"Seriously. What are you going to do when I'm at college? How am I supposed to have fun when I know you're sitting at home alone like a pathetic spinster?"

Emily battled a pang of guilt for allowing Colleen to think she was truly an eternally sexless hermit—a heterosexual one, at that. It was probably ridiculous to keep that part of her life so secret, but since she'd never gotten serious about anyone, she hadn't had a reason to share. She still didn't. Nat wanted to see her again, and she wanted to see Nat, but it was far too early to involve her sister in something she didn't yet understand.

Poking Colleen in the side, Emily said, "You're not supposed to have fun at school. You're supposed to swear off sex and frat parties, study every night, and live the virtuous life of a woman who will one day be an accomplished author."

Colleen scoffed. "Authors need life experience—including sex and the occasional frat party. Otherwise what would they write about?"

"Getting good grades?"

Colleen swallowed her last bite of pizza and slouched so she could put her feet up on the coffee table. "I'll get good grades, don't worry. Believe it or not, I *do* want you to be proud of me."

"I am proud of you."

A wistful look passed over Colleen's face. "I want you to trust me."

"I do trust you." Aware that Colleen knew that wasn't exactly the truth, Emily sighed. "I just want to see my little sister grow up and be happy. That's all."

"Well, I'd like for my big sister to be happy, too." Colleen pinched her elbow, making Emily squeak and pull away laughing. It was a familiar move, one that Emily never managed to anticipate. "That's why I think you need to get laid. If you don't want cock, I'm sure there are plenty of lesbians who'd be thrilled to do you."

Since shortly before her eighteenth birthday, Colleen's favorite pastime had been to say provocative things to try and elicit a reaction. She clearly thought Emily was beyond conservative and seemed to delight in making her uncomfortable. Usually it worked. But memories of sex with Nat made it hard not to smile at Colleen's comment. "You think so? Thanks."

Colleen's eyebrows shot up. "So does that mean you like chicks? I knew it!"

Wow. Emily realized with a start that she'd just initiated the perfect opportunity to come out to her sister. Clearly she was still riding high on her emotional awakening with Nat, because suddenly intimacy felt easier with Colleen, too. Confirming her sexuality didn't require disclosing details, and this conversation was probably long overdue. "I do like women. But I don't have any interest in picking them up in bars. I appreciate your concern, though."

Clearly stunned at receiving confirmation, Colleen blinked. "You're a lesbian."

Emily fought back the satisfied smirk that threatened to escape when she thought back to the sex she'd had that weekend—in the bathtub, on her hands and knees, riding on top, bent over the arm of the couch. "Definitely."

Mouth dropping open, Colleen squeaked, "Like, you've slept with a woman?"

Heat rose on Emily's cheeks. This really wasn't where she'd intended the conversation to go. "I'm not going to talk about this anymore."

Colleen gasped as she made the mental leap Emily had feared she might. "Wait, *this weekend*?"

So much for honesty. Emily had to lie. How would she explain how she'd met Nat? What if things didn't work out between them? What if she regretted the entire episode tomorrow? "Of course not. I'm just telling you, so you know…if I wanted to meet someone, it would be a woman."

"Okay." Colleen studied her for a moment, then folded her arms and giggled. "Well, well, well. Who knew? Mild-mannered accountant by day, ravenous rug-muncher by night."

Torn between disgust and amusement, Emily decided to go with disgust. She really didn't want to talk about her sex life with Colleen right now. Not when she still ached from Nat's fingers and cock. "That's my cue to excuse myself and go read your essay."

"Hey, you know I'm just kidding, right?" Colleen caught her arm before she could stand up. "It's cool that you're a lesbian. Thank you for telling me."

"You're welcome." Emily hesitated, then gave Colleen a tentative hug. "Thanks for thinking it's cool."

Colleen hugged her back, tighter than she would have expected. "It's probably the coolest thing about you."

Laughing, Emily gave Colleen a playful shove as she extricated herself from their embrace. "Nice."

"Well? You're an accountant. An accountant who spends her weekend watching *The Golden Girls*. Need I say more?"

"No, you've said plenty." Emily moved to stand up again. "Let me go get your essay—"

"I thought we were going to watch a movie."

Uh-oh. Colleen's tone had turned petulant. Emily raised an eyebrow. "But you said you wanted me to read the essay."

"Can't you do that after? I don't want to watch this movie alone." Colleen gave her a mischievous smirk. "It has that actress in it—you know, the one with the boobs? I'm sure you'll enjoy that." She paused as Emily chuckled, then said, "Please, it's still early. I want to hang out with you."

Emily took a deep breath and reprioritized. She'd wanted to read the essay now so she'd have plenty of time to call Nat before bed. But Colleen had to come first. She always came first. If she was up too late helping Colleen, she would just have to choose between calling Nat and getting a full night's sleep after an exhausting weekend. Unfortunately, Nat would probably win.

This was exactly why she'd always sworn off relationships—she didn't want any distractions from her responsibilities. But she supposed it was too late not to want what she'd already found. She just needed to make sure Colleen's needs remained her number-one focus. The rest of it, she could sort out later.

Sighing, she settled back against the arm of the couch and gestured at the television. "I *do* kind of love boobs."

Colleen guffawed. "Em, you're awesome. You crack me up."

Emily didn't bother to hide her happiness at the sudden warmth between them. Even if Nat was a distraction, she was also a magnificent catalyst. Without Nat and their transcendent weekend, she wouldn't have come out to Colleen just now. They wouldn't be sharing this closeness, wouldn't be luxuriating in the sisterly bond that seemed harder and harder to find these days. Without Nat, she wouldn't be nearly as content as she was in this moment.

Maybe having Nat in her life could be a good thing, after all.

CHAPTER TWELVE

On the Wednesday after her life-altering weekend with Emily, Nat met her best friend Bridget for their weekly lunch date at their favorite cafe wearing the same shit-eating grin that had been plastered on her face since Sunday night. Bridget took one look at her and popped an eyebrow in surprise. "Who is she? What's her name?"

Nat dropped into the chair opposite Bridget and enjoyed a long, appreciative sip of the glass of lemonade Bridget had ordered for her. She set it down with a contented sigh. "Why did you come to that conclusion?"

"You're glowing." Bridget wrinkled her nose, scrutinizing her carefully. "Like, disgustingly happy. Either you've met a girl or you just landed a job at a Michigan-star restaurant. I assume it's the former."

"That's *Michelin*-star," Nat said lightly. "And her name is Emily."

"Ha!" Bridget sat up straighter. "Where did you meet her? Who is she?"

Nat had been waiting all week for the opportunity to tell someone about Emily. Bridget was her sole confidante and Nat's only real friend besides her boss, Janis Copeland. At thirty-five, Bridget had been an escort even longer than Nat. She was a constant source of sage advice about protecting herself and balancing work with the rest of her life. Bridget understood her better than anyone.

She respected that Nat aspired to more than selling sex and had been the first one to suggest that she consider turning her love of cooking into a new career. Bridget only wanted the best for her. So why was she suddenly intimidated to tell Bridget just how hard and fast she'd fallen?

"Don't get shy now." Bridget nudged her with her foot. "Let's start with where you met."

"She was a client—"

"Ooh." Bridget gave her a knowing look. "Scandalous."

Nat laughed. "Shut up."

"Was this one of your fantasy appointments? What did she have you do?"

Nat had always been open with Bridget about her professional and private life and didn't plan to stop now. Yet she battled a twinge of guilt over the knowledge that sharing such personal information might embarrass Emily, if she and Bridget ever met. Which she desperately hoped they would. "Cone of silence?"

"Of course." Bridget clapped her hands together, eyes shining with excitement. "Was it something kinky? Or is she more mundane—like she wanted to pretend she was meeting a one-night stand at a bar?"

"I physically abducted her from the parking lot at her workplace. Forced her to drive us to the penthouse, where I dominated her for the evening. Talked nasty to her. Spanked her." Nat shocked herself by blushing. "You get the idea."

"*Nice*," Bridget said, nodding appreciatively. "I know you like the kinky ones." The waiter chose that moment to approach with their usual sandwiches that Bridget had ordered. The young man's gaze drifted to Bridget's ample cleavage as he set a roasted vegetable ciabatta in front of each of them.

Knowing that Bridget would enjoy the praise, Nat smiled when she caught the young man's eye as he stepped back from the table. "She has beautiful breasts, doesn't she?"

The waiter's face went slack and he bolted from the table. Bridget laughed, squeezing Nat's wrist as she reached for her sandwich. "That poor kid. You're mean."

"He could stand to be a little less obvious. Show you some respect."

"You're such a gentleman." Bridget took a bite of her sandwich, shaking her head in obvious amusement. "So spill it. Does Emily feel the same way?"

Nat sighed heavily.

"Uh-oh."

"No, it's not that. She likes me. We have chemistry like...well, like nothing I've ever felt before. That's *definitely* mutual." And, blessedly, it had persisted past the weekend. She and Emily had spoken on the phone every night since—one short conversation on Sunday, then two longer ones. The calls always began with thrilling, soul-stirring conversation, and ended in self-induced mutual orgasms. At this point Nat was confident that Emily considered her a very good friend and an exciting lover. What she still didn't know was whether Emily would ever want to consider her as a partner. "She's a little nervous about commitment. Dating, even. Her parents were drug addicts, and they died when her younger sister was eleven and she was seventeen. She's raised her sister since shortly before she turned nineteen. She...has a lot on her plate."

"So you're saying she has issues."

Nat sighed again. "Yeah."

Bridget shrugged. "Well, don't we all?"

"Yeah." Nat paused, then said, "She's an accountant."

Bridget threw her head back and laughed out loud. "Oh, boy. An accountant with commitment issues. She *must* be good in bed."

"She's mind-blowing." The memory of exactly how mind-blowing got a little fuzzier every day, which only sharpened her need. She had no idea when she'd see Emily again, but until then, at least the phone sex was fantastic in its own right. "She's really pretty. Blond, a girl-next-door type."

"Well, I'm not surprised you've got a crush. The innocent-looking ones have always gotten you hard."

"Yeah, well..." Nat took another bite of her sandwich, chewed, then set the rest down on her plate. "I really like her. And everything I know about her so far."

"That's great, Nat. Truly." Bridget crunched on a piece of ice, folding her arms over her chest. "So how does she feel about your job?"

"It seems to turn her on." In fact, telling Emily about some of her more memorable female clients had functioned as surprisingly hot verbal foreplay. Emily loved hearing about other people's kinky fantasies almost as much as she enjoyed playing out her own. "She's a very dirty girl."

"Well, she sounds perfect for you. The all-American girl with a naughty streak." Bridget was beaming. "Have you seen her outside of work yet?"

"We spent the weekend together. Our Friday-night appointment sort of lasted until Sunday evening. But I haven't seen her again since then. We have been talking on the phone, though."

"Every night?"

Nat rolled her eyes at Bridget's teasing tone. "Maybe."

"So is this a fuck-buddy thing or are you two, like, girlfriends?"

"Not girlfriends. Our exact status is...yet to be determined." Nat shrugged, trying to act casual. Judging by Bridget's sympathetic gaze, she was failing miserably. "We're taking it one day at a time."

"But you want to date her."

"Absolutely."

Bridget laced her fingers with Nat's. "That's where those pesky commitment issues come into play, huh?"

"Yeah." Nat dropped her forehead onto her arm without letting go of Bridget's hand. "I think I might get my heart broken."

"You're my hero for even trying." Giving her a gentle squeeze, Bridget returned to her sandwich with gusto. "One of these days I'll decide to get back on that horse, too. Assuming I meet a guy worth half a shit."

Unlike Nat, Bridget had actually had a few boyfriends over the years. According to her, a potential partner's attitude about her job was the single make-it-or-break-it factor as far as whether their relationship would last more than a week or two. Nat had never tried to date after falling into sex work. She hadn't wanted to try to compartmentalize her feelings about what she did for money with a girlfriend in the picture. It seemed too emotionally complicated. She would most likely crave monogamy within a stable relationship, so it hardly seemed fair to ask a girlfriend to be faithful when she couldn't do the same.

Even though she'd dreamed of a new career for a while, she wasn't sure she was ready to take that leap. Besides, it was insane to even consider quitting her job when she'd known Emily only a few days. They weren't even really dating. Yet the thought of continuing to fuck strangers turned her stomach. The past weekend had confirmed something that she had long suspected—sex was *amazing* when real feelings were involved. Knowing that, how could she go back to the way she was before?

"Fuck." She shouldn't be having these kinds of thoughts about a woman she'd just met. It was irrational. Crazy. Only one explanation occurred to her. "I'm falling in love."

Bridget stopped mid-chew. "Whoa. Did Nat Swayne just say *love?*"

Without lifting her head, Nat muttered, "Don't judge me."

"I'm not." Bridget set down her sandwich and pushed her plate aside. "Sweetie, I'm not. I've just never heard you talk this way before."

"Well, I've never felt this way before." Nat straightened with an embarrassed shrug. "I mean, I *really* like her."

"I guess so." Grinning, Bridget shook her head. "Falling in love."

"With an accountant."

"And just when I think life has finished surprising me."

Nat laughed. What else could she do? "Trust me, no one is more surprised than I am."

"I don't know…I'm guessing Emily was probably shocked when her sexy hired stud suddenly fell head over heels for her."

"That she was." The memory of their pleasurable transition from client and escort to lovers warmed Nat, restoring the stupid grin to her face. "Fuck, I'm in trouble."

"Maybe." Bridget scooted her chair around the table until she was close enough to wrap her arm around Nat's shoulders. "Maybe not. Either way, I'm thrilled for you. What've you been telling me for forever now? You need a change. Opening yourself to the possibility of love is a great start."

"Well, let's hope so."

The waiter returned, doing everything possible not to look in their direction. Bridget snuggled closer to her and offered him a friendly smile, which he accepted with a tentative nod. "Can I get you two anything else?"

"I think just our bill." Nat pulled Bridget tight against her side. "Or did you want something else, darling?"

"The bill sounds perfect, poodle."

Nat pinched Bridget's hip after the waiter scurried away. "Really? Poodle?"

"It's endearing. Like you." Bridget kissed her cheek, then scooted back to her side of the table.

Cuddling with Bridget only intensified her need for Emily. The gnawing ache in her chest led her right back into her earlier thought pattern. Was now the time to change careers, whether or not Emily was on board for more than casual sex? She sighed. "What if I can't cut it in the culinary world?"

"You can. Your food is delicious and you know that. I've gained at least ten pounds since you started cooking for me."

Nat raised her eyebrow and leered at Bridget's cleavage. "In all the right places."

"Oh, sure. So you can ogle them, but our poor waiter can't."

"That's right."

Bridget rolled her eyes, but gave her a fond look. "I have no doubt you'll succeed in your culinary career. But you know what? If it doesn't work out, I'm sure Janis would hire you back. You know you're one of her top earners. And a client favorite."

Bridget was right. Janis would probably hate to lose her. Currently she was the only butch escort at the agency, which meant she was always in demand. And she had more regular clients than anyone. If cooking didn't work out, she could go back to escorting. That safety net made her feel marginally better about the thought of putting herself out there. Now if only she could overcome her fear of failure.

"Are you worrying about this right now because of Emily?"

"Kind of." Nat hated to admit that she would make a life-changing decision because of a woman she'd just met, even if that was sort of what was happening. "You know I've been thinking about changing careers for a while. If there's a chance Emily wants to date me—that we could actually have a relationship—I don't want to keep fucking other people. It's not even that I think she couldn't handle that. It's that I can't."

"Just give it a little time. See where things go with her over the next few weeks, and see how you feel about escorting. This *just* happened, Nat. These feelings are intense and brand-new and not something you're used to, but you don't have to make any decisions today. *She's* not making any decisions today."

Heat crept up Nat's face. "I know. You're right. I'm being silly." Her phone rang before Bridget could reply, and even though Emily had never called at noon before, Nat scrambled to check the front display. Face on fire at the way her heart raced at the sight of Emily's name, she ignored Bridget's laughter and answered her phone.

"Hey, sweet girl." She half-turned away from Bridget, too self-conscious to watch her reaction to their conversation.

"Hey, yourself."

Emily's obvious joy instantly restored her good mood. "I was just thinking about you."

"Dirty things, I hope."

Nat lowered her voice. "You have no idea."

"Oh, I think I might." Emily spoke in a bare whisper, leading Nat to believe she might very well be in her office at work. With the door closed, no doubt, but still. "I've been thinking about you, too. *Extremely* dirty things."

She didn't care that Bridget could hear. When she spoke to Emily, her libido always took over. "Is your pussy wet?" She looked up at Bridget's giggle to find their nervous waiter staring at her, bill in hand. Nat took it with a sheepish nod, silent as she awaited Emily's answer.

"Constantly, these days." Exhaling, Emily said, "Colleen just texted me that she's spending the night at her friend Kaysi's house. I was wondering if you wanted to maybe see each other this evening. If you don't have to work."

No longer concerned about her audience, Nat sat up straighter in her chair. She'd never been so happy to have an empty work schedule. "Absolutely. May I buy you dinner?"

"That would be really nice." Emily paused. "And then maybe we could go back to your place?"

Nat warmed at Emily's palpable desire. The thought of being with her again in only a few hours was overwhelming. Though she wanted to take Emily on a proper date, it would be a challenge to keep her hands to herself during dinner. She wasn't sure she would even try. "I think that part goes without saying, don't you?"

"I hoped so." She could hear the smile in Emily's voice. "How about I pick you up at seven?"

"Sounds great." Nat glanced around, relieved that the waiter had disappeared again. Bridget sat gazing at her fondly. Ignoring her indulgent grin, Nat turned away again and murmured, "Do me a favor, darling?"

Emily's shaky exhalation was exactly the reaction she'd hoped to elicit. "Yes?"

"Wear a skirt."

It took Emily a moment to answer. When she did, Nat had to strain to hear her quiet whisper. "Should I wear panties, or no?"

"Yes." Nat paused, savoring the image of playing with Emily beneath her skirt, over her panties. "I want to work for it a little."

"Okay." Clearing her throat, Emily suddenly sounded far more composed. "Done. I'll see you tonight, then?"

Nat imagined that a co-worker might have just passed by, or perhaps knocked on her office door. The thought of Emily in her business attire, soaking wet and ready for her, made her day. "I can't wait."

"Me, either. Bye."

Nat chuckled as she hung up. Then she turned back to Bridget, wrinkling her nose at the amusement written all over her face. "What?"

"Sounds like you just made a date."

"Seems that way." Nat pulled some money from her wallet and set the bill at the edge of the table. "Hopefully the first of many."

Bridget bounced in her seat and clapped her hands. "*So* cute."

Nat was too happy to disagree. "I try."

CHAPTER THIRTEEN

Emily had never been on a real date. At least not one that involved being led to a private table at a small, elegant restaurant by a stunningly dressed suitor who pulled out her chair, then ordered them an expensive-sounding bottle of wine without missing a beat. She folded her hands in her lap—over the form-fitting satin skirt she'd worn per Nat's request—and tried to quiet her nerves.

She could do this.

Nat caught her gaze when the waitress left to fetch their wine. "I know I've already said it a couple times, but you really do look gorgeous tonight, Emily. Breathtaking."

She managed an anxious laugh. "Likewise." In fact, Nat had never looked better. She wore black, well-tailored pants, a crisp white collared shirt, and a dark vest—she was Emily's ideal butch, a veritable wet dream. "Nothing on the menu will compare to how delicious you look."

Nat dragged her chair around the table to sit beside her. Her light, vaguely spicy scent filled Emily's nostrils, stirring a gnawing hunger that wouldn't be satisfied by any of the decadent entrées the restaurant had to offer. Leaning close, Nat planted a kiss where her neck met her shoulder. "I love your skirt."

"Thank you. I don't usually have a reason to wear one."

"A crying shame, with legs like yours." Nat drew away, putting distance between their faces. Beneath the table, her hand landed on Emily's knee and quickly slid upward. "I recommend the roasted lemon and garlic chicken. Or the pumpkin ravioli, if you want to go vegetarian."

The gentle caress of Nat's fingertips along her inner thigh rendered Emily utterly incapable of thinking about food. "Chicken sounds good."

"Are you sure?" Nat tickled a path higher up the inside of her thigh, scratching her nail along the elastic leg of her silk panties. "The ravioli is divine."

"Maybe…" Emily gasped as Nat's fingers rubbed over her sensitive labia, through her panties. She cast a furtive gaze around the restaurant, making sure nobody was watching. "Maybe we could order both and share."

"That works for me." Nat circled the pad of her thumb over her clit. Her fingertips pressed lower, between Emily's swollen lips, and sought out her entrance. "I love sharing with you."

Their waitress appeared, breaking their heated eye contact. She gave them a friendly smile. "Have you two decided yet?"

Nat never ceased the motion of her fingers between Emily's thighs. "We'll have the roasted lemon-and-garlic chicken, and an order of the pumpkin ravioli."

Emily held her breath and tried not to react as Nat settled into a particularly pleasurable rhythm. She stopped listening to the friendly conversation between Nat and the waitress, who seemed oblivious to what was happening under the tablecloth. When the waitress finally walked away after shooting Nat a final, flirtatious grin, Emily sagged in relief.

"Oh, you are *cruel*." She whimpered when Nat retreated, closing her thighs to trap her before she could withdraw her hand entirely. "Don't stop."

Nat wriggled her fingers between Emily's thighs until she spread her legs slightly. Then she resumed her gentle teasing with a contented sigh. "You feel so good. I can't wait until after dinner."

"If you aren't careful, I won't be able to, either."

Kissing her ear, Nat whispered, "That's okay." She hooked her finger in the crotch of Emily's panties and tugged the material to the side. "I can take care of you right now."

"Nat—" Emily inhaled sharply as Nat penetrated her in one swift motion. She gripped the edge of the table, knuckles going white from the effort not to cry out. "Oh...my."

Nat eased away, propping her chin on her hand and doing a perfect impression of a dutiful listener. "Nobody will know. Not if you're quiet and pretend that you and I are having a nice, innocent first-date conversation."

Rocking against Nat's hand, Emily cleared her throat and folded her hands on the table. "What do you want to talk about?"

Their waitress, a pretty brunette who clearly liked Nat, winked at Emily as she returned with their bottle of wine and poured two glasses without saying a word. Emily felt like she should speak, if only to distract from the subtle flexing of Nat's arm and the pleasure she knew was written all over her face. But she didn't trust her voice not to shake.

"Thank you." Nat dismissed the waitress with a polite nod, then picked up her glass with her free hand. She continued to finger Emily with slow, deliberate thrusts as she took a sip. "I hope you like the wine. It's one of my favorites."

Emily lifted her glass and took a tentative sip. The bold flavor surprised her—she hadn't taken a drink in years. "I'm actually not much of a wine drinker."

Nat's hand stilled. "I'm sorry. I wasn't thinking."

"No, it's okay." Emily took another drink, hoping it would calm her racing heart. "It's not that I *won't* drink, I just don't generally choose to."

"Because your parents were addicts."

"Yes." Emily set the glass on the table. Then she closed her thighs on Nat's wrist. "Please don't stop."

Nat curled her finger inside Emily, stroking a spot on the front of her vaginal wall that sent pleasurable shudders through her body. "I wonder what everyone here would think if they knew what I was doing to you right now?"

"That I'm a lucky girl." Emily kept her expression stoic as she studied Nat's face. Her eyes had gone dark and an air of sensual longing softened her rough edges. "And that you're ridiculously sexy." Her attraction to Nat hit her full-on, almost as though she was seeing her for the first time. Adrenaline made her palms sweat. "Honestly, Nat, you could have anyone you wanted."

"Then I guess I'm the lucky one." Nat gave her a chaste kiss on the lips. "Because I want *you*." She moved her thumb up to circle Emily's clit, sliding a second finger inside to join the first. With slow, hard strokes, she rubbed Emily's clit and G-spot simultaneously.

"Oh, fuck," Emily whispered. She turned her face away from Nat, bringing her fist to her mouth in a desperate attempt not to cry out as she came. The rhythmic contraction of her inner muscles around Nat's fingers felt divine and made her thighs quake, which only seemed to encourage Nat to rub her clit more furiously. When the waitress suddenly appeared to deposit their salads in front of them, it took all of Emily's willpower not to scream.

Her orgasm subsided only after the waitress left them alone again. Emily brought her hands to her burning cheeks and fought to regain her composure. "Was it obvious?"

Nat withdrew her hand, readjusting Emily's panties and then the hem of her skirt. Eyes sparkling, she glanced around the restaurant before bringing her fingers to her mouth and sucking them clean. "Would it embarrass you if I said yes?"

"A little."

"And would you regret having let me do it?"

Emily didn't even have to think about that one. "No." She took another sip of wine, then picked up her salad fork with a shaking hand. "That was definitely an experience I'll never forget."

"Me either." Nat stabbed a bite of her own salad, chewing with an appreciative murmur. "And to think, our evening has just started."

Emily watched Nat enjoy her food, once again surprised by the depth of the emotion such a simple act provoked. Even after their perfect weekend, their chemistry continued to sizzle—and only seemed to intensify the more time they spent together. With a woman who looked like Nat, physical attraction was a given. What shocked her was how far beyond sex her desire went. She could easily imagine late-night movie marathons, more trips to the grocery store, and rainy days cuddling in bed. She could even imagine confiding in Nat when she had a hard day with Colleen or simply needed her spirits lifted.

Emily chewed another mouthful of salad, trying not to spin out over the implications of her thoughts. Clearly her feelings for Nat were so much more than casual. Neither of them had admitted that yet, but she supposed it didn't really matter whether they articulated the obvious or not. It was what it was. Closing her eyes briefly, she tried to contend with the rush of panic elicited by her acceptance of cold, hard reality.

Against her better judgment, she was falling for Nat Swayne.

"Are you okay?" Nat put a hand on Emily's wrist, wrenching her back into the moment. "If I crossed a line just now, I'm sorry. I didn't want to wait to touch you again, and from our phone calls, I got the impression that public sex might turn you on. But if I made you uncomfortable..." Throat tense, Nat looked like she might be sick. "I would never want to do that."

Emily shook her head. "Unicorn, remember?" Seeing the confusion in Nat's eyes, she clarified. "I know our safe word, Nat. If you ever do anything I don't like, I promise I'll use it."

Nat held her gaze, then nodded, apparently satisfied. "Is something else wrong?"

She liked Nat too much not to be honest with her. Praying she wasn't about to make a fool of herself, she said, "I'm a little shaken by how strongly I feel about you."

Nat seemed to stop breathing. Hope lit up her eyes, making Emily feel as though someone had just grabbed her heart and squeezed. "Me too," Nat said, then hesitated. "Is that a good thing or a bad thing?"

"I don't know yet." Emily had always assumed that developing feelings for a woman would divert her from her focus. It would set her up for potential heartbreak. But so far, getting to know Nat had only yielded positive results. She was happy, sexually satisfied, and optimistic in a way that felt both foreign and wonderful. She'd also taken an important step toward a closer relationship with Colleen. "So I came out to my sister Sunday night."

Nat blinked in surprise. "Wow. She didn't know?"

"She obviously suspected, but I'd never confirmed it. There's never been a reason to talk to her about my romantic life. I haven't had one." Her rationale seemed a little ridiculous when she tried to explain it now. Not for the first time since Sunday night, she rejoiced that her days of hiding such a fundamental part of herself from Colleen were over. "For a long time I just felt like…well, she's a kid. I'm not going to talk to her about who I'm attracted to. Once she was old enough to understand, I'd kind of sworn off dating anyway, so…" She managed an embarrassed shrug. "Well, it seemed easier not to talk about what I didn't have."

"What changed your mind?" Nat took a bite of her salad, affecting a casualness Emily suspected she didn't really feel. Like she was hopeful for an answer she wasn't sure she would get. "Did you tell her we spent the weekend together?"

"No. She did ask me why I was walking funny," she slapped Nat lightly on the arm when she released an amused snort, "but I couldn't tell her I was sore from hot marathon sex. That would be…ugh." Emily shuddered. "No, the conversation sort of led to a natural opportunity to come out, but instead of doing my normal avoidance thing, I just…took it."

"Congratulations." Nat pushed her salad plate aside and put her hand on Emily's knee. The innocent contact warmed her from the inside. "That must feel amazing."

"It does." With effort, Emily took one last bite of salad before setting down her fork. Chewing gave her a moment to regain her poise. "It's strange, raising your sibling. I might as well be her mother, but she sees me as just her big sister. Yes, I raised her, but now that she's eighteen, she's eager to transition our relationship to one of peers. And I'm…still getting used to that idea." She covered Nat's hand with her own. "Colleen was obviously thrilled that I confided in her. She likes to tease me—about everything, really—but she was cool about it. We had a very nice evening together afterward. It made me feel closer to her—and her to me, I hope."

"That's wonderful, Emily. Really."

"Thanks." Emily fought back the tears that threatened to gather at the gratitude that flooded her body. "Even though I didn't tell her about you, it's because of meeting you that I said anything at all. Last weekend...changed me." Afraid to say too much, she slowed down and considered her next words carefully. "I've always sacrificed my own happiness for Colleen's. Or at least for what I *think* will make her happy. Our 'date' was the first time I'd ever done something just for me. Friday night alone would have changed me, in a way. But spending the whole weekend with you? Well, I can't go back to the person I was before. I'm different now. You know?"

Nat gave her a bashful grin, then stared down at the tablecloth. "Yeah, I know." She seemed pleased by Emily's words, but hesitant to share her own feelings. Scared, even. "So am I."

Nat's reticence made her eager to further lower her own defenses. Exhaling, she admitted, "It is a good thing. Scary, but good."

"For me, too." Nat touched Emily's knee, then turned her hand over so they could entangle their fingers. "Does that mean I can look forward to another date after tonight?"

There didn't seem to be much point in pretending anymore. "Of course."

Pure joy flashed over Nat's face. "Excellent."

Swept away by how good it felt to make Nat happy simply by acknowledging their very real connection, Emily couldn't help musing out loud. "Colleen says she's worried that I'll be a lonely, sexless recluse after she goes away to college. Maybe I *should* tell her about you. Assuming you don't get tired of me after a couple of dates."

"That hardly seems possible." Nat moved her free hand to Emily's face, drawing her closer for a soft kiss. "The more I know you, the better I like you."

Emily kept her face close to Nat's, reluctant to pull away from their easy intimacy. "How in the world have you managed to stay single all these years?"

Nat chuckled. "A combination of having an unappealing job and not meeting a girl like you, I guess."

"I don't mind your job," Emily murmured. Perhaps she would feel differently within a long-term relationship, but for now, the knowledge that Nat was so good that women *paid for it* only served

as an aphrodisiac. Maybe that made her strange—but it was true.
"Not as long as you save your best work for me."

Their food arrived before Nat could answer. Emily held Nat's
gaze as their waitress arranged the plates on the table, not wavering
even when the waitress left with the cheerful instruction to enjoy
their meal. Neither of them moved to start eating.

Finally Nat swallowed, looking almost painfully earnest. "I've
never sold to a client what I've given to you. I promise."

Overwhelmed by the urgency of her declaration, Emily caressed
her hand. "I'm not asking for promises."

"I'm making one, anyway." Nat's voice was resolute. "You are
the *only* woman I think about when I'm alone."

Emily blushed, almost embarrassed by how fantastic that made
her feel. "And when was the last time you thought about me while
you were alone?"

"This morning in the shower." Nat moved closer, whispering in
her ear. "I jacked off thinking about how wet your pussy gets when
I suck on it. How good you taste. And how beautifully red my hand
makes your bottom when I take you over my knee to spank you."

By the time Nat was done speaking, Emily could barely breathe.
She just wanted to go back to Nat's place and fuck. She didn't care
at all about the expensive, delicious-smelling food in front of them.
She felt absolutely no need to go through the motions of a normal
date. It had been only three days since she'd been in bed with Nat—
and maybe only fifteen minutes since Nat last made her come—but
Emily needed her so intensely her whole body ached.

Emily pulled back, arching an eyebrow. "How hungry are you,
really?"

"For dinner?" Nat's eyes flashed. At Emily's nod, she said,
"When the waitress comes back I'll ask her to box up our meals.
Why don't we eat a few bites to tide us over while we wait?"

Emily knew that she had wanted to impress her with a gourmet
dinner, so she was pleased that Nat so easily accepted having her
plans derailed. She definitely intended to make it up to her once they
got back to Nat's apartment. "Thank you."

Nat snorted. "Are you kidding? This is the best date ever."

CHAPTER FOURTEEN

They made it back to Nat's apartment less than an hour later. Nat dragged Emily into the kitchen by the hand, tossed their leftovers into the fridge, then scooped Emily into her arms and initiated a passionate kiss. Her single-minded focus was on getting Emily naked and into bed as quickly as possible. She stumbled across the living room, hands grasping at delicious curves as they continued to make out, then kicked open her bedroom door. As soon as her knees bumped against the mattress, she dumped Emily in the center of the bed and crawled on top of her without interrupting their frantic kisses.

She sat up just long enough to discard her vest and direct Emily's questing hands to the buttons on her shirt, frustrated by all the damn clothing between them. Then she returned to Emily's mouth with a growl of satisfaction. Emily's delicate fingers fumbled open Nat's shirt buttons, moving swiftly from her waist up over her breasts. Eager to feel bare skin against her own, Nat gathered Emily's top in her hands, ready to tug it off the next time they broke for air.

Emily succumbed to the need to breathe first. Gasping, she yanked Nat's shirt off her shoulders, then raised her arms as Nat stripped off her top. They came back together in a clash of teeth and tongues, Nat bare from the waist up and Emily clad in a silky green bra. This kiss lasted a long time and ended only when Nat grabbed Emily's bra cups and yanked downward, then attacked her bare breasts with hungry, sucking kisses.

Emily dug her fingers into Nat's scalp, groaning. "Take off my skirt."

Nat complied without moving from the nipple she was licking, wrestling blindly with the fastening at Emily's hip for an embarrassingly long time. Emily dissolved into giggles just as she managed to unzip the damn thing. Determined to make this their last interruption, Nat yanked Emily's skirt and panties down her legs. She tossed them onto the floor, but when she went to move back on top, Emily pressed a hand against her chest.

"Not until you lose those pants."

Turned on by Emily's commanding tone, Nat stood and thumbed open the button at her waist. "Bossy."

"I want to feel your skin on mine."

Nat stripped off her pants, enjoying the way Emily's gaze tracked her progress. Normally, the more demanding her partner, the slower she went. But holding back was impossible when she wanted Emily so goddamn badly. As soon as her boxer briefs hit the floor, she scrambled back onto the mattress and pressed Emily's thighs apart with her hands.

"Nat…" Emily's plea turned into a throaty whimper at the first touch of Nat's tongue against her labia. Her hands found Nat's face, caressing her tenderly. "Please."

Taking that as encouragement, Nat sampled the juices trickling from Emily's opening. She was soaking wet—probably had been all evening. Her light flavor was at once familiar and long-lost, and she lapped it with enthusiasm.

"Wait." Emily closed her thighs on Nat's head. "Please, come up here and kiss me."

Nat surged upward, capturing Emily's mouth in a deep kiss that she returned with equal fervor. Positioning herself over Emily's body, she entangled their legs so she could rub her swollen clit against Emily's warm thigh. Instantly they fell into a natural rhythm, rocking against each other in pursuit of mutual pleasure.

Beep.

The noise registered on the edge of Nat's consciousness but didn't distract her from trailing wet kisses down Emily's throat to the impossibly soft space between her breasts. Only when Emily froze beneath her did she realize what she'd heard was Emily's phone—and that Emily was most likely trying to decide whether to check it.

Lifting her head, Nat mustered her best mature, understanding smile. "Do you need to get that?"

"I—" An internal struggle played out over Emily's face, then she sighed in resignation. "Yeah, I probably should."

Nat rolled off. She understood. Emily wasn't living the life of an average twenty-five-year-old woman. She had a dependent at home—a teenager, for God's sake—who obviously demanded her attention. Even, Nat mused, when it was inconvenient. She suppressed a sigh as she watched Emily dig through the purse she'd dropped beside the bed, looking for her phone.

When she found it, Emily navigated through the menu in silence, no doubt pulling up her text messages. Avoiding the urge to glance at the display, Nat studied the tension in Emily's body as she read something onscreen. At first she betrayed no reaction. After what felt like forever, she bit her lip, met Nat's eyes, then typed a brief message in reply. Locking her phone, Emily tossed it over the side of the bed.

"Is everything okay?" Nat asked. Though it appeared that Emily hadn't been called away, her heart thumped as she waited for their idyllic moment to end. "Do you have to go?"

"No, I don't think so." Emily took a deep breath. "Apparently she and her friend Kaysi had an argument. Colleen was supposed to stay at Kaysi's place tonight, but she's home now. And wondering where I am."

"What did you say?" Nat's stomach churned slightly in anticipation of her answer. She hated being Emily's dirty little secret, but understood why she didn't feel she should tell Colleen yet. If lying was what it took to get Emily to stay a little longer, she could handle that. For now.

"That I'm working late. She'll believe it."

"So you're sure you don't need to go?" Hopeful that their evening hadn't gotten cut off before it really began, Nat stroked her palm up and down the length of Emily's inner thigh. "Because I do understand, if you need to."

"No, I can stay for a while. If you want me."

"I want you *desperately*." Nat rolled Emily onto her back and returned to her position on top before she could change her mind. "Now where were we?" She pressed her thigh against Emily's pussy, then groaned when Emily mimicked her action. "Oh, yeah. Right here."

Emily lifted her head, kissing the corner of her mouth. "Let's see if we can come just like this."

Beep.

Hesitant to proceed, Nat waited to see if Emily would react to the incoming text notification. Without missing a beat, Emily rocked her hips and rubbed her slick pussy all over Nat's thigh. Nat moaned happily. If Emily felt comfortable ignoring Colleen's messages, she didn't intend to argue.

Beep.

Emily screwed her eyes shut, shaking her head in obvious frustration. "No. She's eighteen years old. She's going to college in two months. She can take care of herself for a few hours."

It sounded like Emily was trying to convince herself. With an iron will, Nat stilled her body once again. "Are you sure?"

"Yes." Emily took a deep breath and opened her eyes. She seemed conflicted, but resolute. "She isn't a little kid anymore, and I texted her that I'll be home soon. She'll just have to deal with it." Emily put her hands on Nat's lower back, pulling her close. "I can't leave you yet."

Nat saw Emily cringe slightly at her own words, so she kissed her again to silence her inner critic. That Emily wanted to be here with her so badly meant more than Nat could explain. Even if they hadn't put any labels on their relationship tonight, she no longer worried that her feelings were one-sided. Emily wanted her, too.

Desperate to feel Emily come, Nat slid her thigh against her pussy, quickly resuming her rhythm. Within moments their mouths came together and their bodies fell back into perfect synchronicity in the silent pursuit of mutual release. The sensation of Emily's supple body beneath hers was so divine that Nat dreaded having to stop for any reason. She hoped she wouldn't have to.

Beep.

This time, Emily didn't react at all.

Emily slipped her key into her apartment door a little before midnight, only to discover it already unlocked. Frowning at Colleen's lack of concern for her safety, Emily opened the door and stepped inside. Colleen was asleep on the couch in front of a blaring television—no surprise there. What shocked Emily into stillness were the three empty bottles of beer on the coffee table, one of them tipped onto its side.

Damn it. She stood frozen beside the couch, not wanting to wake Colleen until she decided how to react. Anger, confusion, and frustration warred for dominance as she processed the scene. What would possess Colleen to do something so stupid? She recalled the series of text messages that Colleen had sent to her earlier, while she was in bed with Nat.

Just got home—Kaysi decided to pick a fight and I'm not dealing with her shit tonight. Where are you?

After she had replied that she was working late and would be home in a few hours, Colleen had fired off a few more irritated messages—ones she had ignored in favor of making love with Nat.

Kaysi is a fucking bitch. Glad she's not going to school with me next year. She's supposed to be my friend, but whatever. I don't care. When will you be home? I'm bored as hell.

Emily sighed. Despite the low-level anxiety Colleen's interruptions had caused, her date with Nat had been phenomenal. So much so that when she'd left Nat's apartment, she felt like she was floating. But now, Colleen's decision to drink in *their* apartment had her rapidly plummeting back to earth. She didn't know whether Colleen had acted out of anger or boredom, but either way, drinking was unacceptable as long as Emily was paying the bills. Frustrated that her good mood had all but vanished, she bent and shook Colleen's leg more roughly than she'd intended.

"Wake up." Emily waited a beat, then smacked Colleen's thigh. "I'm serious, wake up."

"Em?" Colleen struggled to open her eyes. "What the hell time is it? Where were you?"

"It's almost midnight. And you're the one who needs to explain, Colleen. Are you *drunk*?"

Colleen's uneven peal of laughter answered the question for her. "I'm *fine*, Em. Geez, calm down. I drank a few beers. It's not like I was slamming tequila shots."

"You're eighteen years old!" Resentment for her disappearing good mood consumed Emily momentarily, leaving her struggling not to explode. "I should be able to leave you alone for a few hours without having to worry that you'll drink yourself into a stupor. How can I trust you when it seems like every time I turn my back lately, you're getting into trouble?"

"This isn't *trouble*." Colleen rolled her eyes. "It's three beers. God! Do you have any idea how easy you have it with me? I've always been a good kid. But now I'm getting older, and you have *got* to let go a little."

It was true that Colleen had always been a generally good kid. Though she'd had her fair share of emotional struggle—necessitating years of therapy after Emily took custody—Colleen was generally well-behaved. Her indiscretions and rebellions were relatively mild compared to those of many of her classmates. Considering how they'd both grown up, she knew she was lucky that Colleen had never felt the need to really act out. Maybe she expected too much from her sister—maybe she held her to a higher standard than she should. But after everything she'd sacrificed to give Colleen a loving home, it didn't seem like too much to ask her to stay away from substances.

"You just don't get it, Col. It's not about how many beers you drank. It's about the fact that you're underage, you're genetically predisposed to addiction, and you should never drink because you're pissed off at somebody. Dulling your emotions with alcohol isn't healthy." Emily folded her arms over her chest. "It's not okay."

Colleen sat with obvious effort. "Do I get to tell you why I *actually* drank those beers, or are we just going to agree to go with your version?"

Emily forced herself to calm down. This was a very fragile time for their relationship. Colleen's upcoming freedom meant that she could choose to shut Emily out completely if pushed too hard. Emily didn't know what she would do if that happened. Her entire life so far had revolved around taking care of Colleen and making sure she grew up all right. Discovering who she was without Colleen was already going to be a real challenge, but losing Colleen's steady presence in her life would be too much. Her sister was all she had.

"Okay." Emily exhaled slowly. "Why did you drink three beers?"

"Kaysi's brother picked us up a six-pack to split tonight. After we fought, I grabbed half the bottles because I'd already paid for them." Colleen gave her a defensive scowl. "So it had nothing to do with being mad at Kaysi. I would've had them if I'd stayed at her house, anyway. Instead I drank them here."

Emily's temples throbbed. "That doesn't exactly make me feel better." Colleen rolled her eyes and started to speak, but Emily held up a hand to stop her. "Listen, I get that young people—even teenagers—drink sometimes to have fun. I don't love the idea that you went to Kaysi's house to drink, but I accept that it wasn't like you were planning to bang heroin like Mom and Dad. But you didn't drink with Kaysi. You came home, and whether out of anger or boredom, you decided to drink alone. *That* is a problem. If you don't see that, then I'm really worried about you."

"Look, Em, I'm sorry. I know how you feel about me drinking. I didn't think a few beers would be a big deal, but I get that it is, for you. I'm sorry. It was stupid. I promise it's not indicative of a larger issue." She put air quotes around the last part of her sentence, lowering her voice to a sober tone that Emily suspected might be mocking her. Colleen grimaced as her hand covered her belly. "If it's any consolation, I think I'm paying for it right now."

Recognizing genuine discomfort on Colleen's face, Emily sighed. "Listen, I don't like seeing you sick. Not even if you deserve it." She gestured toward Colleen's bedroom. "Go drink some water and take some ibuprofen. I'll clean up, okay? You go to bed."

Colleen gave her a bleary nod. "Thanks, Em." She grabbed the arm of the sofa with both hands, using it to keep her balance as she struggled to her feet. "Why did they make you work so late? Who the hell needs an accountant at midnight?"

"I had some papers to prepare for a big client. A foreign client. Wildly different time zone, you know." Emily trailed off, knowing Colleen wasn't honestly curious enough to challenge her explanation. No need to lie any more than necessary. "I'm sorry I wasn't here when you got home."

Colleen stumbled toward her bedroom. "No worries. I'm a big girl. I was fine."

Sure she was. Emily sat down on the couch after Colleen left, covering her face with her hands. Less than a week—and only one official date—and already Nat had complicated her life. She had always lived by an internal code that dictated she not put anyone or anything above her sister. Yet tonight she'd done exactly that. She'd chosen to get laid instead of being here for Colleen. As a result, Colleen had turned to alcohol.

She'd told Nat that Colleen wasn't a little kid anymore, which was true. But the fact that she didn't feel comfortable leaving her alone for even one night frankly terrified her. Here she was preparing to send Colleen away to college, yet one evening apart had resulted in Colleen making a bad choice—a choice she never would have made had Emily been here to keep her company.

She blinked back the tears that threatened to spill as she considered a possible course of action. The most obvious solution— and the one she refused to pursue—was to cut things off with Nat. That was a simple answer to the problem of not getting distracted.

Unfortunately, it just wasn't an option. She was enjoying the sex too much. Hell, she was enjoying *Nat* too much. Ditching her was out.

She could simply put the brakes on their relationship until Colleen left for college. That was only two months away—doable, in theory. But even that thought caused her physical pain. Two months was a long time, especially when she considered how hard she'd struggled to get through only three days without touching Nat. No. She didn't want to wait.

Or she could stick to her guns and make the commitment to choose Colleen's needs first every time, even if it meant forgoing her own pleasure. That would require stealing time with Nat whenever she could, even if most of their interaction had to take place over the phone. The thought pained her, but it was far preferable to not seeing Nat at all. It wasn't as though they wouldn't have opportunities to get together. Colleen was attending an overnight college orientation a week from Friday. That would be the perfect time to see Nat. Another guilt-free night off.

It couldn't come fast enough.

Chapter Fifteen

Nat closed her eyes and tried not to think about Emily as a gorgeous, silver-haired butch below her nudged her one step closer to orgasm. Deb was one of her oldest clients, and her kink was face-sitting. Every appointment for the past seven years unfolded exactly the same way. Deb would disrobe while Nat watched in silence. Once naked, Deb would lie motionless in the center of her queen mattress. Next she undressed, then straddled Deb's head and lowered her pussy onto her mouth. And that was all she had to do—just sit there and withstand an intensely skillful oral assault that would sometimes last for hours. Deb liked it best when she settled her full weight on her face, allowing her only the occasional break to gasp for air. Throughout, Nat talked dirty and stimulated Deb's clit with her fingers, until finally she allowed Deb to climax with her.

She had to admit, it wasn't a bad way to make a living. Or at least it hadn't been, before Emily.

Though Deb had always been one of her favorite clients—attractive, sexually voracious, and a real gentleman—tonight she could hardly stand the wet, sucking heat of her mouth. It just didn't feel right to be with anyone else now that she had Emily in her heart. The first orgasm Deb had given her this evening had immediately flooded her with shame and regret. She didn't expect the second to feel any better.

Still, she was a professional. She lifted herself off Deb's face slightly, allowing her to breathe. "You like sucking butch pussy, don't you?" She rubbed furious circles over Deb's clit as she rocked her hips slightly, dragging her labia over Deb's nose. "You want me to come all over your face?"

"Please." Deb lifted her head, burying her tongue in Nat's folds. "Give it to me."

Nat lowered herself once more, jerking as Deb latched onto her clit and sucked hard. She missed the softer, more sensuous heat of Emily's mouth. The memory that accompanied that fleeting thought sent pleasure rushing through her lower body, leaving her teetering on the edge of orgasm. She tensed, preparing for her body's betrayal. Amazing how something that felt so good could bring such shame.

"Don't stop," Nat said automatically. She rubbed Deb's clit harder, pulling out the lines that she knew would push Deb over. "I'm almost there. Come with me, now. That's my good boi."

Deb's legs locked as she quaked in release. But her tongue never stopped moving, and though Nat tried to hold back, she was powerless against the shuddering orgasm that rolled through her body. She crawled off Deb as soon as their mutual pleasure ebbed, hoping like hell that her need for space wouldn't be taken personally.

Deb's hard-nippled breasts rose and fell with her deep breathing. She grabbed a corner of the comforter beneath them, wiping Nat's juices from her face. "*Goddamn*, you taste good." Sighing, Deb patted her on the thigh, like a sports buddy. "So come on, talk to me. What's up?"

Nat blinked rapidly. She'd honestly thought she was doing a fine job of acting like she was savoring her work. The very last thing she ever wanted to do was make a client feel as though she hadn't enjoyed their time together. That's what they paid for, after all—a sure thing with an enthusiastic partner. "I'm not certain what you mean."

Deb patted her again. "It's only because I've known you so long. You seem really detached tonight. Distant. I can tell something's wrong. How many times have you been there to listen to me bitch about my life?" She grinned broadly. "Let me reciprocate. Talk to me."

Blushing, Nat shook her head. "Tonight is about you, Deb. You're the one paying for my time, not the other way around."

"That's right, *I'm* paying *you*. So if you feel comfortable talking to me, I'm telling you that I want to listen." Deb rolled onto her side, planting her elbow so she could prop her head on her hand. "Come on. Something's bothering you."

Nat exhaled. It was totally unprofessional to bring her personal life to work. She'd never done it before—well, except for Emily. As often as she'd played therapist to various clients, she'd never crossed the line when it came to revealing her own issues. The thing was, she wasn't sure she cared about being professional anymore.

Hell, she wasn't even sure she cared about being an escort anymore.

"I met a woman." Nat pulled her knees to her chest and wrapped her arms around them. "It's hard not to think about her when I'm working." She grimaced when she realized how that sounded. "No offense."

"None taken." Deb's eyes danced. "Are you in love with her?"

"I'm getting there fast." Nat managed a shaky laugh. "I've never felt like this about anyone before, that's for sure."

"Congratulations." Deb seemed genuinely pleased, although her smile was tinged with sadness. "Does this mean I won't be seeing you again?"

Nat hadn't planned to make a decision right then. She figured she'd go home, weigh the pros and cons, and probably talk herself out of quitting. But instead she said, "I don't think you will." Her heart raced with the enormity of that thought. Sex work was all she'd ever known. She had no idea if she could actually succeed doing something else. But for the first time, she felt ready to try. "I'm sorry."

"I won't lie and say I'm not disappointed." Deb sat and pulled her into a tight hug. Despite what they'd just done—what they'd always done—the embrace was almost platonic. "But I am happy for you. You deserve the very best."

"Thank you." She squeezed Deb gently.

"What's her name?"

Nat grinned. "Emily." Just saying it made her feel all gooey inside.

Deb snorted, clapping her on the back as she broke their hug. "Getting there fast, huh? You sure you haven't already arrived?"

"Maybe." Nat lifted a shoulder. "I haven't known her very long."

"Sometimes you don't have to. That's how it was with Laura." As she always did when talking about her dead lover of fifteen years, Deb lowered her voice. Though Deb had never admitted it, Nat suspected she paid for her services because she craved sex and companionship but simply didn't believe she could ever love another woman. As long as she knew emotions were off the table, Deb could satisfy her needs without worrying about betraying the woman she'd lost to breast cancer. Deb's face softened. "A half hour after I met her, I was in love with her."

"I met Emily a week and a half ago, but I've only had the chance to actually be *with* her for about three of those days." She kept telling herself that she didn't know Emily well enough to truly love her. But that didn't change how she felt. "We have great chemistry and I can feel she cares about me, but we definitely haven't made any plans. Beyond having more sex, I mean."

Deb gave her a sympathetic smile. "Well, tell Emily she's one lucky girl. You're a real catch. And tell her she'd better treat you right."

Of all her clients, only Deb could make her feel quite so girlish. Blushing, Nat said, "I'll be sure to pass that along."

Deb rolled out of bed chuckling. Without a trace of self-consciousness, she picked up her boxer shorts and pulled them on. "Does Emily have a problem with you being an escort?"

"No." Embarrassed to admit it but committed to continue the openness between them, Nat said, "She started out as a client. Our first session just sort of...kept going. For two days."

Deb failed to suppress an amused grin as she tugged a sleeveless athletic shirt over her head. "Stud."

Nat puffed up her chest. "That's right." Laughing, she climbed off the bed and began to get dressed. "We just connected, you know? I don't think she has a problem with my job, but I'm finding it difficult to be with other women when I only want Emily. I can't stop thinking about her."

Grimacing, Deb said, "I'm sorry. You should have told me. I hate the thought that I made you do something that was uncomfortable." *Damn.* She turned to Deb with an apologetic look. "I'm sorry, that's not it at all. I don't want you to think that what we just did wasn't completely wonderful." She stepped closer to Deb, placing her hand on the slope of her breast, over her heart. "Being with you has *always* been wonderful."

Deb closed the distance between them, kissing Nat's forehead as she would a child's. "Flattery will get you everywhere." She sat on the edge of the bed. Since she showed no sign of tiring of hearing about her love life, Nat joined her on the mattress. "So what will you do? I assume you're not independently wealthy."

Nat shrugged, shy about admitting her dream to Deb. Not because she thought Deb would mock her, but because she still wasn't certain she had what it would take to succeed in the culinary field. "I like to cook. Love it, actually. I've been working on my skills for years now, trying to work up the courage to change careers." She exhaled. "Emily isn't the only reason I want to quit, but she is the perfect inspiration to finally pursue a dream I've had for a while now."

Deb studied her face carefully. "A lot less money in a culinary career than sex work, I imagine."

"Very true." Money didn't matter much to Nat. It never had. That made it easy to save most of what she earned—enough to handily accommodate a major decrease in income. "I don't need a lot of money to make me happy. Cooking is my real passion, and I want to pursue it even if it means harder work for less pay."

"It does." Deb nodded, as though she'd made a decision. "I've never told you what I do for a living."

"No, you haven't." Deb had always kept the details of her personal life closely guarded, preferring to speak only in generalities, except when she confided in Nat about how badly she missed Laura. Curiosity piqued, Nat said, "Are you going to tell me now?"

"Talk about serendipity—I happen to own and manage a restaurant. Right now we serve breakfast and lunch only, but I recently decided to extend our hours to include dinner service as well." Deb's voice rang with pride. "I'm actually looking to hire a new sous chef. It wouldn't provide the kind of pay you're used to, but I can promise you'll get good, solid culinary experience. My head chef Armando has high standards, and he's an excellent teacher."

Nat's heart pounded and all her insecurities flooded back. "That would be an amazing opportunity, Deb, but you don't even know if I can really cook or if I'm just delusional."

Deb chuckled. "Come by the restaurant next week. You can prepare a couple of your favorite dishes for me, and we'll talk." She waggled her eyebrows. "If you're even half as good at cooking as you are at fucking, you'll be just fine."

Anxiety took hold. "I've never worked in a kitchen before. I'm not even sure I'll know what to do."

Deb sobered. She scooted closer, taking Nat's hand between her own. "Do you know how much you've done for me over the past seven years? Every three months, you've reminded me what it's like to *feel* again. What it's like to pleasure a woman. It may seem like a little thing, but it's not."

Nat shook her head, caressing Deb's handsome face with her hand. "It doesn't seem little."

"I'd be honored to have the chance to do something for you now. I'm sure I'm not the only client you've made happy over the years. Frankly, it's long past time for you to be happy, too." Deb kissed Nat's palm. "If working in a restaurant would make you content, well, I'm just pleased I happen to own one."

Nat laughed. "Me, too. Assuming you decide I've got what it takes." She hesitated. "I don't want you to give me a job out of pity, okay? If my cooking sucks, I want to know. If I need to work on my skills, I will. Whatever it takes."

"I promise to be honest with you. But I'm not worried. I have faith."

Nat wished she could say the same. "Whether or not you end up being able to offer me a job, it would be great to get some feedback from someone in the industry. That would mean a lot."

"Good." Deb smiled. "So does Emily know about your upcoming career change?"

"She knows I want to cook, but I haven't told her it may be sooner rather than later." Nat hadn't dared speak to Emily about her growing unease with her job. She didn't want Emily to read more into her feelings than she was ready to reveal. "I figure I'll wait until I have something to tell her. When it's not just an idea anymore."

"Well, hopefully it'll be more than an idea soon." Deb shifted so she could withdraw her wallet from her back pocket, then fished out a business card with a flourish. "Here's my number at the restaurant. Call me tomorrow and we'll set something up for next week."

Nat took the card, humbled by the offer. "Thank you." She studied Deb's face. "You're sure you wouldn't feel awkward working with me?"

Deb waved off her concern. "I trust you to be discreet. You can expect the same from me. If I do ever become your boss, I assure you that our sexual history will be nothing more than a distant— albeit pleasant—memory."

It was sweet for Deb to be concerned, but honestly, it hadn't occurred to Nat to worry. She was a teenager the last time she had a job that didn't involve occasionally sleeping with her boss. "I appreciate that." She had a sudden thought. Sheepish, she said, "So...maybe it's time I tell you my real name."

Amusement deepened the lines at the corners of Deb's mouth. "You're not really 'Sean'?"

"Nat Swayne." She offered her hand in greeting. "It's a pleasure to meet you."

CHAPTER SIXTEEN

"Tell me something you'd like to do with me. One of your own fantasies."

Nat sighed as Emily's sultry tone washed over her. She wished they were acting out their fantasies together instead of simply talking about them on the phone. It had been a week and a half since she'd last touched Emily, a week and a half of calls like this one. As much as she cherished their conversations—falling in love a little more with each one—she craved Emily's physical closeness so keenly it hurt. Tonight marked the end of their lengthy separation, as Colleen had an overnight college-orientation session. Unfortunately, Emily wanted to wait until Colleen called to confirm that she'd reached campus before they met.

Waiting for a teenager to check in was torture.

At least talking served as effective foreplay. Nat considered Emily's question, then said, "I want to restrain you—with rope. I know a number of different bondage positions. We could experiment to find which you like best." Hearing an almost imperceptible hitch in Emily's breathing, she paused to allow her imagination to take over.

After a brief silence, Emily murmured, "What would you do to me once I was restrained?"

"Touch you everywhere. Lick you. Put my fingers inside you. Use a vibrator to tease and torture your pussy until your entire body is shaking." Nat slipped her hand into her boxer briefs but didn't dare touch her clit. She wanted to save herself for tonight. "I would force you to come over and over again, all while you're powerless to stop it. I would only stop when you literally cried out for mercy."

The only sound from Emily's end of the line was heavy breathing. Then a shaky exhalation. "Put that on our list. *Definitely.*"

Nat grinned. One pleasant result of all these phone calls was "their list"—an ever-expanding collection of sexual fantasies they wanted to try together. Given the length of the list and the diversity of its contents, she doubted their sex life would ever be boring. "Done."

"I expect Colleen to call or text any minute now. She should be there already." Emily let out a frustrated whimper that raised the hair on Nat's arms. "I'm sorry."

"I understand."

Nat *had* to understand. Emily had been devastated about Colleen's solo drinking party during their last date, and when she'd called to tell her about it, her internal conflict over where Nat fit into her busy life had been plain to hear. Sensing that the only way to convince Emily to give their relationship a chance was to demand absolutely nothing from her, she had decided to do just that.

Colleen's three beers had resulted in Emily taking a step back from their contact, only initiating phone calls when Colleen wasn't home or had already gone to bed. She'd also announced that until Colleen left for school, their dates would be few, only scheduled when Colleen was away—for more than just an evening with a friend. It was painful not to be with Emily when her very existence consumed Nat's waking thoughts and invaded her dreams, but she couldn't ask Emily to choose time with her over time with her sister. She could only hope that come August and Colleen's move onto campus, Emily would decide to turn her attention toward satisfying her own needs. And Nat's.

Emily exhaled. "You have no idea how much it means to hear you say that. I never thought I'd be able to date because I didn't think I'd find a woman who wouldn't want more than I could give. But you're perfect, Nat. You really are."

Hearing those words from Emily reminded her why she endured the pain of separation. Nobody had ever called her perfect—not in a way that made her actually believe it. She wanted to be perfect for Emily, because she believed that despite the complications, Emily was perfect for her. She wanted so much more from Emily than secret phone calls and occasionally meeting for sex, but she was willing to wait.

Nat allowed the full scope of her growing feelings for Emily into her tone. She didn't want to scare Emily away, but at the same time, she had to let Emily know how much she cared. "I just want to be with you, Em. I'm willing to do whatever it takes to make that possible. Whatever makes you feel comfortable."

"I just want to be with you, too." Emily's voice wavered with emotion. "In bed and out. Desperately."

Nat closed her eyes and allowed her fingers to roam closer to her clit. She couldn't remember ever feeling so content and hopeful for the future. Her crazy-intense feelings seemed to be reciprocated. Tonight she was going to be with Emily, and on Tuesday she had an interview with Deb and her head chef Armando at Deb's restaurant. For the first time in her life, things might just be falling into place. As scary as that possibility was, it also thrilled her.

Eager to get Emily even more excited for their date, she murmured, "Would it turn you on if I made you come where other people could watch? There's a club in the city where I've taken clients before. One woman had me fuck her with a strap-on while a crowd of men and women watched. Another client preferred to have me lick her pussy—not for an audience, but in a corner of the club where we were visible but not easily seen."

Emily giggled nervously. "I don't know if I'd like that." She inhaled sharply. "But judging from how wet you just made me, it's entirely possible."

Nat groaned. "*Don't* touch your pussy. That belongs to me."

"But it feels *so* good." Emily made a quiet, keening noise, signaling her disobedience. "And you aren't here."

"Emily." Forcing a note of stern admonition into her voice, Nat secretly hoped Emily would give her a reason to deliver a swift punishment later. "Consider this your warning. If you don't stop fingering your pussy right now, I'll make you very sorry when I see you later."

"How will you do that?"

Nat loved the coy challenge in Emily's tone. "I'll have to take you over my knee, darling. And I won't be as nice about it as I was the last time."

Emily released a shuddering whimper. "Good."

Nat broke down and dragged her fingertip over the length of her slick labia, careful not to let Emily hear her reaction to the sheer pleasure the touch elicited. "I'm warning you, stop. Take your hand out of your panties."

"I'm not wearing panties."

Groaning at both the admission and the pleasure from her own hand, Nat said, "You are in *so* much trouble."

Emily gasped. "Hold on a second." Nat stilled her fingers, listening to a slight commotion on the other end of the line. "Colleen just texted. She's at campus and checked into her room."

Nat removed her hand from her briefs. "Excellent. Do you want to come over here?"

"No, I want you to come to my place. I want you in *my* bed tonight." The sudden emotion in Emily's voice caught her attention, and she listened intently to what Emily was telling her. "When we're apart I want to remember you here, in my space. With me."

Gooseflesh rose on Nat's arms. "Okay. Give me your address and I'll be there soon."

"You'd better. I'm not sure I can wait much longer to have you."

Pleased by the urgency in Emily's words, Nat rolled off her couch and stood, buttoning her jeans with one hand. "You'll have to wait. That's part of your punishment for disobeying me." She walked to the kitchen and lifted the lid of the slow cooker on the counter, inhaling the savory aroma of the minestrone soup she'd prepared earlier. "Also, I'm bringing dinner. We'll eat first, then deal with your transgression."

Emily let out a quiet, frustrated noise. "As much as I can't wait to try more of your food, I was kind of hoping we could—"

"Nope." Nat made sure Emily couldn't hear her smile as she transferred the soup into her favorite Dutch oven. "Remember when I told you not to play with your pussy? And you did anyway?"

"It's been a week and a half, Nat. *A week and a half.* You must want me as much as I want you."

Delaying sex would only make the end result more pleasurable. Besides, she wanted to reduce Emily to mindless desire, begging for release. It would drive Emily crazy, but Nat knew she would love every second of it. "Of course I want you. And I'll have you. But first we'll eat dinner."

Emily sighed. "Just get over here. *Now.*"

Nat suppressed a chuckle. "Yes, ma'am."

CHAPTER SEVENTEEN

While Emily couldn't believe that Nat actually made them sit down and eat a meal instead of running directly to the bedroom, Nat's homemade minestrone soup blew her away. Paired with crusty sourdough bread, it was comfort food of the highest order, and once again, she couldn't remember the last time she'd eaten so well. The only thing that kept her from going back for a second helping was the knowledge that overeating would be a colossal mistake. This would be their only chance to be together for who knew how long, and Emily didn't want anything to spoil the mood.

Pushing her empty bowl aside, Emily reached over the table and took Nat's hand. "That was amazing. I know you're shy about cooking for other people, but you shouldn't be. You are *definitely* a bona fide chef."

Nat flushed with obvious pride. "That means a lot. I'm glad you enjoyed it."

"It's a real turn-on," Emily said, rubbing her thumb over Nat's knuckle. "Actually."

Nat pushed her own bowl to the side and captured Emily's hand between her own. "You're dying for me to take you to bed, aren't you?"

As though Nat had to ask. Emily had greeted her at the door with a searing kiss, dressed only in a black satin-and-lace babydoll. She'd purchased the lingerie the previous weekend, specifically to appeal to what she knew of Nat's tastes. It had been her hope that the sight of her wearing the form-fitting lingerie would prove too much for Nat's resolve, and she'd decide to forgo dinner and take her straight to the bedroom. Instead Nat had kissed her forehead, fondled her ass, then asked her to fetch two bowls for their soup. Emily had eaten the entire meal barely clad while Nat sat across the table looking just as delicious as the food in a pair of blue jeans and a thin army-green T-shirt that pulled tight over her chest.

Emily glanced down at the cleavage she was showing off, lovingly framed by the babydoll, then tilted her head and smiled. "What gave you that idea?"

Nat released her hand and wiped her mouth with her napkin, drawing the moment out. "We can go to bed now, if you'd like. As long as you understand that you'll need to take your punishment before I can allow you to come."

Squeezing her thighs together, Emily fought not to squirm on her chair. "I'm ready." She was more than ready. She'd been fantasizing about this spanking since Nat had threatened it. "Do what you have to. I understand."

A grin spread across Nat's face. She stood and walked around the table, offering her hand. "You're being very brave."

"Thank you." Emily allowed Nat to pull her to her feet. "And just so you know, my 'transgression' was worth whatever you're about to do to me." In truth, she had barely touched herself. She wasn't about to spoil the pleasure of allowing Nat to release all her pent-up desire. But she'd been happy to let Nat believe that she was shamelessly masturbating, hopeful that Nat would take the role-playing opportunity and run with it. And, thrillingly, she had. "Even if you don't plan on being as 'nice' this time."

"Be honest, darling. You don't want me to be nice." Nat tugged her closer, dropping her hand to grab her ass. "Do you?"

Shivering, Emily whispered, "No." The threat of a not-so-nice spanking had triggered her darkest, most wanton desires. Nat always gave her exactly what she wanted, and tonight she wanted her limits tested. "What would be the fun in that?"

"I'm glad we agree." Nat cupped Emily's breasts, rubbing her nipples through the sheer fabric. "Show me your bedroom, bad girl."

Biting her lip, Emily led Nat through her apartment by the hand. She'd never brought someone home before. It was strange to have Nat in her space, walking among her things. Strange, but wonderful. It made Nat's presence in her life feel more real somehow. She took a deep breath, then opened her bedroom door. Allowing Nat to be here was the ultimate show of trust. These four walls enclosed her sanctuary, the one place where she could escape the outside world. Even Colleen rarely entered her bedroom. To let Nat inside meant more than she would ever admit aloud.

"This is awesome." Nat's voice rang with affection, drawing Emily's attention to the way she gazed fondly around the room. "This place is *you*, Emily."

She had no idea what specifically Nat was talking about—her collection of math books crammed into the bookcase, the random assortment of unique and whimsical abacuses that she hunted for at flea markets, or the ratty patchwork quilt on her bed that she'd had since she was sixteen—but she didn't really care. The adoration on Nat's face made her feel like the most special person in the world. Never had she experienced even a fraction of the warmth and acceptance that Nat gave her so freely. It was a feeling like no other.

"Thank you." Looking around, Emily tried to decide what the décor would suggest about her. "Are you saying I'm a geek?"

"I'm saying you're my dream girl. My stunning, geeky, *sexy* dream girl." Nat let go of her hand and walked deeper into the room. She grinned over her shoulder. "I'm glad you invited me over. I'll be able to imagine you in here the next time you touch yourself when we're on the phone."

Emily blushed. "Nat..." She was unsure what to say. She was wet, impatient, anxious, and desperate to receive her punishment, but she didn't want to beg for it. She wanted Nat to simply know what she needed and give it to her. "I'm glad, too."

Amusement dancing in her eyes, Nat sat on the edge of the bed. Then, like a mask had dropped over her face, she was all business. "Take off the lingerie."

Emily's heart rate accelerated as she bolted into action. She didn't question, didn't tease. They both knew what she wanted, and pretending otherwise would only serve to delay the release Emily craved. She yanked the top over her head, then stripped off her skimpy panties and kicked them aside. Once bare, she stood in front of Nat and basked in the now-familiar sensation of having a fully clothed woman stare her down.

"Turn around," Nat said. "Let me look at you."

Emily pivoted in a full circle, aware of Nat's scrutiny the entire time. She remembered the first time Nat had asked her to put her body on display. How hesitant she had been. What a difference a little trust made. Tonight she was willing to do whatever Nat commanded without hesitation. Anything to please her. She was safe with Nat because Nat cared for her deeply. Even with all that remained unspoken between them, Nat wore her devotion on her sleeve.

Completing her turn, Emily stood quietly and awaited the next instruction. She assumed she shouldn't approach until asked.

Nat planted her hands beside her hips, leaning back slightly. The movement pulled her shirt tighter over her breasts, outlining her hard nipples. "Tell me why you're being punished, Emily."

"Because I touched myself when you told me not to." Emily shifted her weight from one foot to the other, feeling naked in every way. "I disobeyed you."

Nat raised an eyebrow. "That's right. You disobeyed me. Why would you do that, darling?"

She gave the first answer that came to mind. "I missed you."

Nat continued to stare at her, unwavering in her silent censure.

Shifting again, Emily mumbled, "And I was horny."

"And you enjoy the consequences."

They wouldn't be playing this game if she didn't like it. Yet the accusation embarrassed her slightly. "Maybe."

Nat smiled. "We both know you like getting taken over my knee and spanked like the naughty slut you are. Don't we?"

Emily gritted her teeth. "Yes."

"Rub your pussy. Show me what you thought was worth disobeying me. *Don't* make yourself come."

Fighting to suppress her own smile, Emily set her feet apart and dropped her hand between her legs. She looked straight into Nat's eyes as she stroked her clit, groaning at the incredible wetness that gathered on her fingertips. Nat dropped her gaze, then grabbed the crotch of her jeans in her fist as though holding back her own orgasm.

"Does that feel good?" Nat's attention was riveted on her hand.

"Of course."

Nat's mouth twitched. "Show me how wet you are." Emily held out her shiny fingers for inspection, but Nat shook her head. "No, show me your cunt."

Emily closed her eyes and spread herself open. The heat of Nat's stare scorched her flesh. "Like this?"

"You're so beautiful." The mattress creaked slightly under Nat's weight. "Look at me, please." When Emily opened her eyes, Nat said, "Taste yourself for me."

Emily ran her fingers through her folds, then brought her hand to her mouth. She made a show of licking each digit, murmuring in approval. Though Nat obviously tried hard not to react, Emily delighted at the way her throat tensed and she moved forward on the bed.

Nat beckoned her closer. "Now give me a taste."

Emily dragged her fingers through her wetness before offering them to Nat. She gasped when Nat lunged and caught her fingers in her mouth, sucking hard. When Nat released her moments later, she wobbled on unsteady legs.

"Get into position, slut." Nat grasped her forearm, dragging her onto her lap. "Let me see that pretty bottom before I turn it red."

Emily scrambled to lie over Nat's thighs, resting her upper body on the mattress so her ass was within easy reach of Nat's hand. She turned her head toward the door and picked a spot on the doorframe to study, trying not to anticipate the first blow. Nat touched her gently, simply caressing her buttocks, as Emily steadied her breathing and waited.

"This will be a harder spanking than you got last time, only because I think you can handle it." The first *smack* came as a surprise, forcing a quiet gasp from her mouth despite her best efforts to remain silent. She clamped her lips shut, determined not to give in to the urge to cry out. "How was that?"

"Go harder."

Smack. Nat's hand glanced off her other cheek, then went back to the first for a slightly harder blow. She knew Nat was taking her time and warming her up. So far the spanking felt no more intense than her first, but Nat had just gotten started. As though confirming that thought, Nat gave her two more slaps, then a third that was loud and painful, landing on already tender flesh with a resounding *crack.*

Emily cried out in genuine discomfort. At once the spanking stopped and Nat rubbed gentle circles over her abused flesh. "Was that hard enough for you?"

Nodding, Emily braced for more. "Yes, mistress."

Nat delivered four more licks, alternating cheeks as she increased the force slightly. Emily winced every time Nat's hand connected, but wiggled her bottom in anticipation of the next blow. Her pussy literally dripped with excitement, pain sharpening her arousal to dizzying heights.

"Ask me for more," Nat demanded.

"More, please, mistress." Clawing at the comforter, Emily hung on tight as she awaited the next onslaught. She both dreaded and welcomed the pain and the rising emotion it elicited. "*Harder.*"

"Tell me our safe word." Nat rubbed her bottom again.

Aware that this was simply a formality, Emily answered, "Unicorn."

"This is going to hurt, darling."

"I know." Emily took a deep breath. She wanted to feel the ache of Nat's hand on her skin for days, long after she'd gone. And she wanted to know how much she could take, because it wasn't even close to not being pleasurable anymore. "Do it."

Nat wasn't lying—the next round of blows *hurt.* Gone was her gentle lover, and in her place was a strict disciplinarian. Nat delivered the licks precisely and efficiently, never striking the same area twice in a row, but never allowing Emily to catch her breath, either. Within moments she was on the verge of tears, which she suppressed valiantly, until finally her entire body trembled with the effort to hold them inside.

The blows ceased and Nat once again soothed her bottom by lightly rubbing her cheeks. "That's my good girl." Nat grabbed

Emily's hand, prying her fingers away from the comforter. "Feel how hot your ass is."

Emily reached blindly for her bottom, cautiously touching her burning skin. She could only imagine what she must look like. The thought made her blush. "Yes, mistress."

Nat knocked her hand away, then yanked her legs apart. The cool air hit her exposed pussy, making her very aware of just how soaked she was. She jumped slightly when Nat slipped her fingers between her labia, giving her a few vigorous strokes. "Look at how wet and open that pussy is for me." Nat pushed what felt like two fingers inside as deep as she could go, taking Emily's breath away. "This is supposed to be a punishment. You could at least *pretend* not to like it."

"I'm sorry, mistress." Emily held her bottom lip between her teeth, struggling not to moan as Nat wiggled her fingertips and tickled her inner walls. "I can't help it."

Withdrawing, Nat placed her free hand on the back of Emily's neck and used the other to deliver a light slap to her exposed pussy. Emily hissed at the sting of the contact, which swiftly turned into burning pleasure.

"Do you like that, too?"

"Yes, mistress." Emily whimpered as Nat delivered a harder slap that landed directly on her labia. "I like it, mistress."

Nat smacked her pussy three more times, just hard enough to make her jump and tense up, never crossing the line into true discomfort. Emily breathed in through her nose and out her mouth, proud of the way she was taking Nat's punishment. She could feel Nat's arousal heighten with every blow.

Nat reached beneath her, sliding her fingers up so she could rub soft circles over Emily's clit. "What do you think, darling? Have you learned your lesson?"

Wiping at the tears that had already gathered in her eyes, Emily considered saying yes only briefly. But she wasn't ready to concede defeat. She wanted to make Nat proud. "No, give me more."

Nat chuckled and continued to gently frig her swollen clit. "That's a lot of bravado for a woman whose ass looks very sore indeed. Are you sure?"

"Yes, *mistress.*" Determined to withstand as much as Nat was willing to dish out, Emily placed her hands back on the comforter and grasped the material in her fists. "Just a few more. A little harder."

"All right. I'm going to give you five more licks. The last two will be the hardest." Sliding her hand from between Emily's legs, Nat gave her bottom a vigorous rub, easing the lingering ache. "And when I'm done, I'm going to make you come. Can you handle that?"

Emily nodded, finding her focal point on the doorframe. Aware that Nat was about to test her limits in a way she'd never done before, she steeled her nerve and waited. Her control had almost slipped during the last barrage, but she desperately wanted to hold it together now.

"Answer me." Nat gave her a feather-light swat on the bottom, teasing. "Can you handle that?"

"I can, mistress."

"Good girl." Nat pulled back and delivered a sharp swat to red-hot flesh. Emily gritted her teeth and grimaced at the searing pain, then cried out when the second blow came, low on her buttocks and more powerful than the first. She was grateful for her prone position, because her legs had turned to jelly. If she were standing she would have fallen already.

Smack.

The third blow jolted her and Emily keened loudly, tears spilling from her eyes. Instinct kicked in and she let go of the comforter, reaching behind her to block her ass from Nat's assault. She'd warned that the last two would be the hardest. All of a sudden Emily wasn't certain she could take any more.

Nat captured her wrists and dragged them over her head, pinning her down with incredible strength. Tears rolled down Emily's cheeks as she surrendered with a choking sob. She knew she could call out *unicorn* and Nat would immediately become the tender lover who would kiss her tears away. But not only would her pride not allow her to give in, it was exhilarating to simply *feel* so much.

"You can do this, baby," Nat murmured, then walloped her so hard it took her breath away. "My beautiful girl." Emily's breath came back in a rush when Nat hit her again, rocking her whole body forward with the force of her hand.

"*Fuck*," Emily rasped, then burst into loud, unashamed sobs.

Two things happened at once—Nat let go of her wrists to gather her into a loving embrace, and the expanding pressure in her chest dissolved as the weeks of pent-up tension escaped. Boneless, Emily clung weakly to her shoulders as Nat carefully maneuvered her onto her back. Then Nat climbed on top of her and peppered soft kisses across her tear-stained cheeks. "I'm very proud of you," Nat whispered, pulling back to stare into her eyes. "You did so well."

Emily's heart felt as though it might burst at the sight of Nat's gorgeous face filled with such tender reverence. She was overwhelmed with a myriad of sensations—the roughness of the comforter against her bruised buttocks, the softness of Nat's T-shirt pressed into her bare breasts, the absolute safety of being in Nat's arms—but what stood out above everything else was her absolute certainty that, in this moment, she was exactly where she was supposed to be. The thought chased away her fears, leaving behind one immutable truth: she was falling in love with a woman who might actually love her back.

"Nat." Emily could barely talk through her tears. "I—"

Nat silenced her by entering her slick, open pussy with a cautious thrust. Emily tipped her head back and moaned hoarsely at the intrusion, almost grateful not to have to finish her thought. She didn't trust herself not to spill her heart completely.

Suddenly Emily's bedroom door burst open, crashing against the wall so hard they both jumped in surprise. Colleen stepped into the room, her eyes fierce and dark, with their largest kitchen knife gripped in her white-knuckled fist. Her free hand flew to her mouth as she took in the sight of the two of them on the bed. The shock on her face faded fast, replaced by swift and furious anger.

"Get the fuck away from her!" Screaming, Colleen brandished the knife like she was ready to use it. "Get your filthy fucking hands off my sister."

Emily winced as Nat withdrew her fingers quickly, then she pushed Nat off to the side, putting her body between her sister and her lover. She wrestled with the comforter in a clumsy attempt to hide her nudity, then gave up when she became hopelessly tangled. It wasn't as though she had any modesty left to preserve, anyway. "Colleen, for God's sake, put down the knife. Everything's okay."

"Like hell it's okay!" Steely-eyed, Colleen darted her gaze between Nat and Emily like she was just waiting for the provocation to strike. "I heard him hit you. You were crying." She took a step closer, chest heaving. "You're *still* crying."

Emily rubbed the heels of her hands over her face, wiping away her tears. She could only imagine how this must seem. Deciding to address the most obvious misconception first, Emily said, "This is my friend, Nat. *She* wasn't doing anything I didn't want her to, I promise. Regardless of what it sounded like."

Nat sat, holding up her hands in supplication. Her skin had gone ashen. "I swear I would never hurt Emily. I care about your sister very much."

Colleen's face twisted into a snarl. "Yeah, obviously."

When it became clear that Colleen wasn't planning to lower her guard, Emily covered her breasts with her arm and bent to fish her teddy off the floor. "Seriously, Colleen, please calm down and give me the knife. We've already established that I wasn't being attacked."

Colleen gasped as Emily stood and half-turned to pull the teddy down over her breasts. "What the fuck did you *do* to her?"

Emily knew what Colleen was talking about even before she saw her sister's horrified gaze riveted to her ass. Humiliated, Emily tugged on the hem of her teddy to try and cover the red marks Nat had left on her skin. "That's none of your business. All you need to know is that it was consensual."

"*That* was consensual?" Colleen lowered the knife, curling her lips in disgust. She searched Emily's face, then took an unsteady step backward. "That's fucking sick." Glaring at Nat with pure murderous rage, she spat her words through her teeth. "You get off on hitting women? Is that it? Well, I don't know how the hell you talked Emily into going along with your fucking *perversion*, but you should be ashamed of yourself. You pathetic, fucking *dyke*."

"That's *enough!*" Emily stalked over to Colleen and carefully pried the knife from her fist. She opened her top dresser drawer and tossed the knife inside, then slammed the drawer shut. "Colleen, I'm really sorry you're seeing me like this. *Really* goddamn sorry. But you're talking to a woman I care about, a lot, and you're being completely unfair. Nat didn't talk me into anything. Let's just leave it at that." Blushing at the disbelief on Colleen's face, Emily glanced over her shoulder and met Nat's guilty gaze. "Please."

"Yeah, fine." Colleen tightened her hands into fists at her sides. "I come home and hear what *sounds* like my big sister being raped, but we'll just leave it at the fact that she's actually just a disgusting, fucking pervert."

"Hey." Nat finally stood, walking to Emily's side to rest a hand on her lower back. "This is an incredibly embarrassing and uncomfortable situation—for *all* of us—but being nasty won't make it better. So show your sister a little respect. She's a grown woman who has nothing to be ashamed about."

"Respect." Rolling her eyes, Colleen extended her middle finger and shot Nat the bird. "Yeah, whatever. Have fun being beaten and fucked, Em. I'm going to bed."

For the first time since Colleen came barreling into the room, Emily realized that something must be wrong. "Wait, why are you home? You're supposed to be at campus for orientation. What happened?"

Colleen's nostrils flared. "Don't try to turn this around on me. I'm home, you got caught, deal with it. I know I told you to get laid, but I didn't expect you to go out and become a goddamn *whore*."

Nat flinched, but Emily simply pointed at her bedroom door. "Go to your room. We'll talk about this later when you're not so emotional."

"No, I don't think so." Colleen ran a hand through her hair, wild-eyed and crackling with anger. "I've got nothing to say to you. You *disgust* me."

Until that moment, Emily hadn't had the presence of mind to feel anything beyond abject embarrassment. The venomous words sliced into her heart anew, unleashing agony like she'd never felt before. The one thing she'd always been able to count on was that her little sister looked up to her. Losing Colleen's respect was one of the worst things she could imagine.

Gathering her willpower, Emily kept her voice steady. "I'm sorry you're upset. I still say we both need some time to cool down."

With an angry grunt, Colleen spun on her heels and stomped out of the room. Seconds later, the walls shook with the force of her slamming bedroom door. Numb, Emily walked to her own bedroom door and closed it with a quiet *click*.

Nat came up behind her and touched her waist. "I'm so sorry. *So* sorry."

Emily shook her head. "It's not your fault. It's mine, I..." She tried to decide where exactly she'd gone wrong. "I shouldn't have invited you over here."

Nat inhaled shakily, sending a shard of pain into Emily's chest. "I apologize for getting involved in the discussion. I know it wasn't any of my business, and I realize this was pretty heavy for an eighteen-year-old, but I just...didn't like her talking to you that way."

Trembling, Emily turned and wrapped her arms around Nat's waist. She buried her face in Nat's shoulder, unsure what to do next but desperately needing comfort. Gentle hands stroked circles over her back, calming her instantly. "I'm sorry about what she said to you."

Nat shook her head. "She was upset. I understand."

"I'm mortified." Emily fiddled with the hem of her teddy with one hand, trying to cover herself without leaving Nat's embrace. "I can't believe she heard us. I can't believe she *saw* us."

"I can't believe she thought I was a man." Pulling back with a teasing smile, Nat gestured at herself. "What about *this* isn't feminine?"

That pulled a giggle out of Emily, almost against her will, but she sobered quickly. Things were fucked up, badly, and she had no idea how to fix them. Stepping away from Nat, she walked to her dresser and pulled out a pair of pajama bottoms and a cotton camisole. "Seriously, I could have lived the rest of my life without Colleen knowing that I like being spanked."

"Obviously it's not what you would want to share with your sister, but I hope you know it really isn't anything to be ashamed about." Still fully dressed, Nat had nothing to do except stand and stare. She seemed uncharacteristically timid, as though she was afraid of saying the wrong thing. "Believe me, I've seen a lot of kinks. Ours isn't even close to truly deviant."

Since meeting Nat, she hadn't questioned her desires even once. She'd fantasized about domination and submission, bondage, spanking, and all manner of kinky sex for years now, but until their appointment, her thoughts had always made her a little embarrassed. Having a lover who got off on giving her exactly what she wanted had changed all that. Unfortunately, Colleen's revulsion threatened to conjure up all her old insecurities, and then some.

Emily turned, folding her arms over her chest. "I'm sorry, but you can't stay." She blinked—that had come out much harsher than she'd intended. "I mean…we can't exactly go back to what we were doing, and—"

"I understand." Nat gave her a genuinely sympathetic smile. "I'm sorry we can't finish, of course, but I agree that it's best if I go." She started to take a step forward, then stopped. Uncertainty poured off her tense frame, and she looked so nervous that Emily's heart ached. "I'm glad we got to spend a little time together, though. I hope…I hope we can see each other again soon. Even if we just meet for lunch some day. Or a cup of coffee."

Emily's chest tightened at the restraint in Nat's posture and tone. Nat was clearly terrified to ask her for anything, which broke her heart and flooded her with relief at the same time. "I'll call you, okay?"

"Okay." Nat took another step closer and opened her arms with a tentative smile. "Hang in there, sweetheart. Even if she's a little grossed out, Colleen will get over this. I promise."

Emily managed a humorless chuckle as she stepped into Nat's embrace. "I hope so. I'd hate to think that I managed to get her to eighteen relatively intact, only to ruin her forever because I couldn't wait another couple of months to get laid."

Nat stiffened slightly, then released her with a kiss on the forehead. "I'm here if you need me. To talk, or whatever. All right?"

Aching at the distance growing between them, Emily caught Nat's hand before she could leave. "Wait."

Nat laced their fingers together, nervously. "Do you want me to stay?"

Emily shook her head. "Before Colleen walked in…what we did…"

Throat moving, Nat whispered, "Yeah?"

"It was everything I wanted. You were perfect."

Nat sagged with obvious relief. "I just wish I'd had the chance to give you more pleasure with that pain."

Emily's chest tightened. She had no idea when they would be together again. Right now she wasn't thinking past dealing with the fallout from tonight. She needed to see how Colleen recovered from interrupting them before she even thought about making another date with Nat. Heart rending, she said, "Next time."

Nat's smile faltered slightly at the obvious catch in Emily's voice. "Next time." She kissed Emily's hand, then walked to the door. "Sleep well, darling."

"You too." Emily put her hand over her eyes as soon as Nat left the room, holding her breath as she listened for the sound of the front door closing. When it came, she bit her lip to hold back the tears that threatened to escape at the sense of loss that swept over her. In the span of ten minutes, she'd gone from experiencing the most profound connection imaginable with another human being to feeling completely alone and ashamed. And she had no idea what to do next.

She decided to start with clearing away their supper. There was a reason compulsive cleaning was her go-to coping mechanism. Her parents had kept a filthy house when she and Colleen were children, and early on she'd figured out that tidying up not only made her feel better, but also gave her the illusion of being in control of her life. With that in mind, Emily washed their dishes and put away the leftover soup, then scrubbed every inch of the kitchen until each surface gleamed. When she finished, she leaned against the fridge and exhaled.

She couldn't stop thinking about Colleen, wondering how she was feeling. Had her anger dissipated at all? Even knowing the smart thing would be to give Colleen more time, she decided to go knock on her bedroom door. She needed to know why Colleen wasn't where she was supposed to be, whether or not she wanted to talk about what she'd seen. No matter what Colleen thought about her right now, Emily was still responsible for her wellbeing.

Colleen didn't answer her first knock. Or the second. Refusing to believe that she was actually sleeping, Emily tried a third time. "Colleen? I want to talk to you."

"Go away."

Ignoring the grumpy retort, Emily opened the bedroom door. Colleen sat on the floor with her back against the bed, face streaked with tears. She wiped at them angrily as their eyes met. "Get the fuck out of my room."

"Why are you home, Col? You're supposed to be at orientation. You texted me as much."

Colleen glared at her. "The orientation session doesn't start until nine o'clock tomorrow morning. I'll get up early and drive myself there."

"But you were supposed to stay overnight in the dorm."

"*You* were supposed to be home alone watching *The Golden Girls.*" The disillusionment on Colleen's face made her feel two inches tall. "Guess it's a night of shattered expectations."

"Tell me why you aren't where you said you would be. *Now.*" Even as strong-willed as Colleen could be, they'd never had a standoff of this magnitude. Emily's legs trembled as adrenaline coursed through her already over-stimulated body. "I'm not messing around, Colleen. Just tell me so I don't think the worst."

"I lied, okay?" Shouting now, Colleen spat her words like bullets. "I was going to spend the night with a friend instead. But it didn't work out, so I came home. I wasn't unsafe, I'm not drunk or high, and the rest of it isn't any of your business. So just drop it."

"A boyfriend?" As far as she knew, Colleen wasn't dating anyone. Meeting a boy for casual sex was definitely something Colleen would lie about. "What friend?"

"I'm not talking about it." Colleen threaded her fingers through her hair, staring at the floor. "You have no right to judge me. *None.*"

"I'm not 'judging' you. I'm trying to figure out why you aren't where you told me you were going to be."

"Who cares? I'm not. Get over it."

Emily's frustration threatened to boil over at Colleen's indignant tone. "*Enough* with the attitude."

"No, *enough* with acting like my mother!" Colleen's voice rose to an ear-shattering volume. "You're *not* my mother! Okay? I don't *have* a fucking mother. So give it a rest." She leapt to her feet and stalked over to Emily, shoving her shoulder with one hand. "What I *have* is a sister who lets a scary butch dyke treat her like a punching bag." Emily stumbled as Colleen shoved her again, knocking her against the doorframe. "You like that? Does this get you hot?"

Emily grabbed Colleen's wrist tightly. "Stop it."

"Get out of my room!" Colleen screamed in her face, taking her breath away with the intensity of her anger. "It makes me sick to look at you. So get the fuck away from me!" With that, she grabbed Emily by the shirt and forced her backward, out the door.

Emily nearly fell but regained her balance quickly, whirling to stare at Colleen in disbelief. "You're grounded."

Colleen laughed. "You're *delusional.*" She slammed the door in Emily's face.

Stunned, she stared at the painted surface that separated her from the little girl she'd raised, who now looked at her like she was a stranger. All because she'd invited a woman over for sex. Kinky sex. Shame swept through her, quickening her escape back to her own bedroom. She went straight into the bathroom and turned on the shower, eager to wash away the night.

She'd never felt so dirty in her life.

CHAPTER EIGHTEEN

After leaving Emily's apartment, Nat drove straight to Bridget's place without even thinking about what she was doing. She was parked in her driveway before it occurred to her that Bridget could very well be working. Her schedule was a lot busier than Nat's these days. The thought that Bridget might not be home threatened to shatter what little composure she had left. She dug her cell phone out of her pocket and dialed with a shaking hand.

Bridget answered on the second ring. "Hey, stud. Shouldn't you be making sweet love with the elusive Emily?"

She refused to cry over the phone, no matter how badly her eyes stung and her throat burned. "Yeah, that didn't work out. Are you busy?"

"Not unless watching reality TV reruns with a tub of ice cream counts as being busy." Despite the light-hearted comment, Bridget sounded concerned. "Is everything okay?"

"No, not really. Can I come inside?" Nat got out of the car without waiting for an answer. She knew what Bridget would say.

"You're here? Of course." Bridget opened the front door as Nat walked up onto the porch. They hung up and Bridget greeted her with a tight hug. "What happened?"

Kissing the top of Bridget's head, Nat said, "Do you mind if we sit down?"

"Of course not."

Nat squeezed and released Bridget, then walked into her living room and collapsed on the couch. Eager for comfort, she rested her head on Bridget's lap as soon as she sat down. The immediate, gentle touch of soft fingers on her scalp loosened Nat's control and unleashed the tears that had been threatening to fall since she left Emily.

"Did you guys break up?" Bridget spoke cautiously, as though she feared having her question answered. "Talk to me, Nattie. Please."

Warmed by the silly nickname, Nat said, "I'm not sure we can break up when we're not actually in a relationship."

"Did you have a fight?"

Nat shook her head. Her vision blurred as tears finally forced their way to the front. "Remember I told you how I moved in with my best friend's family for a few months after I left home?"

"Sure. Until your friend's mother walked in on you going down on her daughter and kicked you out." Bridget bent and kissed her temple. "A twist of fate that eventually led you to me, by the way."

Right now she couldn't look back at that experience with any sort of fondness. Because of that day, being caught by Tracey's mother, she'd ended up out on the street selling her body to men in order to survive. It had been the single most devastating experience of her young life, even worse than the epic fight with her father that left her homeless in the first place. Tonight's confrontation with Colleen had been no less terrifying.

"Until tonight, that was the most mortified I've ever been." Nat paused, willing her voice to stop wavering. She sounded so very small and weak—like the teenager she'd been. She was stronger now. This wasn't the same situation at all. "Emily's younger sister came home unexpectedly and interrupted us."

Bridget made a quiet, sympathetic noise. "Embarrassing, but I'm sure she'll get over it. You said she's eighteen, right?"

"It wasn't like she just caught me going down on her sister, though. She thought I was attacking Emily. She heard the tail end of a pretty hard spanking, including some tears." Nat let her own tears flow, too exhausted to hold them back anymore. It wasn't like Bridget would judge her, and her chest felt like it would explode if she didn't let some of her agony out. "It all happened so fast. I've got my fingers inside Emily, and she's staring at me like she honest-to-God loves me, tears streaming down her face, when Colleen busts in with a big-ass knife, ready to kill."

"Oh, no."

"So of course immediately I flashed back to that day at Tracey's house, the way her mother looked at me..." Nat pulled her knees to her chest, shivering. "But tonight was even worse. Emily's sister thinks I'm a sick freak who gets off on hurting women, and she's disgusted with Emily for 'going along with my perversion.' I have *no* idea what Emily is thinking right now, except that it was a mistake to invite me over tonight."

By this point Nat was struggling to enunciate through her rising sobs. She wasn't a crier. It simply didn't happen. But the thought that Emily might call off whatever it was that they were doing—which seemed like a real possibility now that Colleen hated her—flooded her with a soul-crushing sadness that made it impossible to pretend she wasn't dying inside.

"Sweetie, breathe." Bridget slipped her hand under Nat's shirt, rubbing along her spine. "What did Emily say before you left? Did you have a chance to talk?"

"She said she'd call me." Cringing at how pathetic she sounded, Nat rolled over and buried her face in Bridget's stomach. "I guess we'll see."

Bridget sighed, stroking her side with one hand, her head with the other. "That doesn't mean it's over."

Nat took a deep breath, then exhaled slowly. This was ridiculous, crying over something that hadn't actually happened yet. And even if it did happen, it would hardly be the worst thing she had ever faced. Her childhood had been nothing but misery—resented by her father from the time she was born, beaten, hated, and finally thrown out. Then losing Tracey, cast out onto the streets to fuck old men, unfaithful husbands, and creeps who weren't interested in having sex with someone they had to view as a fellow human being, all so she could put food in her belly—*that* was real trauma. Losing a woman she'd known mere weeks? In the overall picture of her fucked-up life, having Emily dump her should register somewhere near the bottom of her list of soul-destroying moments.

Yet she had never felt this level of despair. She ached inside.

"Give her a few days to smooth things over with her sister. Everything will seem less overwhelming once everyone has a chance to sleep on it." Bridget tickled the back of her neck. "Don't you think?"

"I hope so." Nat used the corner of Bridget's shirt to dry her tears, then sat up and shook off her despair. Bridget was right—this would take time to sort out. Getting weepy wouldn't change anything. Determined to focus on more positive thoughts, she said, "I have a job interview on Tuesday. For a sous-chef position at a client's restaurant."

"What? That's amazing."

She needed to work on her confidence if she really intended to pursue a new career, so she threw back her shoulders and fought the urge to play off the interview as a lark. Doing well was more important than ever after tonight. Given Colleen's venomous labeling of Emily as a "whore," Nat doubted that her current career would help change the poor first impression she'd made. "If I get an offer, I'm going to quit escorting. At least while I see how it goes."

"This is so exciting." Bridget clasped Nat's hand between her own. "I know how nervous you are, whether or not you show it, but I believe in you. And whether or not you get this job, I'm proud of you. I'm sure Emily is proud of you, too."

"I haven't told her yet."

"Why not?"

Shrugging, Nat said, "I don't want her to think I'm doing it because of her. Also, I didn't want to tell her and then not get the job. That would be embarrassing." And as much as she was trying not to worry about the worst-case scenario after tonight, she couldn't ignore reality. "Besides, it may not matter what she thinks anymore."

"Regardless of what happens with Emily, this is a great thing. It's been a long time coming." Bridget tickled her wrist, coaxing out a reluctant smile. "If your dance card is open, I'd love to take you out to celebrate afterward. We can do whatever you want."

As low as she felt at that moment, Nat couldn't imagine celebrating anything. But she nodded anyway, grateful for Bridget's enthusiasm. "It's a date."

"Excellent." Patting her thigh, Bridget beamed in an obvious effort to lift her mood. Even if it didn't exactly work, Nat loved her for trying. "Do you want to spend the night?"

"Would that be okay?" If she went home to her empty apartment, she'd stay awake for hours staring at her phone, willing it to ring. Emily wouldn't call. Not tonight, at least.

"Silly question." Bridget waved her hand in the direction of her bedroom. "If you want to take a shower, I've got a pair of your boxers in my underwear drawer. I have *no* idea how that happened, by the way."

"You're my safe haven. Seems only right to store a change of underwear here."

Bridget giggled. "I guess so." She grabbed Nat's hand as she stood to take her up on the offer. "Nattie?"

"Yeah?"

"You're a catch and Emily would be lucky to have you. If she doesn't realize that, it's her loss." Bridget stroked her thumb over the side of Nat's hand. "Even if it doesn't happen with her, you *will* find someone who sees how special you are."

Touched by the sentiment even if it failed to ease her pain over the prospect of losing Emily, she kissed the crown of Bridget's head. "You know I love you, right?"

Bridget grinned. "Of course I do. Just like you know I love you back." She swatted Nat on the rear. "Now go take a shower. We've got some bad TV to watch."

CHAPTER NINETEEN

Emily didn't call that weekend. Or text. By the time Monday evening rolled around, Nat was so paralyzed with missing her she could do nothing except sit on the couch and stare blankly at the television with her phone clutched in her hand. Her interview with Deb and Armando was tomorrow morning and she really should be practicing knife skills or preparing somehow, but she couldn't think about anything but what it meant that Emily hadn't contacted her yet.

Things with Colleen must still be bad. Colleen had been so full of anger that night, her revulsion for Nat palpable and terrifying. She knew Colleen always came first for Emily, so the fact that she hated Nat so badly made it hard to imagine a happy ending. She didn't believe Emily would choose to alienate Colleen so she could pursue a relationship with the sex worker she'd just met. Emily's devotion to her sister was one of the things Nat loved most about her, so she couldn't fault Emily for her priorities.

"But she *is* eighteen. And she'll be living her own life soon." Nat spoke to the phone in her hand, as though Emily were on the other end. "What will you have then, Em?"

Her phone remained silent. Emily wasn't going to call.

"*Fuck.*" Nat set it on the couch cushion and dropped her head into her hands. It hurt to be apart from Emily. Didn't Emily feel it, too? "Obviously not," she said.

Normally she would force herself to hang back and wait for Emily to make the first move. Tonight it wasn't so easy to play it cool. She was nervous about tomorrow, and although Bridget had spent the weekend offering steady encouragement, what she really wanted was the simple reassurance of hearing Emily's voice. She glanced at her cable box. It was ten o'clock, when they'd normally talk.

Knowing she might be making a mistake, she dialed Emily's number and held her breath as her phone rang. Her heart beat so hard she could feel it thrumming in her chest, and her stomach turned over in anticipation. Emily picked up just as she decided that she would have to leave a voice mail.

"Hey."

Nat sat up, ramrod tense. Now that Emily had answered, she almost wished she hadn't decided to call. "Hey. I'm sorry, I shouldn't have called like this."

"No, it's fine."

Emily spoke in a near-whisper, so it was difficult to discern her tone. Nat wasn't sure whether she was pleased or upset by her decision to call, which made her confused about how to proceed, or even what to say. She decided to stay as neutral as possible until Emily gave her more to go on. "How are you?"

Emily sniffled. "I really miss you." She made a small, sad noise, then fell silent.

Nat could feel Emily struggling not to say more. "I miss you, too. I figured you'd call when things had cooled down a bit, but I can't stop worrying about you." *About us*, too, but Nat left that part unspoken. "I wanted to check in and make sure you're okay." Nat hesitated. "And that Colleen is okay."

"She's still angry." Emily laughed without humor. "At least I think she is. She went to her orientation on Saturday morning, didn't come back until late, and has either been out or locked in her room since. She hasn't spoken to me, except to make snide little remarks."

Nat hung her head, rubbing her hand over her scalp. She couldn't remember the last time she'd felt so low. "I'm so sorry, Em. That's my fault."

"No, it's not." Emily's voice wavered. "You were only doing what I asked you to." Guilt rang through in her words, raising the hair on Nat's arms. "I've been thinking about it a lot, and I should have known that Colleen's behavior has been unpredictable enough lately that even a 'guaranteed' overnight is anything but. We should never have been at my apartment. So it's not your fault, okay? I don't blame you at all."

Nat wished that actually made her feel better. "I know you don't have a lot of time left before she leaves for school, and that you want to make the most of it. The thought that our relation—" She stopped, wary of describing what they had in such definitive terms. Doing so might scare Emily away. "The thought that meeting me has jeopardized this time for the two of you kills me. If I can do anything to fix this, tell me. I'll do it."

"There's nothing you can do." Emily fell silent, then sighed heavily. "She can't stay mad at me forever. Not over this. Right?"

"I can't believe she's stayed mad this long."

"She's always been strong-willed, so I guess I'm not shocked. But yeah…she's never been this upset with me before." Emily sniffled, then whispered, "Sorry. I didn't call because I wasn't sure what to say. It was a long, lonely weekend, and I thought about calling you constantly, but at the same time…I don't know. I guess I'm just feeling overwhelmed. And confused."

Confused. That didn't sound promising. "I get it. I hope my call doesn't make things worse."

"No." For the first time since she picked up, Emily's tone shifted and Nat heard familiar affection in her voice. "I meant what I said. I miss you. It's nice to hear your voice."

"Yours, too." Heart rate finally slowing, Nat stretched out on the couch and allowed Emily's presence to soothe her jangled nerves. "How was work today?"

"Same as always. I had a hard time concentrating, honestly. My mind is going a million miles an hour."

"Do you want to talk about it?" Nat was desperate for some insight into what Emily was considering. Did she plan to keep seeing Nat, or was whatever they had over? Did she think Colleen would ever accept her? If not, was that a deal-breaker? Trying hard not to allow her insecurity to show, Nat said, "Whatever you're thinking about, I'll listen. And I'll support you however I can."

"Thank you."

Nat tried not to read too much into Emily's refusal to elaborate. Emily wasn't used to confiding in others, and this situation was suddenly a big, complicated mess. No doubt she had some very tough decisions to make—decisions that would impact Nat's state of mind more than she cared to admit. But she wouldn't interrogate or push Emily in any way. She couldn't make up Emily's mind for her, and begging her for reassurances wouldn't lead anywhere good. The situation with Colleen had created so much emotional turmoil between them that she hesitated to add to it in any way.

Emily cleared her throat. "Enough about my fucked-up life. How are you? How's work?"

Nat cringed. She hadn't booked an appointment since Deb had offered her the interview. She'd told Janis that she simply needed a break, but honestly, if she got the job at Deb's restaurant, she would never do another escorting appointment. Janis didn't know that yet. Only Bridget knew, and that's the way Nat had planned to keep it until after she knew whether she got the sous chef position. Choosing her words carefully, she said, "Work is work."

There. That was sufficiently vague.

"Did you have any appointments over the weekend?"

She should just lie. It would be easier. But she couldn't—not to Emily. "No. I spent most of the weekend with my friend Bridget, watching God-awful reality television. I'm still working to restore my faith in humanity."

"Anything interesting coming up this week? Something kinky, maybe?"

Nat closed her eyes. She sensed that Emily wanted to live vicariously through her, since they presumably wouldn't be having sex anytime soon. If she were smart, she'd make something up— she knew Emily well enough to come up with a fantasy that would really get her going. But it wasn't worth potentially getting caught in a lie. Not to mention that it didn't feel right pretending to fuck other women when that was the last thing on her mind. "No. I'm actually…taking some time off."

"Oh." Emily sounded perplexed. "Is everything okay? You're feeling all right?"

"Everything's fine." Nat weighed the pros and cons of just coming clean. She hadn't wanted to tell Emily about the interview until she knew the outcome, but now that Emily knew she wasn't working, withholding the truth sure felt a lot like lying. Taking a leap of faith, Nat said, "I have an interview tomorrow. For a job."

"Tomorrow?" Now Emily was clearly shocked. "What kind of job? Another escort agency?"

Nat was surprised by how much it stung that Emily hadn't assumed she might finally be pursuing her dream of becoming a chef. That was probably her own fault for not displaying more confidence in her culinary abilities, but still—it would have been nice if Emily had reacted with excitement instead of confusion. "No. It's a sous chef position, at a restaurant in Marin."

"Really? Wow." Emily didn't sound excited in the least. On the contrary, she radiated anxiety. "When did this happen?"

"I set up the interview last week. I would've told you sooner, but…" Nat was unsure what to say. *But I was worried you would think, correctly, that I was doing it because of how I feel about you?* "I didn't want to jinx it."

"You never mentioned that you were planning to change careers right now. Not even three weeks ago, I was only the second person you'd ever cooked for. I mean, I know you told me a culinary career had 'crossed your mind', but you never indicated that you were planning to do it anytime soon." Her heart sank as Emily spoke. She'd hoped for advice, encouragement, *something*. Not the panic in Emily's voice. "What changed? Why now?"

"An opportunity presented itself. I decided to give it a shot."

Silence. Then Emily said, in a tight voice, "This isn't because of me, right? Because I would never expect you to quit your job. Seriously. And I *really* don't want you to make any big decisions on my account."

Nat bristled, both at the lack of support and the implication of Emily's words. "I told you before that I can't sell my body forever. That I wanted to cook someday." She debated hiding her hurt feelings for only a moment, then decided not to. It was one thing not to ask Emily for promises, but if being together came at the cost of suppressing all her emotions, Nat wasn't sure it was worth that. "Honestly, Em, I thought you'd at least congratulate me for trying. But I mean, don't worry...I probably won't get the job, anyway."

"I'm sure you *will* get the job. Your food is incredible." Emily's compliment should've given her a boost, but not like this, delivered with an undercurrent of dread. "This just...seems really sudden. Very rash. And the timing...well, it's hard not to worry that you're doing this because of me. Because of...whatever we've been doing."

Nat didn't understand how Emily could manage to make her feel even worse than she had before she called. Tired of apologizing for the depth of her feelings, she said, "Would it really be so awful if you *were* the reason I didn't want to fuck other women anymore?"

Emily inhaled sharply. "Oh, Nat."

She knew she'd made a mistake the moment she heard the despair in Emily's voice. "It's not like I wasn't already planning to try and make a change. I didn't decide I wanted to be a chef because I met you. You've just given me a reason to try."

"I don't know what to say."

Nat assumed that most women would be pleased that their lover wanted to be faithful. The exhaustion in Emily's voice made it clear that her fidelity was anything but welcome. "I'm sorry that I'm having a hard time fucking other women now that we're together. The last thing I want to do is upset you, but I can't help how I feel. I've never...cared for someone before. It turns out that escorting doesn't work for me when I do. That doesn't mean I expect anything from you in return."

"That's what you say now." Emily sounded like she was on the verge of tears. "But how could you not?"

"I've *never* asked you for more than you can give—not before, and not now." Nat's frustration bubbled over, fueled by her disappointment over the direction their conversation had taken.

"Don't turn this around on me. Don't act like I'm the one who's sabotaging this thing."

Emily drew in a breath as though she was about to fire back a retort, then stopped, exhaling. "Nat."

"What?"

Sniffling, Emily whispered, "I can't do this anymore."

Nat stared up at the ceiling, hollowed out by her mournful tone. She had a bad feeling about where this was heading, but she refused to make it easy on Emily. She refused to let her throw away what they'd found without argument. "Can't do what?"

"Whatever it is we're doing." Emily sounded so heartbroken that her first instinct was to wrap her up in her arms until she was better. Except she was the reason for Emily's misery, apparently. "Seeing each other."

"Fucking?" Nat cringed at the bitterness in her voice. Sometimes it felt like sex was all Emily wanted from her and Nat's desire for more was merely an inconvenience. Then other times, she seemed to reciprocate Nat's feelings. In those moments, it seemed as though they both realized they'd found something special. This was the moment of truth. Time to find out what Emily thought was going on between them, even if it destroyed her. "That's what we've been doing, right? Fucking."

Emily took a deep, shuddering breath. "You know it's more than that."

Nat's chest expanded until she felt like it might burst open. "So is that the problem? That it's more than fucking?"

Through her tears, Emily whispered, "Right now…yes."

"Right now, I understand. But what about after Colleen leaves for school?"

Emily's quiet sobs spoke louder than any answer she might have offered.

Nat closed her eyes. All of a sudden she felt very foolish. "Colleen hates me. So I guess that's that."

"Don't blame this on Colleen." The fire in Emily's instant, impassioned response made Nat's stomach clench. "This is *my* decision. Based on what's right for me—and for you."

"Don't tell me that not seeing you again is what's right for me." Nat lost her own battle with her tears. She hated being so weak with Emily, but she was done holding back. Emily was breaking her heart and Nat was going to damn well let her know it. "I've never dated anyone before, either. Never truly believed I would find someone who was worth it. But you are, Em. You're so worth it. Sometimes, I swear it seems like you feel the same way. That's why I don't understand what's happening right now. Or why you're doing this."

"What's happening is that I'm telling you I'm *not* worth it. I'm not giving you what you deserve. You're amazing, Nat. I mean... absolutely incredible." Emily's voice broke. "You should be with someone who can spend every night with you, someone who can return your feelings without hesitation...someone who's capable of even being in a relationship."

"How do you know you're incapable if you've never tried?"

Emily barked a joyless laugh. "Just trust me."

Arguing only made Nat feel more pathetic, but she wasn't ready to concede defeat yet. "There's something very real between us. You can't deny that."

"I'm not denying it." The raw pain in Emily's voice sent a shiver through Nat's body. "You're right, we do have a connection. One I don't want to lose. But I just don't see a future for us...not the kind I know you want."

"What *can* you see for us?" Nat wasn't sure she wanted the answer to that question, but she had to ask. "You say you don't want to lose our connection. Do you see any way we can avoid it?"

"I don't know." Emily hesitated. "Do you think it's possible for us to go back to something uncomplicated? Something casual?"

Nausea rose in Nat's throat. "What, like an appointment? You want to just book a couple hours with me when the mood strikes?"

Emily was quiet for a long time. Then, wearily, she said, "If that's an option, maybe it's the best way to keep things less personal but still see each other occasionally. I could pay you, of course."

Emily's words hit her like a punch in the gut. Was that all she had been? A good lay? It shouldn't come as a surprise, she supposed.

That's all she'd ever been to every woman she'd fucked. Why should Emily be different?

Yet Nat had thought she was.

Hardening her heart, Nat said, "Okay, then. I guess there's nothing more to say."

"Nat, wait. I didn't—"

"No. You want to keep things impersonal, fine. I understand, even though I wanted more than that with you. But, hell, I'm available to anyone with enough money...right? So if you want to fuck me again, you can do what everyone else does. You know, if it's not going to mean anything, anyway." Nat swallowed, forcing back the urge to throw up. Emily had just ripped her heart into pieces, and all she wanted to do now was hang up so she could mourn in private. "It's safer that way, right, Em?"

"Nat, please—"

"If you want to make a date, just call Janis. I assume you've still got the agency's number." Hand shaking, she put her thumb on the phone's End button. "I've got to go. I'll see you when I see you, I guess."

She hung up before Emily could reply.

Shit. Emily dropped her phone over the side of the bed, closing her eyes when it hit the floor with a soft *thump*. That wasn't how she'd envisioned their conversation unfolding. After spending the entire weekend isolated from Colleen and struggling with her attraction to Nat, she hadn't resolved anything by the time Nat finally called tonight. As selfish as it felt to still want to see Nat when it clearly conflicted with her responsibility to Colleen, she couldn't bear to think about never being cradled in Nat's arms again. Seeing Nat's name flash on her phone had made her happier than she'd been since the moment before Colleen caught them.

Yet she'd just broken up with Nat. Hadn't she?

Emily rolled onto her side and buried her face in her pillow. Their conversation replayed in her head, over and over. She'd been so comforted to hear Nat's voice, even though it killed her to realize how badly she craved Nat despite the clear harm their relationship had caused to her fragile bond with Colleen. She felt guilty for wanting Nat, as though she had no right to anything of her own if it made Colleen uncomfortable. That probably wasn't fair to herself, but she'd always put Colleen first. Always.

Like that time their parents disappeared for two weeks when she was eleven and Colleen was four. That first night their folks didn't come home, she had calmly made dinner for Colleen from the meager contents of the pantry, then put them both to bed. She called in to her school the next morning, disguising her voice as best she could, and made up a story about a family emergency. Even at that age, her biggest fear was being separated from Colleen if child protective services were called. So she'd simply decided to hold down the fort until their parents returned. With no money and very few groceries, she'd had to get creative. She went without, eating only one small meal a day so Colleen could have more. When their parents finally returned twelve days later, they'd offered only mumbled apologies and a box of Ho-Hos. Emily felt guilty even eating one, knowing Colleen would have less.

She exhaled. Colleen was nearly an adult and needed to learn to fend for herself, so things were different now. But that didn't mean it was easy to let go of old habits.

Still, no matter how wrong it felt to keep seeing Nat, she hadn't intended to break up with her. At least that hadn't been her plan when she'd answered the phone. As confused as she was, she hadn't had a plan. If Nat hadn't dropped that bombshell about her job interview, she might have just as easily succumbed to the lure of phone sex. Instead she'd panicked when Nat confessed that she was planning to quit escorting in favor of pursuing a career that she'd seemed to regard as a distant dream only weeks ago.

She could have praised Nat for her courage. Congratulated her for landing an interview. Wished her luck. Of all the reactions possible, selfish dread was probably the worst. Unfortunately, it had been her first, instinctive response. Given that Nat had been doing sex work for more than ten years now, it was impossible not to interpret her decision to change careers only weeks after they started seeing each other as evidence that Nat was making a commitment to her, even if she wasn't ready to do the same. The thought that Nat might rush into a major life change because of her had sent Emily into a tailspin. She was a twenty-five-year-old woman who had never had a relationship because her entire world revolved around taking care of her little sister. She wasn't the type of person Nat should ever consider upending her life to please, to say the least.

Even if Nat had pursued an interview because of her, it wasn't *only* because of her. She did know that. But once she realized that she'd hurt Nat's feelings, and that she was offended, Emily had made a snap decision that she regretted almost instantly. It was bad enough that Colleen was upset with her. When she realized how badly she'd hurt Nat, it was simply too much. Tired of the guilt and the uncertainty, she'd decided to try and end things right there.

Except she'd faltered. Unable to conceive of never seeing Nat again, she'd stupidly taken the bait and suggested that they could continue to meet for sex. To fuck without emotion. She should have known that Nat would get even more upset. It was a moronic suggestion, but one she'd felt compelled to make after considering how awful it would be to never touch Nat again.

Emily dried her face with her comforter. What was done was done. There was no point in regretting it now. She wished she hadn't said what she did about making an appointment—the pain in Nat's voice would haunt her forever, she suspected—but maybe that was for the best, too. Now Nat wouldn't attempt to dissuade her from this solitary course of action. Why try to win back someone who'd basically suggested that the only thing you were good for was sex?

Fuck. She should be relieved. She didn't have any more choices left to agonize over. No more fear of falling in love and being loved back. Nat probably hated her for what she'd just done. But that was best, right? Nat deserved better than her, and Colleen needed her full attention, anyway. Problem solved.

Sure. Except for the gaping hole in her heart.

CHAPTER TWENTY

Stomach roiling, Nat waited for Deb in a rear office of the upscale restaurant where she'd just completed her first culinary interview. It had gone well, as far as she could tell. Armando had demonstrated the preparation of one of their breakfast dishes—eggs Benedict—and a lunch plate—fish tacos—then asked her to recreate each dish on her own. After successfully completing that task—and drawing smiles from both Armando and Deb when they tasted her efforts—Armando had set her loose to create an entrée that she would want to put on the dinner menu. She'd prepared a mushroom risotto that had earned her a clap on the back from Deb and warm praise from Armando.

And to think, she'd nearly called to cancel. After her conversation with Emily the night before, the thought of subjecting herself to criticism and risking failure had been spectacularly unappealing. But it was true what she'd told Emily—she wanted to cook. It would be idiotic to throw away an honest opportunity to turn her passion into a career. So this morning she'd woken up, cried in the shower, then gave herself a long pep talk before driving to the address Deb had given her, ready to do whatever it took to impress them.

Hopefully it had worked.

Deb walked into the office wearing a broad grin. "So. You can *cook*, Nat Swayne."

Shy under the enthusiastic praise, Nat struggled to make eye contact. "Thank you."

"With that said, I'd like to talk to you about coming to cook for me." Deb sat in her leather office chair, sighing as she put her feet up on her desk. "But first, let's discuss the salary, because I suspect it may be a potential deal-breaker."

Nat blinked, stunned by how casually Deb had seemingly offered her a job. "Wait, just like that?"

"What do you mean?" Folding her arms over her chest, Deb tilted her head in obvious amusement. "You nailed the interview. We brought in another candidate last week who had three years' kitchen experience under his belt, and he didn't perform half as well as you did. The fact that I'm thrilled to be able to help you make this change aside, you deserve a chance. I'm in a position to give you one." She winked. "By the way, I *loved* the risotto. I definitely want to put it on our new dinner menu."

Nat's chin trembled. She was overwhelmed with emotion, unable to respond. In her wildest dreams, she'd never expected today to go so well. She wasn't sure what to do next, so she concentrated on fighting back the tears that threatened to escape. "The salary is irrelevant. It's not as though I have any experience, anyway."

Deb raised an eyebrow. "You may change your mind when I give you a number."

Nat shook her head. "I've made a lot of money for a number of years now. All I've ever done is stick it in the bank." Her heart thundered at the realization that she was really going to do this. She was going to change her life. "Believe me, the salary isn't a deal-breaker. It doesn't even matter."

"So does that mean you accept?"

Nearly paralyzed by an excruciating wave of doubt, Nat barely managed to look Deb in the eyes. "I've never worked in a kitchen before. I'm not sure I'll know what to do."

"You'll learn." Deb's expression softened. "And you've got to start somewhere, right?"

Nat nodded. Her fear receded as anticipation took hold. "When do you want me to start?"

"As soon as possible. Whenever you can give notice, I suppose."

"I haven't scheduled an appointment since ours. All that's left is to talk to my boss and make it official." She tried not to imagine how that might go. Janis Copeland was a genuine friend, and while Nat hoped she would be pleased for her, she couldn't be sure. She was a big earner for the agency, and her departure would disappoint a number of regular clients. "I'll do it this afternoon."

"Perfect. How about you come in later this week to take care of some paperwork, and we bring you in for your first shift next Monday?"

"Sounds good." Nat planted her hands on her knees and took a deep breath. What had just happened was so big she could hardly fathom how to react. She wasn't even sure the reality had actually hit her yet. This would probably be the happiest moment of her life, except for the fact that all she could think about was how badly she wanted to share it with Emily. Forcing away a sweeping sense of loss that threatened to shatter her composure, Nat extended her hand over the desk. "Deb, thank you for this. I promise I'll make you proud."

Deb gave her a firm shake. "No, thank *you*. I'm the one hiring a passionate, talented chef for a meager salary." She kept hold of Nat's hand, meeting her gaze soberly. "As for making me proud, you already have. You impressed both of us back there. Armando thinks I'm a brilliant recruiter for managing to find you. He has no idea how that happened, by the way. Honestly, after that performance, I'm hoping that once you spend a few months working under Armando during breakfast and lunch, you'll be ready to run point on the dinner shift." Clearly amused by Nat's surprise, Deb shrugged and released her hand. "The sous-chef salary may not be great, but there's room for you to grow. I have every confidence that you'll take this opportunity and make the most of it."

Nat's chest swelled with a wonderfully painful mixture of pride and the stunned disbelief that someone in a position to start her culinary career recognized her potential. She'd never been a good student in school, nor a talented athlete or musician. Although she knew she was a skilled lover, that didn't make her feel particularly special. Cooking did. And this was the first time in her life she truly felt like she was worth a damn.

Except, that wasn't true. The first time was with Emily. Emily, who was the reason she was sitting here now, experiencing her second major triumph. Alone.

Nat was horrified when her tears finally spilled over. Refusing to succumb to her emotion, she affected her toughest butch persona, swiping at her eyes and throwing back her shoulders. "I appreciate that. You won't be sorry."

"I know."

Nat left the restaurant, still reeling from the swift turn her life had taken. The urge to call Emily and share the good news was overwhelming, but she knew she wouldn't get the reaction she wanted. Besides, she was angry with Emily. More than that, she was hurt. Stunned. When Emily suggested that they might continue seeing each other professionally, her callous disregard for Nat's very real emotions hit her like a semitruck. As though she could simply turn off her feelings and fuck Emily with cold, professional distance. The fact that Emily would even suggest such a thing made her feel very small, and very cheap. Like she was only good for one thing.

Emily wasn't the first person to make her feel that way. But she would damn sure be the last, if she had any choice in the matter.

With that in mind, she drove to the penthouse where the Xtreme Encounters agency was headquartered. It doubled as Janis Copeland's second residence, after the small apartment she kept in Marin. Nat had no doubt that she would find Janis at the penthouse in the middle of the day. She was a shrewd businesswoman who was deadly serious about building her little empire. Which was why she probably wouldn't be pleased with what Nat needed to tell her.

Nat parked her car and walked to the front entrance, holding her breath as she pressed the buzzer. Janis's voice came over the intercom within seconds.

"Yes?"

"Janis, it's Nat. Do you have a few minutes?"

Rather than answer, Janis buzzed her in. Nat took the stairs two at a time in an effort to burn off her nervous energy. It worked. By the time she reached the fifteenth-floor penthouse, she was too exhausted to wallow in her anxiety.

Janis opened the door just before she could knock. Attired in a designer dress that probably cost more than Nat would spend on clothing over the course of her entire life, Janis wore her auburn hair perfectly coiffed, as though she'd just stepped out of the salon. Fifty-two years old, she managed to be both regal and sexy without seeming to try. "Oh, my. Did you really just run up fifteen flights of stairs?"

Panting, Nat managed a short nod. "May I come in?"

"Of course." Janis stepped back, openly scanning her body as she staggered inside. "Do you want something to drink?"

"Please. Would you like something, too?" Nat followed Janis into her office, walking to the bar and setting up two glasses. She always served Janis. Falling into their familiar routine comforted her slightly, even as her heart ached at the knowledge that things were about to change.

"Why don't you make us a couple of vodka martinis?" Janis approached from behind and rested a hand on Nat's hip. "You look like you need one."

The scent of Janis's light, expensive perfume triggered a Pavlovian urge to turn around and slide her hands beneath the skirt of her classy, well-mannered boss. Janis would be willing—she always was—and right now, the allure of touching familiar curves almost overpowered her. Even if she didn't feel for Janis what she felt for Emily, they did care about each other. And being inside someone she cared about just might help her feel less alone.

Doubtful, but it could work. After Emily, Janis was the closest thing she had ever had to a real lover. She had initiated their first encounter shortly after she was hired, mostly because her first pimp had conditioned her to expect that fucking the boss was just another part of the job. But to Janis's credit, she quickly shut down Nat's clumsy attempt at seduction, letting her know that although she was attracted to her and would happily play, those duties weren't in her job description.

Nat had fucked her anyway. And had kept fucking her, sporadically, over the past eight years. In a way, Janis Copeland was her longest-term relationship. But while she enjoyed the sex and genuinely cared for Janis, there was no love in their coupling—just friendship, attraction, and a mutual desire for occasional pleasure.

As tempting as it was to fall back into old habits, Nat finished making their martinis. "I do need a drink. We may both need one, in a minute."

Janis took the glass from her hand without breaking eye contact. "Uh-oh. Does this have something to do with all those appointments you had me cancel?"

Nat told herself that the lump in her throat was simply a result of her already volatile emotional state. That she wasn't going to lose it now, with Janis. "Yeah, it does. Listen, I actually need to talk to you about something. About..." She took a quick gulp of alcohol in a desperate attempt to calm her nerves. "I'm sorry, this is hard."

"Let me make it easy on you, then." Janis took her hand and led her to the vintage loveseat on the other side of the room. She tugged Nat down to sit beside her, then gave her a bittersweet smile. "You quit. Am I right?"

Nat blinked away her rising emotion. "Yes."

"Well, damn." Janis took another dainty sip of her martini, with a rueful shake of her head. "I can't say I'm entirely surprised. But I will miss you, and so will your clients."

"I know." Nat tossed back the rest of her drink, then set her glass on the coffee table in front of them. "You've always been good to me, Janis. And just so you know, I'm not going to work for another agency, and I'm not branching out on my own."

Janis raised an elegantly sculpted eyebrow. "Early retirement? Or a career change?"

"Career change." Blushing, Nat said, "I've just been hired as a sous chef at this little restaurant downtown. The Vine Street Station—have you heard of it?"

"Oh!" Janis's face lit up. "My brother-in-law took us there for breakfast once. They have wonderful omelets. It's very quaint, a charming little place." She set down her drink, covering Nat's hands with her own. "You cook? I didn't know."

"Not many people do." Nat shrugged. "I've mostly kept it secret."

"I'll say. So what inspired you to go from secret chef to shopping for a new career?"

Nat really didn't want to talk about Emily. She was barely hanging on to her composure as it was. "I'm almost thirty. It's time."

Janis scoffed, dragging her gaze along Nat's torso. "Almost thirty? You've never been sexier. Trust me, you've got plenty of miles left on you."

"Maybe. But I'd rather spend them doing something that truly fulfills me."

With a long, drawn-out sigh, Janis scooted closer and traced a fingernail along the exaggerated curves of her pinup-girl tattoo. "So you're saying that being the best lay I've ever had isn't fulfilling?"

Nat chuckled, nipples tightening under Janis's teasing caress. Those painted red nails got her every time. "No, it definitely is. Just not in the same way."

"I do understand that." Janis exhaled, then gave her a mock glare. "Well, I'm pleased that you're following your dream, even if I really will miss you. And not just because you're the most popular escort working for me. If you ever want a job in the future, or even if you just want to moonlight, let me know."

"Thank you." The hair on the back of her neck stood on end as Janis's hand moved to her chest, seizing an erect nipple between two perfectly manicured fingers and twisting lightly. Normally this would be when she'd kiss Janis, but as much as she craved the warmth of a female body, only one woman could truly satisfy her needs. Fucking Janis wouldn't make her feel better, not really. "Jan—"

"Oh." Janis dropped her hand from Nat's chest, easing away. She studied Nat's face, then chuckled. "I see." Her eyes sparkled with amusement. "You've met someone."

"Stop being so perceptive," Nat grumbled, though she was honestly grateful that Janis could so easily read her body language.

She respected Janis too much to want to forcefully push her away. "Honestly, we kind of broke up. Like, last night. So as much as I love being with you, and as good as I know it would feel..."

"You're nursing a broken heart." Janis stared at her with quiet, tender sympathy. "Oh, honey. I'm really sorry."

Nat lifted a shoulder, ready to brush off Janis's concern, but instead her chin trembled and tears streamed from her eyes before she could stop them. She shook her head and lowered her face, embarrassed to let Janis see her so undone. "Whatever. It was probably doomed from the start."

"But you obviously care about her a lot." Janis went from seductive to maternal so quickly that Nat struggled to adjust. When Janis pulled her into a tight hug, she tensed for a moment before surrendering to the warm safety of her arms. Janis kissed her temple, as though Nat were a child. "Do you love her?"

She was glad Janis couldn't see her face. Red eyes, tear-streaked, with her bottom lip quivering uncontrollably, she knew she looked pathetic. Ridiculous. Heartbroken. In other words, exactly how she felt. "Yeah, I love her. Doesn't look like she feels the same way, though."

"Well, then she's a fool. That's the only explanation for letting someone like you go." Janis's hand, which had been rubbing her back, stilled suddenly. "Was she upset about you being an escort? Is that why you've decided to change jobs?"

"No, she wasn't upset. In fact, she was unhappy that I was planning to. She thought I might be doing it because of her, and apparently that smacked of taking our relationship too far, too fast." Nat pulled away, taking deep, regular breaths in an effort to calm down. "I've wanted to be a chef for a while now, but I didn't think I was ready. Meeting Emily gave me the push I needed to try. But she didn't like hearing that." She fell silent, anger building as she thought back on their conversation the night before. "Anyway, what's the big deal about not wanting to fuck other women? It's not like I asked her to marry me."

"I'll say it again, she's a fool." Janis patted her knee sympathetically. "So her name is Emily? Where did you meet her?"

Nat cringed. "Technically, you introduced us. Her last name is Parker. Abduction fantasy. You met her when she came in for her client evaluation."

Gasping, Janis brought her hand to her chest. "Oh! I *knew* you were going to like that one."

"Yeah, I did. Very much. And then it got...complicated."

"So she broke up with you *because* you decided to become a chef?" Janis frowned. "Why?"

"It wasn't just that. Honestly, she told me from the start that she wasn't looking for a relationship. She's raising her younger sister, she's busy, she's scared..." Nat shrugged, trying to act less affected than she was. "I think the last straw was when her sister walked in on us when we were in a...delicate situation. Her sister freaked, and then Emily freaked. The job interview just gave her the excuse she was already looking for, I think."

"That *does* sound complicated."

Chin trembling at Janis's obvious sympathy, Nat swallowed back the angry words that sat on the tip of her tongue. Then she spit them out. "And then Emily has the gall to suggest that maybe we can still meet for *appointments*. You know, something impersonal. Something that won't threaten to upset the neat order of her life. Because obviously a whore like me can just turn off her feelings and fuck, right?"

"Nat, sweetheart..."

Shaking her head, Nat exhaled harshly. "It doesn't matter. I'll get over it." Even as she said the words, she didn't believe them. "It wasn't meant to be."

"You don't sound so sure of that."

Nat nodded, then cursed as she dissolved into fresh tears. "That's because I'm not."

CHAPTER TWENTY-ONE

Emily tried not to let her gaze stray to the time displayed in the lower right corner of her computer monitor, content to pretend that it wasn't already six o'clock in the evening. That was hard to do when the office was so eerily silent, the regular hum of productivity having quieted an hour ago. Only her boss Denny remained, but he would also leave soon. He had a seven-year-old son, so despite his workaholic tendencies, he never stayed too terribly late. She used to be the same way, mostly, but since the break-up with Nat and the new distance between her and Colleen, she no longer had any reason to rush home. Her loneliness only intensified when she wasn't keeping busy with work.

A knock on her door startled her into awareness. Denny held onto the doorframe with a sheepish smile on his face. "Sorry, I didn't mean to frighten you."

"I'm fine," Emily said automatically. That was her standard response to everyone. She was always fine—even when she really, really wasn't. "Heading home?"

"In a few minutes." Denny stepped inside her office, holding up a ledger she'd worked on that morning for one of their biggest clients. "Emily, is everything okay?"

Emily swallowed as her throat went dry. She wasn't sure why he was asking, but it couldn't be good. "Of course. What do you mean?"

"Well, I just caught a transposition error. And a reversal of entries."

Heat crept up her face. Two mistakes? She usually double-checked her work, so she couldn't remember the last time she'd let even one error slip through. "I am *so* sorry."

"No worries, mistakes happen. That said, they don't usually happen to you." Denny held the ledger against his chest, clearly nervous about the conversation he had initiated. "I've noticed that you've seemed a little...distracted lately. So I thought I'd ask."

Emily tensed at Denny's tentative attempt to get her to open up. He was a nice man, with sandy-brown hair that was graying at the temples and glasses that made him look both handsome and intellectual. From the way he talked about his son, he seemed like a good father. She had mused once or twice about how her life would have been different with a dad like him, but they'd never had a personal conversation before, despite his general air of kindness.

"I'm fine. Just...some stuff going on at home." Emily folded her hands on her desk to stop them from shaking. She hated talking about herself with co-workers, even the ones she genuinely liked and respected. "I promise I won't let it interfere with my work again."

"I'm not trying to reprimand you. Or pry." Denny stepped closer to her desk, seeming to gain a little confidence. "You're excellent at your job, Emily. We're lucky to have you. I just want you to know that if something is bothering you, if you need to talk, I'm a pretty good listener. And...I hope I'm not overreaching." He exhaled as his nerves visibly resurfaced. "I'm sorry, I don't mean to make you feel uncomfortable. I just figured...if I could do something to help. If you need some time off, or whatever...Just let me know."

Time off was the last thing she needed. Work was the only thing keeping her mind off the mess she'd made of her life. Still, Denny was obviously trying to be helpful. She forced a smile. "I really do appreciate that, but it's not necessary. My younger sister and I had an argument, and it's been weighing on me. I'm her legal guardian, so the occasional major clash sort of comes with the territory, I guess."

Denny's gaze softened. "Being a parent isn't easy. How old is she?"

"Eighteen. Leaving for college soon."

"How long have you had custody of her?" Seemingly emboldened by her willingness to open up, he rested the ledger casually against the chair on the other side of her desk.

Never having had a conversation like this at the office, Emily wasn't entirely sure how much she should say. She absolutely, wholeheartedly did *not* want to over-share. But they were both just people, it was after hours, and it felt damn good to talk to someone who wasn't upset with her. "Since she was twelve. It took me a year after our parents died to get her out of the foster-care system. First I had to turn eighteen, and then I had to prove I could care for her."

"Wow. *Eighteen?*" Denny looked at her with new respect. "I don't know how you did it. I mean, I know she wasn't a baby or anything, but when I became a father at thirty-five, I worried that I wasn't possibly mature enough to take care of another human being. When I was eighteen…I was in college, drinking beer and chasing girls."

Emily always felt jealous when people spoke about college as a time of freedom, fun, and personal growth. Those had been the hardest years of her life. "I took most of my college classes online and studied at night when Colleen was asleep. I worked during the day, when she was in school." Embarrassed by the growing sympathy in Denny's eyes, she shrugged. "It was worth it. The alternative was foster care. I only spent a couple months in a foster home, but it was enough to know that Colleen was better off with me."

Denny exhaled and shook his head. "I already knew you were an impressive accountant. Now it turns out you're an all-around impressive human being. I'm not sure I could have done all that."

Emily waved him off. "I did what I had to." Not taking care of Colleen had never been a real option. "Anyway, I appreciate your concern, but we'll be okay. We're sisters. She can't stay mad at me forever."

"Pretty soon she'll realize what you sacrificed for her. I'm sure she'll always be grateful, once she's grown up enough to understand."

She would be lying if she denied hoping that was true. Since Colleen was born, she'd done everything possible to give her the childhood, and then the adolescence, that she'd never had. She didn't want Colleen to have to worry about what they would eat, or where they would sleep, or how to pay bills with parents who spent all their cash on heroin. Every sacrifice was worth it if it meant Colleen's biggest worries could be grades, boys, and getting into college. She felt like she'd mostly succeeded on that front, even if Colleen had rewarded her with some questionable behavior. Unfortunately, she was starting to understand that the cost of Colleen's happiness was her own youth and joy.

Somewhere along the way, sacrificing for Colleen had become second nature to the point where it didn't seem to matter that her sister wasn't a child anymore. Emily had just destroyed her first real opportunity to love someone because it took time away from Colleen and because catching them together had upset Colleen so badly. Naturally she wanted Colleen to appreciate how much she had sacrificed to make her happy—including Nat.

To be fair, her fear of investing her emotions in something she couldn't control had also played a large part in the way she'd sabotaged things with Nat. She'd figured that worrying about Colleen was exhausting enough. Being in a romantic relationship would stretch her already strained mental and emotional resources to the breaking point, especially once the honeymoon phase wore off.

Emily tightened her hands into fists. Although she kept telling herself that losing Nat made things easier, clearly that wasn't true at all. Nothing felt easy anymore. Nat had insinuated herself into her life with startling ease, and although she'd only had their regular phone calls for a few weeks, she missed knowing Nat would be there when she needed to talk. Or when she needed to feel another person's heartbeat pounding against her chest.

Denny cleared his throat, breaking her out of her introspection. "Well, try to do something nice for yourself. Take it easy." Sheepish, he bobbled the ledger in his hands. "After Seth was born, my wife was so focused on taking care of the baby that she forgot to ever do anything for herself. She went on that way for months, until one night I came home to find her sitting on the kitchen floor, crying, with a burned pot roast on the counter above her. After that I instituted a mandatory four-hour time-off break for her on Wednesday and Sunday evenings. Having permission to focus on her own needs every once in a while seemed to make all the difference in the world."

Emily gave him a rueful smile. "I'll keep that in mind."

"Anyway. If you do decide you want that day off, let me know. You've certainly earned it." Denny tapped the corner of the ledger on her desk. "I'm heading out. You should, too."

"I will." Emily nodded at her monitor. "Right after I double-check the expense report I just prepared."

Denny grinned. "I'll see you tomorrow. Drive safe."

"Thanks." She watched Denny's back as he walked away, relaxing only when he exited the office through the big glass doors. Finally alone, she fought back her embarrassment as she reviewed their conversation in her head.

Though it was true that her argument with Colleen humiliated and upset her, it was the breakup with Nat that had really shattered her world. She could hardly think of anything else. Even the awkwardness of living with someone who thought she was a deviant somehow wasn't as bad as not having Nat's warm presence to come home to—whether it was her voice or her body. Colleen would forgive her eventually, but Nat would disappear, receding into her memories as the ultimate what-if. Nat would be the regret to haunt her for the rest of her life.

Emily leaned back in her chair and closed her eyes. If she hadn't pushed Nat away, maybe *that* would have been her regret. Raising Colleen until she was eighteen, then promptly alienating her with her choice of a sex partner—how could she feel good about that? Of course, she'd feel worse if Nat was only just a sex partner. And she clearly wasn't.

That was precisely why her "I'll just hire you to fuck me" suggestion had been so colossally, stupidly bad. So hurtful. So destructive. So precisely the opposite of doing something for herself and focusing on her own needs.

So *typical.*

CHAPTER TWENTY-TWO

When Emily got home from work at eight o'clock that night, she was surprised to find Colleen waiting in her regular spot on the couch. Since their blowup a week and a half ago, Colleen had spent almost all her time at home locked in her room. They'd spoken no more than necessary. The friendship Emily had been so excited about after her coming out had simply vanished. Although she knew that the tension would eventually blow over and Colleen would forgive her, she hadn't expected it to happen anytime soon.

Yet Colleen greeted her with a tentative smile. "Hey, Em. Are you hungry? I ordered Chinese. It should be here in about ten minutes."

She couldn't even think about food. Her stomach had been in constant turmoil since Nat hung up on her the night they last spoke. "No, thanks. I'm not feeling well."

Colleen's smile faded. "Well, do you want to watch TV with me while I eat? You can pick the show. I'll even watch *The Golden Girls* or one of those other ridiculous eighties sitcoms you love so much."

Apparently she'd been forgiven. Instead of the relief she had thought she'd feel, anger bubbled up in her chest. Now that she'd gotten her way and Nat was gone, Colleen was ready to make nice. Meanwhile Emily was miserable and alone. Trying hard not to lash out, she walked past the couch without meeting Colleen's worried gaze. "Honestly, I'm tired. I may go straight to bed."

"Wait."

Emily stopped. As mad as she was, she couldn't walk away. With her back to Colleen, she said, "What?"

"Emily, look at me."

Irritated, she turned and stared Colleen down. "What?"

Colleen shrugged, as though she were both embarrassed and annoyed by what she was about to say. "I'm sorry."

Tears stung Emily's eyes. "Just like that?"

"Cut me some slack, Em." Colleen came up on her knees, turning to peer over the back of the couch. "It scared the hell out of me to come home and hear what sounded like someone beating you. When I heard you crying out, I went into this kind of trance. I've never been so terrified in my entire life, but I grabbed that knife and I was *ready* to kill whoever was attacking you." She paused, taking a deep breath. "I didn't know you were sleeping with anyone. You've never let on that you're anything but the world's most boring lesbian. So it didn't occur to me that I might be interrupting something consensual. Not only because it sounded violent, but because that looked like a *man* on top of you. I thought your life was in danger. I really did. I thought…" She shuddered. "It doesn't matter. The point is that I was really, honestly afraid. So maybe I overreacted a little once I realized you were okay. I shouldn't have shoved you…or said what I said. So I'm sorry about that. I am."

"I'm sorry, too, that you were scared." Emily had placed herself in Colleen's shoes more than once since that night. If she'd walked into the apartment and overheard the same thing, she would've also burst into Colleen's bedroom with a knife. That part was understandable. So was Colleen's embarrassment and anger when she realized that Emily's life had never actually been threatened. "I understand why you got upset. You had no reason to think I would choose to do that with someone. I wish you still didn't, honestly."

"Me too." Colleen twirled a lock of blond hair around her finger. "Kaysi told me I was being too judgmental. That people like different things, and as long as two adults agree on what they want, and nobody gets seriously hurt, it's really nobody else's business. She also said she likes it when her boyfriend smacks her ass in bed, and that it's not as fucked up as I think." Blushing, she said, "Then she Googled erotic spanking and showed me how many millions of search results come up. So I guess she's right. Maybe I'm the fucked-up one."

Emily softened at the humiliation in Colleen's expression. "You're not fucked up. That stuff's not for everyone."

Colleen looked down at her hands. "Yeah. So anyway, I'm sorry about what I said that night. About you being disgusting and stuff. I…didn't mean it."

Disgusting was the least of the insults Colleen slung that night. One thing had bothered her more than the rest. "You said a lot more than that."

Colleen lifted her gaze. "Like what?"

"About Nat. You called her a dyke. Twice."

"You know I'm not homophobic." Straightening in defiance, Colleen narrowed her eyes. "I don't have a problem with you being a lesbian. I was just upset."

"I know you were upset, and I understand, but that was really out of line and hurtful. You were out of control." As much as she appreciated that Colleen had initiated an apology, she wanted to make damn sure she understood the implications of her actions. "We were all embarrassed about the situation, but your reaction turned an awkward moment into a complete nightmare. It was unacceptable."

"Fine. It was unacceptable." Colleen started to roll her eyes, then stopped. Sighing, she studied the fabric beneath her hands. "Look, I don't want to get into a whole discussion about this, but I…" Her voice broke, and she cleared her throat. "There was a man in my last foster home. He was an asshole. He got angry a lot, he was abusive, and sometimes he said and did things that…made me very uncomfortable. When I walked in and saw you guys that night, it just sort of took me back there. And I freaked. I know I said some horrible things, and maybe I even meant some of them at the time, but all I can say now is that I'm sorry. I was there, but I wasn't there. Part of me was somewhere else. You know?"

Colleen's revelation knocked the wind out of her. It confirmed something she'd always suspected but had never known for sure.

Post-foster-care Colleen had been a different girl than the eleven-year-old she'd lost to the system while she fought for custody. Only a year had passed, but there had been a definite shift. Of course Emily had asked her about it, but Colleen refused to talk about her time in her foster home. That's why she'd gotten Colleen into therapy as soon as she could afford it—almost two years later.

Two years, her baby sister had suffered with the repercussions of abuse alone. And that was assuming that she had ever chosen to discuss this with her therapist.

Emily struggled to swallow. "Colleen—"

"I told you I don't want to talk about it."

"Okay." Numb, Emily walked to the sofa and sat down. She still wasn't interested in TV night and Chinese, but her legs were shaking too badly to keep standing. If Colleen didn't want to discuss it, she wouldn't force her. She wasn't even sure she wanted to know. Still, she hated the thought that Colleen had been keeping such a terrible secret. "Did you tell your therapist?"

"I did. And I'm fine." Colleen played with her hair. "It was just…that night, the memories were intense. And the fear that I might lose you was very real. When I realized that you'd willingly put yourself in that situation, that I'd been terrified for nothing, I snapped." She fell silent, giving Emily a tentative look. "Plus I had a really bad night before I even got home. Flashing back to that man pushed me over the edge. But still, I am sorry. I shouldn't have called your friend a dyke. I knew it would hurt both of you and that's exactly why I said it."

Just like that, the last of Emily's resentment dissolved. Guilt took its place. She pulled Colleen into a tight hug. "No, *I'm* sorry."

Colleen grabbed her shoulders. "Stop." Drawing back, she stared at Emily with gravity beyond her years. "This is why I didn't want you to know. I didn't want you to feel like it was your fault, because it wasn't. Nothing that happened to us was your fault. You were seventeen, with no full-time job and no way to take care of a little kid. There was nothing you could've done that you didn't do. I always knew that. So it took a little while for you to get me back. Some siblings wouldn't have even tried."

Tears spilled onto Emily's cheeks. "I just wish I could've spared you from that."

"Blame Mom and Dad." Colleen flashed her best gallows-humor grin. "I always have."

Emily nodded, then retreated to her side of the couch. With her anger gone, she wasn't sure how to feel. Self-recrimination was a no-brainer, considering what Colleen had just revealed. Flattered, that Colleen had finally trusted her enough to tell her. Frustrated, because she'd pushed Nat away for reasons that seemed less and less important now that she and Colleen were talking again. So many emotions swirled around inside her, threatening to explode.

"Are you okay?" Colleen nudged her with a sock-covered foot. "I didn't tell you that to upset you. I wanted you to know that I wasn't being an asshole that night just for the hell of it."

"I know you weren't." Emily released a shaky breath. "And I don't know how I am."

"Em—" The doorbell rang. Colleen held out her hand in a silent plea for Emily not to get up. "This will only take a second. Don't go anywhere."

"All right." Emily closed her eyes, resting her head against the couch cushion while Colleen paid the delivery boy. She wanted to crawl in bed and stay there forever. Now that she knew exactly how her encounter with Nat had impacted Colleen, she felt lower than low. And still, what she craved more than anything was a simple phone call with Nat or, better yet, being held in her strong arms. It was the only thing that she knew would ease the pain in her chest.

Colleen touched her arm. "Em."

Startled, Emily sat up. "I was just resting my eyes."

"Looked more like you were upset." Ignoring the cartons of food on the coffee table, Colleen sat cross-legged on the couch and searched her face. "Please don't be sad. I told you I'm fine now."

"It's not that." Emily hesitated, then admitted, "Well, not entirely."

"Then what?"

"I'm just…tired."

"No, you're sad," Colleen said. "It's obvious. You've been moping around here for days. I was hoping that apologizing would help."

"It does."

Colleen tilted her head. "But something else is wrong?"

She met Colleen's eyes. "I don't want to talk about it."

Colleen nodded. She turned to the coffee table and opened the container of lemon chicken with a happy sigh. Never having had enough patience for chopsticks, she grabbed a fork and shoveled a bite into her mouth. Unladylike as ever. Without tearing her attention away from her food, Colleen said, "So your friend? Nat?"

"What about her?" As hard as she tried to keep her voice even, she knew she sounded upset and defensive. With effort, she relaxed her shoulders.

"Are you dating her? I mean, is she your girlfriend or something?"

"No." Emily paused, fighting to bring her rising emotion under control. "I'm not seeing her anymore."

"Oh." Colleen chewed in silence, then gave her a sidelong glance. "Was it because of what happened that night? 'Cause she seemed like more than just a fuck buddy. The way she defended you and everything."

A fresh tear escaped from Emily's eye and tracked its way down her cheek. She wiped it away with a casualness she didn't feel. "It's complicated. That's all."

"Complicated how?" Colleen stopped chewing. "Wait, did Nat end it, or did you?"

Emily didn't respond. The answer was too complex to boil down. She'd used her obligation to Colleen as her main justification for running away, but honestly, her flight response was more about her own fear than anything. Nat had been willing to take whatever she could give, as long as their relationship meant *something*. Colleen had been the most convenient excuse for why she had nothing to offer, but she wasn't the real reason Emily had run away. If she'd truly wanted to make things work with Nat, Colleen's initial impression of her girlfriend wouldn't have been a deal-breaker. If she had been brave enough to take a chance on another person, she would never have given up fighting to make it work—just like she'd never given up on taking care of Colleen.

Growing visibly upset, Colleen said, "Did she break up with you because of me?"

"No, it wasn't like that." Emily struggled with how to explain her relationship with Nat without admitting that it had started as sex with a stranger that took an unexpected detour into genuine attraction. But she didn't want Colleen to worry that she'd ruined a long-term relationship when Emily had been avoiding making a commitment from the start. "She knew I wasn't looking for anything serious. That I have too much going on to devote time to a girlfriend."

"Like what? You barely leave the house except to go to work." Colleen's eyes narrowed. "Wait, you mean me?"

"Well, you're part of it, obviously."

"Why is that obvious? It's not like I'm a little girl anymore. You don't exactly need to be home to supervise me every second." In a huff, Colleen shoveled a bite of chicken in her mouth and chewed angrily. "Don't blame your lonely spinsterhood on me."

Emily flinched at the harsh words. "I'm not. But I've taken care of you since the day you were born, and now you're getting ready to leave for college. There's nothing wrong with wanting to spend as much time as possible with you while you're still living with me. That doesn't mean I blame you for the fact that I'm single."

"Whatever. I'm not saying I think you *should* date that proto-butch or anything, but it's pretty lame to act like *I'm* the one keeping you from doing so."

Even though she'd just come to a similar conclusion, Emily was rankled by Colleen's obvious irritation. It wasn't as though raising a teenager made it *easy* to date. Losing her tenuous hold on her control, she lashed out. "You don't think you make dating more difficult for me? The one night I tried to go out to dinner with Nat, I came home to find you passed out drunk on the couch. And then when I finally had a night to myself and invited her to our place, you burst in unexpectedly because you'd lied to me about where you were going to be. Why *wouldn't* I feel like you're a legitimate complication in my life? I've sacrificed everything for you. Why not a relationship, too?"

Colleen set down her fork and pushed her food away. Then she sat back on the couch, folding her arms over her stomach. Tears streamed from her eyes as Emily watched in silent horror. "I never asked you to sacrifice everything for me."

Emily winced. She never should have thrown that in Colleen's face. Even if she was angry, it wasn't Colleen's fault. "No, you're right. You didn't. And you didn't have to. I wanted to."

"I don't want you to be sad. I don't want you to be alone." Colleen scrubbed away her tears without looking at her. "Haven't you been listening to me? I really am worried about what will happen to you when I go to school. Don't you think I realize that you pretty much live for me? How do you think that makes me feel about growing up and leaving?" Colleen finally met her eyes. "Honestly, that's why I've been such a bitch lately. I guess I thought it might make you not miss me as much when I'm gone."

Snorting, Emily murmured, "No matter how obnoxious you are, I'll still miss you."

"Yeah, I kind of know that." Colleen picked at the knee of her pajama pants. "Seriously, I hate the thought that you might honestly believe you can't have a girlfriend because of me. If you had someone—and I'm not saying it has to be Nat, mind you—but if you had *someone*, then at least you wouldn't be so lonely. You'd have someone else to look after."

"I'm not sure *that's* what I want."

"Well, someone to look after you, then."

Emily smiled at the memory of Nat making her the crepe for breakfast. *When's the last time someone took care of you?* If that's all there was to being in a relationship, it would be easy to buy into Nat's vision of them together. Unfortunately, she wasn't naïve enough to think that the shine of new love wouldn't eventually wear off. At the end of the day, her life was far from exciting, and Colleen would always be an essential part of it, no matter how old she was or where she lived. Considering where she'd come from, she felt like she was doing well on her own. Did she really want to give someone else the power to determine something as fundamental as her happiness?

She snorted quietly. Like she hadn't already. It had been almost two weeks since she'd spoken to Nat, and she hadn't felt genuinely happy even once in that time. Surely the pain would lessen eventually, but she wasn't certain her regret would. She nudged Colleen's foot with her own. "You're right. It's not your fault that I don't have someone. It's mine. I'm scared to death at the thought of being in a relationship."

"Why?"

"I don't want to fall in love with someone only to have her disappoint me." Emily swallowed the lump in her throat. "I'm not used to depending on anyone but myself. I'm used to being in control. The idea of giving my heart to someone—with no way to stop her from stomping on it if she wants—terrifies me."

"You think Nat will stomp on your heart?" Colleen tried and failed to suppress a giggle. "I mean, she *did* stomp on your ass pretty good. But you seemed to enjoy that."

"Shut up." Face burning, Emily said, "I think Nat would treat me like a queen—at least at first. It's what happens when she realizes what a boring control freak I really am that worries me. It's not that I think she'll treat me badly. Just that she'll leave at some point, and then I'll have to start all over again. But with a broken heart."

"Oh my *God*, that's depressing." Colleen came up on her knees, reaching to smack Emily's thigh. "Snap out of it! Are you seriously telling me that you're choosing to be sad and mopey because if you tried to be happy, maybe it wouldn't work out? What are you so afraid of? Obviously it's not being alone, *or* sad and mopey. You already are."

Emily screwed up her face in what she feared was a hopeless battle not to lose her composure. Colleen was blunt, but she was also right. "I know. It doesn't make a lot of sense."

"It really doesn't." Colleen's expression softened. "You've always been the best sister—and the best *mother*—so I know you would be an incredible girlfriend, too. Nat, or whoever, would be stupid to let you go. The right woman won't." She smirked. "No matter how boring and controlling you can be."

Emily wasn't sure what surprised her more: Colleen's kind words or that she sounded like she genuinely believed in true romance. "The right woman, huh? You think there's someone out there for everyone?"

"I think there's someone for you."

"Oh, my. Can it be that I actually managed to raise a starry-eyed optimist?"

"No, you raised someone who believes there are people in this world who will love you so much they would do anything for you." Colleen's nostrils flared as she struggled to hold back what appeared to be a crushing wave of emotion. "And I *don't* believe that you can't depend on anyone but yourself. Why would I?"

Colleen's heartfelt words left Emily caught between laughter and tears. To hear such hope and youthful idealism from Colleen made every moment of struggle, every sacrifice, worthwhile. From the day Colleen was born, all Emily had ever wanted was to give her what she'd never had. Apparently this was what success looked like.

Hoping to capitalize on Colleen's obvious moment of gratitude, Emily said, "Please tell me where you were the night you were supposed to stay on campus. I promise to try and not get upset about whatever you tell me. I just want to know. You said you had a really bad night so I need to make sure you're okay."

"I'm okay." Colleen took a deep breath, then threw her hands in the air as though admitting defeat. "Remember Jason Komanski?"

"Of course. The boy you dated last year, who took you to his senior prom?"

"He lives on campus. I was supposed to crash in his room after this party at the frat he's pledging—except he spent the entire time we were there talking to this slut in a permanent state of nip slip. Meanwhile one of his frat buddies was being drunk and obnoxious and grabby, and Jason didn't even bother to stop talking to that bitch to tell him to back off. So I left." Colleen folded her arms over her chest in her classic defensive posture. "I didn't have anything to drink, I swear. I wasn't ready for another hangover."

"All right. I believe you." Though her instincts screamed at her to lecture Colleen about the dangers of frat parties, it wasn't the right move at that moment. "Thank you for telling me."

"Yeah." Colleen snorted under her breath. "It's embarrassing. I slept with him after prom last year, and even that wasn't enough to keep him interested."

Emily closed her eyes. She wished she hadn't just heard that. "Guess we're even on things we don't want to know about each other."

"Guess so." The amusement in Colleen's voice told her that she'd chosen to make that disclosure on purpose. "We were safe, by the way."

"Good to know. Still traumatized." Finally opening her eyes, Emily couldn't help but return Colleen's smile. "You know, he's an idiot. And you're way too good for him."

"Yeah, that's what Kaysi said, too."

"I always knew I liked that girl." Emily frowned as a thought occurred to her. "Wait, I thought you and Kaysi had fallen out?"

Colleen's expression turned sheepish. "Our fight was about me spending the night with Jason. She thought I was an idiot for going up there and rewarding him with sex since he pretty much never texts me anymore. When he pulled that shit at the party, I couldn't exactly stay mad at her for being right. Luckily, she forgave me for the way I lost my shit with her when she tried to warn me. She understood. The beauty of unconditional friendship, I guess."

"I guess." Emily had never had unconditional friendship before—probably because she'd always told herself that she had no time for that, either. In just a few weeks, Nat was the closest she'd ever come to having a real friend. Unfortunately, she didn't know whether Nat would so easily forgive her if she worked up the nerve to apologize.

And she wasn't certain she was brave enough to find out.

Sighing, Emily picked up a pair of chopsticks from the coffee table. She still wasn't hungry, but she had to eat at some point. "Hey, Colleen?"

"Yeah?" Colleen offered her the container, watching as she captured a piece of chicken between her chopsticks. "Show-off."

"Let's make a deal. No more lying. You're eighteen years old, and you're right—you *are* growing up. So if I promise to treat you like the young adult you are, will you promise to act like one? That means trusting me not to be unreasonable or to overreact when you tell me what's going on in your life." Emily paused. On a night of confessions, it only seemed right to admit her deepest fear. "I don't want to lose touch with you just because you don't live with me anymore. I know I'm not your mother, but the way I feel about you, I may as well be. I would hate for you to become a stranger now that you don't have to listen to me anymore."

"I'd never let that happen. I have always and will always need you in my life, even if we do argue sometimes. And I promise— no more lying." Colleen met her gaze. "Now will you promise me something?"

Emily hesitated, then said, "Sure."

"Promise me you'll call Nat and ask her if she wants to try again."

CHAPTER TWENTY-THREE

It wasn't that easy, of course.

If she had simply told Nat she didn't have time to date, that would be one thing. She could call, tell her she'd reconsidered, and as it turned out, she *could* make time in her schedule to fall in love. But she'd done something so much more cowardly than that. She'd selfishly turned Nat's good news into a deal-breaker. Then she'd suggested that things would be so much simpler if only they could go back to playing high-priced escort and loveless, pathetic client. She'd trivialized their very real connection by implying that all she needed from Nat was emotionless sex.

And she'd done it knowing—*knowing*—that wasn't true.

Emily wasn't even sure she could forgive *herself*. If she'd lost Nat forever because she'd been too afraid to try and keep her, it would stand as one of the most foolish missteps of her entire life. Still, as scared as she was to find out whether she'd ruined her chance with Nat, she had to try to apologize. Time—and her conversation with Colleen—had put a lot of things into perspective. Pushing Nat away had been a spineless move. She was more miserable now—and less present in every aspect of her life—than she had been even with the "distraction" of dating.

Funny how breaking things off with Nat had accomplished exactly the opposite of what she'd intended. Without Nat, she seemed to be worse—as a sister, as an accountant, maybe even as a human being. Objectively, it made sense to see if she could actually make a relationship work. If she could, she would be better off. If not, she'd be in exactly the same boat as she was now. That Colleen had not only given her blessing but also outright encouraged her to pursue Nat gave her the courage she needed to swallow her pride and send Nat a text.

Did you get the job?

It was short, to the point, and not nearly as apologetic as she felt, but Emily told herself it was prudent to keep her message brief until she knew whether Nat would even respond. No sense pouring her heart out to an unsympathetic audience.

When the response came, forty minutes later, the single word revealed nothing about Nat's mood.

Yup.

Emily smiled as her eyes filled with tears. She should have been there to reassure Nat before her interview, then to congratulate her once it was over. But she hadn't. Fingers shaking, she texted back.

I'm so proud of you, Nat. You deserve it.

Then she waited. And waited. An hour later, Nat still hadn't replied.

Unwilling to give up that easily, Emily sent another message. Something unambiguous, she hoped.

I miss you.

Her phone beeped not five minutes later. The two sentences on-screen reached into her chest, grabbed her heart, and shook it like a wolf does its prey.

This is my personal number. If you want to make an appointment, call Janis at the agency.

All right. Obviously Nat was still upset. Emily bit her lip and debated what to do next. She hadn't wanted to actually contact Janis and pretend like she and Nat were nothing more than escort and client, but if that was the only way Nat would see her, so be it. She would play whatever game Nat wanted if it meant she could apologize face-to-face. The upside to making an appointment was that Nat would be professionally obligated to meet her.

The downside was that she would have to dip into her savings account to make it happen. Emily snorted. She *must* be falling in love.

Surrendering to that thought, Emily looked up the number to the Xtreme Encounters agency and dialed.

Exhausted after a long day at her new job, Nat rested on her couch and stubbornly refused to wonder how Emily would respond to her last text message. She'd thrown down the gauntlet, telling Emily to call Janis and make an appointment, and she damn well knew it. But Emily couldn't have it both ways. Either they had a professional relationship or a personal one. Emily had chosen professional, and if she wanted something deeper, she was going to have to do a hell of a lot better than impersonal, vague text messages.

In a perfect world, Emily would reply back that she didn't want to make an appointment—that she wanted to apologize. She'd say that she'd made a terrible mistake, and that she was sorry, and that Nat hadn't been crazy to feel like they had the sort of chemistry that could overcome any obstacle. She would beg for another chance, and Nat would *feel* her sincerity, so of course she would forgive her.

That was the best-case scenario. Worst-case, Emily could take her terse instructions as a hostile good-bye and disappear from her life forever. Despite her lingering anger, that wasn't what she wanted. She could still see a future with Emily—she could practically *taste* the life they would make together. It wasn't that she didn't want Emily back. She just wanted to feel like she was the one being chased, at least for a little bit. She needed to know that Emily was willing to work to win her back.

That was assuming Emily even wanted her back in that way. It was entirely possible that Emily simply craved a casual, paid encounter. Maybe she missed the sex but still wasn't ready to offer more. Maybe she honestly believed Nat was capable of fucking her without loving her, which meant she was crazy as fuck on top of being the most perfect woman Nat had ever met.

Nat's stomach flip-flopped when her cell phone began buzzing its way across her coffee table. It took her a moment to realize that she had an actual call and not just a reply from Emily. She rolled onto her side and grabbed her phone before it fell off the edge of the table. Her throat went dry when she saw Janis's name on the display.

She rolled onto her back and answered, heart pounding as she stared up at the ceiling. "She actually tried to make an appointment, didn't she?"

"She did." Janis's warm voice managed to relax the tension in her shoulders, allowing her to exhale slowly. "I told her I'd have to get back to her. I didn't *even* want to guess what you would prefer I tell her."

"She texted me a few hours ago. Congratulated me on the new job, told me she missed me." Nat hesitated. "To be fair, I told her to make an appointment. I think maybe I was hoping she'd just apologize instead. Or call me. Or something."

"Well, she did what you told her to do. Now what?"

"I don't know." Nat tried to imagine meeting Emily for fantasy sex. She still wanted to fuck Emily—nothing had changed in that respect. But she was so hurt and so angry she honestly didn't know how to be near Emily without losing her cool. If it turned out that all Emily wanted was a good, hard fuck, Nat would be shattered. "What did she say?"

"That she'd like to see you as soon as possible. She wants to pay for the entire night."

Nat winced. She'd returned her portion of Emily's money for their first appointment, but the agency had kept its cut. Now Emily was prepared to pay thousands of dollars for the opportunity to be with her again. She battled a wave of guilt at the thought of Emily parting with her hard-earned money just as she was getting ready to pay for Colleen's college. "We're not taking her money."

"I know that." Janis's haughty tone conveyed her distaste that Nat would even go there. "She sounded very nervous. I didn't let on that I knew about you two. When I asked her what she wanted, I could sense that she struggled to answer."

"And?"

"She wants you to punish her. She wants, and I quote, for you to 'take what's yours.'"

Nat's breath hitched as her mind began running through various ways she could do exactly that. She tried not to dwell on the implications of Emily's choice of words, too afraid to believe that she'd really had such a dramatic change of heart. "Oh."

"Wet?"

"You can't imagine."

Janis chuckled. "Sure, I can." She cleared her throat. "So should I set something up?"

"Yes," Nat said, then shook her head. "No. I mean, I don't know."

"Yes, you do."

Nat sighed. "Of course I want to see her again. But if I show up and all she wants from me is a good fuck, I don't think I'll be able to handle it."

"But at least then you'd know." Janis paused. "If this was just about sex, don't you think she'd ask for someone else? Someone uncomplicated?"

It wasn't as though Nat had a real decision to make. Of course she would go. "All right. Tell her any evening this weekend works— after six o'clock. But I don't want her to come to my place. Until she tells me otherwise, this is all business."

"I'll let you use one of the agency's apartments. Mine, if I have to."

Relieved, Nat said, "You're a good friend."

"I sure try. Anything else you want me to tell her?"

"Ask her to repeat our safe word: *unicorn*. Make sure she remembers." Nat shivered as she began to plan their encounter. "She may need it."

CHAPTER TWENTY-FOUR

Emily's hand trembled as she knocked on the door of a top-floor apartment. She checked the time on her cell phone and then the address Janis had given her. Nat had agreed to meet her on Saturday night at eight o'clock, and for three days now, Emily had worried about what would happen when she saw her again. There was so much she wanted to say. She doubted she would remember any of it once Nat was standing in front of her. Just thinking about the possibility of touching Nat made her feel dizzy, like she might pass out. She wished Nat would answer the door so she could go sit down.

Next to Colleen's custody trial, no moment had ever felt so important. For all the academic achievements and career triumphs Emily had racked up, nothing had ever truly fulfilled her like one weekend with Nat. If she'd lost the chance, however slim it might have been, to somehow try and turn that magical weekend into months or even years, she would be devastated. Now that she had opened herself to the idea of being with Nat, the thought that she might've thrown away the relationship they could've had crushed her. It would take baring her soul to convince Nat to take her back, and even if that wasn't always easy for her, she was ready to do it now.

She just hoped she would have the chance before passion swept them away. She desperately wanted to know where they stood before they jumped into bed, but if Nat initiated sex, she would be powerless to resist.

Even with her safe word.

Emily shivered, then knocked again. She was a little early, but hopefully Nat would forgive her for that, too. She was too impatient to wait in her car for another five minutes. The anticipation was killing her. She needed to know whether Nat could forgive her. She needed to apologize.

A warm body pressed against her back, making her gasp. Strong fingers covered her mouth and muffled the sound. "Don't." That one word, whispered next to her earlobe, turned her insides to liquid. "Don't make this any harder than it has to be."

Emily closed her eyes and sagged against Nat's chest. She wasn't sure whether Nat was playing a role or pleading with her not to bring emotion into what they were about to do. Hopefully it was the former, because the latter was impossible. She'd been foolish to ever think for even a moment that she could allow Nat to touch her without it meaning something. It meant *everything*.

As Nat dropped her hand from her mouth to her throat, Emily murmured, "Nat—"

"No." Nat tightened her fingers ever so slightly on Emily's neck. Her other hand pressed a key into Emily's palm. "Unlock the door. We're not here to talk."

Emily angled her head, fitting the key into the lock without leaving Nat's possessive grip. Somewhere below them, a chorus of loud male laughter shattered the quiet. The reminder that someone could interrupt them heightened Emily's sense of danger and unleashed an embarrassing flood of wetness between her legs.

"Go inside." Reaching past her hip, Nat grabbed her hand and forced her to turn the knob. She pushed open the door and walked them into a large foyer in one smooth motion. Then she locked the door with a quiet *click*. Emily barely had a chance to look around the lavishly decorated apartment before Nat caught her wrist and tugged her backward into a crushing embrace. "You want to be punished? You got it."

There was so much Emily needed to say, but as she feared, she had neither the time nor the presence of mind to find the words. Nat dragged her over to the couch, yanking her shirt and bra over her head and tossing them onto the floor. Emily turned, hoping for a kiss, but Nat seized her chin before she could bring their mouths together.

"No." Nat grasped her shoulders and turned her around, forcing her over the arm of the couch. Emily fought against her instinct to struggle and surrendered to Nat's will. Her feet came off the floor as Nat held her by the back of the neck, pushing the side of her face into the cushion. "This is what you wanted."

Emily whimpered as Nat reached beneath her and worked open the button on her pants. She opened her mouth to initiate the conversation they desperately needed to have, but couldn't speak. Nat's hands were strong and already so familiar, and she had missed them more than she'd realized. Now that those hands were on her again, she was hesitant to do or say anything that might make them stop. If Nat couldn't forgive her, this would be their last time together. She didn't want to end it before it even began.

So she lay helplessly as Nat undressed her—cold, efficient, and without any discernible affection. Nat unzipped Emily's pants quickly, not bothering to be gentle as she shimmied them down her hips and off. Her panties followed. When Nat grasped her thighs and forced her legs apart, Emily came up on her elbows just to regain the illusion of control. The cool air in the apartment hit her exposed labia, making her uncomfortably aware of the fact that she was literally dripping with arousal.

Nat gave her a hard smack low on her left buttock, then repeated the action on the other side. "You can't tell me I'm not giving you exactly what you want. Not when you look like *this*." She spread Emily wide open, using her free hand to pat her labia—gently at first, then harder until Emily gasped and pulled away. "You just want to get fucked, don't you? That's all a girl like you *really* needs."

Emily's breath caught in her throat. Nat hadn't said or done anything she hadn't said or done before, yet everything about this experience felt different. She sensed a hard edge to Nat's words, despite her flat tone. Her fingers were as skillful as always, sliding over her folds, circling her clit, teasing her with the promise of penetration. But there was no love in Nat's caress. It felt even more impersonal than their first time.

Emily needed more. She needed all the things she had taken for granted before—the intimacy, the connection, the palpable adoration in Nat's touch. When Nat dragged questing fingers up to circle her anus, Emily planted her hands on the couch and tried to regain her footing. All of a sudden, she didn't want to let Nat take her like this. Without that thread of love and trust between them, it wasn't the same. "Wait."

Nat pushed her back onto the couch cushion without ceasing the motion of her fingertip around her tight opening. "Silly girl." She reached beneath Emily's chest with the same hand that had forced her down and cupped a breast in her palm. "You know that won't work."

Emily bit her lip. She didn't want to use their safe word. It felt like admitting defeat. So she said the only other thing she thought might make Nat stop—which was also the most important thing she had to say. "I love you."

Nat went still. She kept her hands on Emily's body, but the stimulation stopped immediately. "What?"

"I mean, I think I…" Emily wasn't sure whether it was crazy to conclude that love was what she was feeling. They'd known each other for less than two months. Was it possible to fall in love so quickly? She didn't even know what it felt like. But if this wasn't it, what was? Exhaling, Emily went with what her heart was telling her. "I'm in love with you."

Nat's hand fell away from her bottom. She exhaled, an audible hitch in her breath. "Don't tease me, Em."

The fearful hope in Nat's voice made Emily dizzy with relief. Perhaps it wasn't too late, after all. She glanced over her shoulder and met Nat's eyes. Still spread out on the couch, she felt vulnerable and exposed in every way. She hoped Nat could see that, too. "I'm not. I wouldn't—never about that."

A tear fell from Nat's eye and tracked its way down her cheek, in stark contradiction to her steely gaze. Emily held her breath, aware that this was it—the moment that would determine whether they had a future together. She'd just given Nat the power to destroy her. All she could do now was hope that she wouldn't.

❖

Emily loved her. Stunned by the declaration, at first Nat wasn't sure how to react. She'd spent the past two weeks in complete agony because of Emily's inability to share herself, and now here they were—Emily posed and spread open on the couch like a porn actress, breathily confessing her love just as Nat was ready to give her a cold, uncaring fuck simply to prove a point. There were so many ways she'd imagined this appointment could unfold, but somehow she'd never anticipated how this would actually feel. Sickened by what she'd almost done, she hurried to pull Emily off the couch and onto her feet.

Turning so they were face-to-face, Emily searched Nat's eyes, nostrils flaring. "I'm so sorry. I was selfish, and a coward. Telling you that I would pay you to keep having sex with me…was inexcusable. It was disgusting." She shook her head and looked away. "It was also stupid. Sex isn't enough. Not with you."

"For me, either." Nat had spent the last twenty-four hours steeling her heart so she could somehow try and fuck Emily without loving her—as though that was even possible. Allowing the wall she had erected to come down was more difficult than she'd thought it would be. "What's changed?"

"Nothing, really." Clearly self-conscious, Emily folded her arms over her bare breasts and lifted one shoulder in an embarrassed shrug. "Me. I realized how idiotic I was being. I'm miserable without you."

"Me too." Nat softened when Emily shivered. She took off her jacket and wrapped it around Emily's shoulders, helping to cover her chest. "Here."

Emily pulled the jacket closed and dropped a quick kiss on her cheek before she could back away. "Thank you."

Dizzy at the sensation of Emily's lips against her skin, Nat tightened her fists at her sides and put some distance between them. She wasn't ready to drop her guard just yet. "What about Colleen?"

The smile Emily gave her was tinged with pain. "We're good. We had a long talk, she apologized for overreacting that night, and she also…" Her voice wavered. "She helped me understand her frame of mind when she found us. Fortunately, her best friend helped her decide that I'm not an irredeemable pervert, and as it turns out, she's more worried about me being sad and lonely when she goes away to school than she is about me dating you."

Nat exhaled shakily. She was so close to crumbling and just pulling Emily into her arms, but she needed to be sure that Emily was saying what it seemed like she was saying. "I thought you were incapable of being in a relationship."

Emily's smile vanished. "I know I said that, but I guess I'm hoping it's not really true." She fidgeted with Nat's jacket, tightening it around her shoulders. "I don't want it to be. I'm *better* when I'm with you. I'm happy."

The last of Nat's hurt and anger faded away. She took Emily's arm and led her to the sofa, sitting down and pulling her onto her lap in one swift motion. Hugging her tight, she kissed Emily's lips. She'd forgotten how soft they were. Between kisses, she murmured, "I forgive you."

Now sobbing, Emily struggled to match Nat's kisses through her tears. Her entire body trembled. "Really?"

"Of course. I love you, too."

Emily broke away to bury her face in Nat's neck. Nat rubbed her hand up and down Emily's spine, memorizing the sensation of having the woman she loved back in her arms. She tried not to think about the beautiful, naked curves beneath her leather jacket, or the hot, moist folds that she knew were pressed against her blue jeans. Now that Emily's wall had crumbled, Nat just wanted to make love to her. However, she sensed that Emily was still trying to process being forgiven.

"I'm so proud of you for getting that job." Emily fisted her hands in Nat's shirt, bringing them even closer together. "I hate that we fought right before your interview. I can't imagine how difficult—"

Nat cut her off with another kiss. "You were scared. It happens." Pressing her forehead to Emily's, she murmured, "Just promise me you're really back. I don't think I can handle having you run away again."

Emily shook her head and reinitiated their kisses. "No, you're stuck with me." She shifted so she could straddle Nat's thighs, sitting on her lap so they were face-to-face again. "I'll do my best not to screw this up. I have no idea what I'm doing, but I'm ready to try. I want to try, with you."

Nat's heart swelled until she felt like her chest might split open. "You'll be wonderful." She cradled Emily's cheeks, pulling away to stare into her eyes. "Does this mean you're my girlfriend?"

Emily broke into the goofiest grin, and from the way Nat's face ached, her expression probably matched. "I guess it does."

"And does *that* mean I can make love to you now?"

Emily shrugged off Nat's jacket and let it fall to the floor. Nat lowered her gaze and admired the breasts she'd tried not to notice earlier, when she'd been attempting emotional distance. Soft, plump, and topped with nipples that always seemed to be hard, Emily's breasts made her salivate like a horny teenager every time she saw them.

Emily curled a hand around the back of Nat's neck. "Kiss my nipples."

Slowly, deliberately, Nat dropped a wet kiss on one, then the other. She sucked the stiff peak into her mouth, reaching between Emily's thighs to cradle her mound. Emily sighed and tightened her grip on her neck. Savoring the incredible heat of slick flesh against her fingers, Nat circled Emily's clit as gently as she could.

"Oh, Nat." Emily groaned, rocking her hips in a slow, sensual rhythm. She keened softly when Nat took a nipple between her teeth and bit down. "Go inside. I need you inside me."

In no mood to tease, Nat slid her index and middle fingers into Emily, driving them as deep as she could go. Emily clutched at her shoulders and cried out, a smile playing across her face as she adjusted to the invasion. Nat took as much of Emily's breast into her mouth as she could, never stopping the motion of her thumb against her swollen clit. When Emily's thighs began to tremble, Nat rubbed faster, desperate to hear her come.

"I love you," Emily whispered, moving her hand to rest on Nat's head. "I love you, Nat. *I love you.*"

Overcome by the intensity of Emily's words, Nat released her breast with a salacious nibble and looked up into her eyes. "I love you, Em. You feel so good wrapped around my fingers. So tight. So beautiful." She was babbling, but that was okay. They would have time for eloquence later. Right now she needed Emily to know that the emotional weight of this moment was mutual. "I will do *everything* to make you happy. Anything."

"Just you." Emily gasped, rising and falling on her fingers. "I only want you."

Tangling her free hand in Emily's hair, Nat brought her down for another passionate kiss. She licked Emily's bottom lip, then bit it lightly. "Come for me, baby. Let me hear you."

Digging her nails into Nat's scalp, Emily rode her fingers until she climaxed with a series of achingly feminine moans. Nat dropped her hand to press between Emily's shoulders, keeping her upright as she came down from her high. Emily's body twitched with each stroke of her thumb against her sensitive clit, but rather than pull away, she only cuddled closer.

"I'm so stupid," Emily said in a tearful whisper. She dropped a hand between her legs, holding Nat in place. "I almost lost you."

"No, you didn't." Without removing her fingers from Emily, Nat shifted their bodies so they lay on the couch, belly to belly. She used her free arm to gather Emily into a tight hug, alarmed by the raw emotion pouring from the woman in her arms. "Don't cry. I've got you."

Nat closed her eyes as Emily snuggled against her chest and took deep breaths. She played with the fine hairs on the back of Emily's neck, pleased when that seemed to help calm her down. After some time, Emily exhaled shakily.

"I really want you and Colleen to meet. Properly, this time." Drawing away, Emily gave her a tentative smile. "Maybe you could come over for dinner soon."

Nat beamed. Being invited into Colleen's life told her more about Emily's intentions than any number of declarations of love ever could. "How about I make Colleen's favorite meal? What is it?"

"She says the best thing she ever ate was chicken satay at this little Thai place downtown." Emily traced her finger over Nat's lips, returning her smile. "But if you made her homemade Thai or Asian *anything*, she'd be totally impressed."

"Chicken satay it is."

Emily replaced her finger with her mouth, giving Nat a slow, deep kiss. "She's going to love you once she gets to know you."

Slight anxiety rolled through Nat's stomach at the thought that she might not. She appreciated Emily's confidence, but worried what the consequences of her relationship with Colleen not living up to Emily's expectations might be. "I hope so."

"She will. And even if she doesn't, for some crazy reason, what matters is that *I* love you." Emily lifted her thigh, allowing Nat to finally remove her hand. Then she slid her own hand between their stomachs, deftly opening the button on Nat's jeans and slipping inside. Allowing her legs to fall open, Nat groaned when Emily stroked her clit carefully. "What matters is that you're mine."

Nat's inner muscles clenched at the words. The strength of her reaction to the idea of belonging to someone surprised her. She should hate the thought, but she didn't. In fact, she couldn't think of anything she wanted more than to belong to Emily Parker—body and soul.

Eyelids heavy with the pleasure of having Emily's soft, delicate hand working inside her shorts, Nat struggled with a sudden, intense desire to let Emily possess her completely. It was a privilege she didn't allow even those she trusted—not Janis, not even Bridget during the couple of appointments they'd worked together—and so it was the perfect way to give herself to Emily completely. She had no idea if Emily understood just how significant that act would be. "Baby, wait."

Emily froze, then removed her hand from Nat's jeans. "Do you want me to use my tongue instead?"

Nat caught Emily's wrist, keeping her close. "No, I want your fingers." Uncharacteristically shy, she cringed as heat rose on her cheeks. "I just...think we'd be more comfortable in bed."

"Okay." The look of adoration on Emily's face helped calm her racing heart. "I definitely want you to be comfortable, because I'm about to give you the best sex of your life."

Nat had no doubt that Emily would do exactly that. Instantly, her anxiety eased. Need took over. She extracted herself from their embrace, then helped Emily onto her feet. "Again."

"Pardon?"

"You're about to give me the best sex of my life...again." Unable to resist touching Emily's naked skin, Nat ran her hands down her back to settle on her ass. "I want to try something new," she said, squeezing gently. "If you're up for it."

"I'll try almost anything at least once." Emily entangled their fingers and led her toward the bedroom. "Whatever you want."

Nat watched Emily's hips move as they walked. "You really are the perfect girl." The comforting warmth of Emily's hand helped bolster her nerve for what she was about to do. When they reached the king-sized bed, Nat took a deep breath and slowly removed her shirt, enjoying the way Emily's eyes stayed riveted to her body. "That's why I want to give you something I haven't wanted to give anyone in a long time."

Emily lifted her gaze to meet Nat's. Then she touched Nat's cheek, rubbing her thumb over her bottom lip. "Only if you really *are* comfortable."

"I promise I'll tell you if I'm not."

Dropping her hand, Emily curled the tips of her fingers in the waistband of Nat's jeans. Her abdominal muscles tensed as Emily's knuckles brushed against her bare skin. Emily's throat moved, but she never broke eye contact. "You want me to go inside you."

Nat exhaled. Nodded. "Yeah."

"I guess I assumed you didn't enjoy that."

"I haven't, with other people." Sheepish, she murmured, "With men." Relieved by the lack of judgment in Emily's gaze, Nat lifted a shoulder, allowing a brief smile. "I've enjoyed it on my own, though, a few times. And I...I want to know how you feel inside me."

Emily wobbled slightly on her feet. "Me too."

Nat glanced down at Emily's hand in her pants, then raised an eyebrow—an attempt at cockiness she didn't really feel. "Come on, then."

"Yes, mistress." Biting her lip, Emily unbuttoned and unzipped Nat's jeans, then knelt on the ground to remove them. She tugged off her boxer briefs next, leaving Nat bare. Then she planted her mouth between Nat's legs. The sudden motion took Nat by surprise, sending her tumbling backward onto the bed.

Without breaking her stride, Emily crawled forward and pressed Nat's thighs apart onto the mattress. She went back to work with a sensuous moan, licking up and down her slit slowly.

Nat echoed her moan. "Oh, fuck." She put her hand on the back of Emily's head, enjoying the sense of control she got from holding her in place. "That's so good."

She could feel Emily smile against her wetness. Her slim hands slid up to rest on Nat's stomach, then moved higher, covering her breasts. Nat lifted her head so she could watch, thrilled by the sight of such a beautiful woman pleasuring her so enthusiastically.

Soon Nat's thighs began to quake. She tugged Emily's hair. "Stop before you make me come."

Emily gave her one last kiss on her clit, making Nat shudder. Rising, she crawled onto Nat's prone body and straddled her hips. Nat bit her lip at the scorching heat of Emily's pussy on her stomach. She wanted to roll Emily over and plunge inside her tight warmth, but she resisted, just as badly wanting the fire within her own belly sated. Emily rocked against her as she bent to capture her mouth in a kiss that carried Nat's own distinctive flavor.

Breaking away from their kiss, Emily whispered, "You're in charge. Tell me what to do."

Nat wrapped her arms around Emily's back and gently placed her on the mattress at her side. Then she took Emily's hand, bringing it to her mouth so she could kiss her knuckles. "Start with one finger." She uncurled Emily's index finger and sucked it into her mouth. "Go slow."

Emily propped herself on her elbow. She bent for another kiss, setting her hand on Nat's stomach before sliding it lower, between her legs. Taking a deep breath, Nat allowed her knees to fall open. She wasn't entirely certain why she was so nervous. Emily wouldn't hurt her. And it wasn't as though she hadn't been fucked more times than she could count. Of course, those had been some of the most painful, humiliating experiences she'd ever had. That made her tense about the prospect of letting it happen again, no matter who was preparing to penetrate her.

Yet this was different. This was about *her* pleasure, not her partner's. She wasn't just a warm, wet hole to Emily. From the way Emily cautiously dipped her fingers into her folds before touching her clit in a feather-light caress, it was clear that nothing would happen without her consent. If she didn't like it, Emily would stop. Because Emily loved her.

Nat relaxed. She played with Emily's hair, gazing into her eyes. "That feels so good."

"So do you." Emily kissed her bottom lip as she slid her finger lower to gently probe at Nat's opening. "You're so wet."

Indeed she was. Confident that Emily would give her nothing but pleasure, Nat covered Emily's hand with her own. Emily inhaled as though she might speak, but before she could say anything, Nat guided her finger inside. She closed her eyes at the delicious sensation of her inner walls tightening around Emily, then groaned at the way Emily writhed against her side with a satisfied moan.

"Nat, baby, look at me."

She opened her eyes, curious about the tremor in Emily's voice. Seeing a trace of uncertainty in Emily's eyes, Nat stroked her cheek and grinned. "Don't stop."

Emily hummed against her upturned lips. "Never." She withdrew her finger, then cautiously thrust back inside. Nat savored every delicious movement, every wiggle of Emily's fingertip against her sensitive inner walls. It was all she could do not to start whimpering and begging for more.

Embarrassed by how close she was to losing control completely, Nat decided to regain the upper hand. She took a fistful of Emily's blond hair and tightened her grip just enough to command Emily's attention.

"Tell me what you want." Emily stroked her clit with the pad of her thumb, finger-fucking her slowly. "I'll do whatever you say." "Just stay here with me." Nat held Emily's face inches from her own, kissing her over and over as Emily thrust gently inside her. Despite how vulnerable this act made her feel—or perhaps even because of it—Nat's arousal was at a dizzying peak. She couldn't remember the last time she'd wanted to come so badly. Even knowing that she would lose control didn't stop her from craving that release with all her heart. "Don't let me go."

Emily curled her free arm beneath Nat's shoulders, pulling their bodies together. "I won't."

Nat pressed her face into Emily's neck and held on tight. Emily rubbed her expertly, concentrating more on her clit than on pounding into her. It was so perfect, exactly what she wanted, and actually trusting Emily enough to lead her through this experience was the most powerful aphrodisiac imaginable.

The climax rolled through Nat's body in increasing waves, stealing her breath and curling her toes. Even though she'd desperately wanted to draw things out, she couldn't stop. She convulsed around Emily's finger, feeling every contraction. When she finally pulled back, she met Emily's gaze and allowed her to watch her face as the pleasure eventually began to ebb.

"That was incredible," Emily whispered. "Are you okay, sweetheart?" She kissed just below Nat's left eye, then the right, making Nat aware that she was crying.

It figured. She didn't like showing weakness in bed, but she was willing to forgive herself, under the circumstances. At least she was pretty sure Emily didn't think less of her for it. "I'm perfect."

"Truer words." Grinning, Emily kissed the corner of her mouth, then shifted, laying her head on Nat's chest. She sighed, curling her arm around Nat's middle and cuddling close. "I liked being inside you."

"I liked it, too." Nat kissed the crown of Emily's head. "Maybe we can do that again sometime."

Emily licked Nat's erect nipple, which jutted out mere inches from her lips. "We can do whatever you want. Pretty much whenever you want." She lifted her head, offering Nat a flirty wink. "Consider me your ready and willing sex slave."

Oh, the things she was going to do to Emily tonight. Suddenly Nat was very glad she'd thought to bring her cock, paddle, and other toys. *You never know when you'll need the tools of the trade.* Her mind going wild with the possibilities, she tugged Emily on top of her body and grabbed her ass in both hands. "You really are my dream girl."

"Ditto." Emily shifted her hips, smearing her wetness onto Nat's belly. "So, best sex ever?"

Nat chuckled. "For the moment." She raised both hands, bringing them down sharply on Emily's bottom. The quick inhalation the twin smacks elicited was fuel for the fire burning in Nat's belly. "But I'm ready to try and top it."

"Me too." Emily squealed as Nat rolled them over, then dissolved into giggles when Nat pinned her hands over her head. "Mistress."

CHAPTER TWENTY-FIVE

Six months later

"I can't believe Colleen is bringing home a boyfriend. Already." Emily glanced at the front door, resisting the urge to call Colleen's cell phone to see how close she and her friend were. She'd told them that dinner was at six o'clock, and it was almost five after. "She practically just got on campus and already there's a guy."

Nat sampled a bite of the chicken satay she'd pulled off the stove, then blew on a second forkful before offering it to Emily. She chewed, smiling at the familiar flavors. It was Colleen's favorite, so Nat made it every time she came home from school to visit. "Delicious. You spoil her."

"She's a good kid."

Abandoning her watch over the front door, Emily stepped into the kitchen and stood behind Nat, wrapping her arms around her waist. She rested her cheek on Nat's strong back, closing her eyes and sighing. "You're right. She is. So tell me to stop worrying about her and this boy."

"Stop worrying about her and this boy." Nat set down the wooden spoon in her hand and turned within Emily's embrace, hugging her back. "He sounds like a good kid, anyway. She said he's also a writer, but an artist, too. Apparently he publishes a graphic-novel series online—something about zombies. Anyway, he sounds more like a geek than a frat boy, and if you ask me, that's a good thing."

"You're right, it is." She fell silent for a minute, then wrinkled her nose. "Zombies? Really?"

Nat shrugged, giving her a sheepish grin. "Zombies are cool. I kind of want to read his stuff."

Emily rolled her eyes. "Great. Now I really am the boring, lame one in the family. Is that it?"

Nat's eyes lit up at her characterization of their situation as *family*. Emily knew they would. The best part was that she meant it. Somehow, in less than a year, Nat had become an indisputable part of their unconventional family unit. Even Colleen genuinely liked her.

Kissing the corner of Emily's mouth, Nat murmured, "You're not boring." She dropped her hand to the waistband of Emily's jeans, then carefully slipped inside to barely graze the edge of the tender area that still ached from the sting of her favorite paddle the night before. "Quite the opposite."

"I'm glad you think so."

"I know so." Nat pulled away at the sound of Colleen's key in the front door. "I'll be happy to remind you how *not* lame and boring you are as soon as they leave."

"I'll take you up on that," Emily said as she stepped out of the kitchen, grinning at the wink Nat shot her on the way out. She walked to the front door just in time to greet Colleen and the boy whose hand she was holding. He was slim, Asian, and wearing dark, thick-framed glasses—not at all Colleen's type, as far as she knew, yet Colleen was absolutely glowing as Emily got her first look at them.

"Em!" Colleen released her boyfriend's hand and gave Emily an excited hug. "I want you to meet Kenji. He lives down the hall from me in the dorm...and we have a creative-writing class together. Ken, this is my sister Emily."

Emily tried to keep an open mind as she shook Kenji's hand. He seemed well-mannered enough, but she had yet to meet anyone she thought was good enough for her sister.

He gave her a warm smile. "It's really nice to meet you. Colleen talks about you all the time."

Colleen poked Kenji in the side. "Shut up." The adoring grin he directed at Colleen looked very genuine and eased some of Emily's apprehension. A hand landed on the small of Emily's back at the same time Colleen glanced over and lit up. "And this is Emily's girlfriend, Nat. She's the one who's about to blow your mind with her chicken satay. Nat, this is Kenji."

"At least she's not building your expectations to unreasonable levels." Nat shook Kenji's hand, chuckling. "It's good to meet you, Kenji."

"You can call me Ken." He fiddled with his glasses, looking very unlike the jocks and frat boys Colleen had dated in high school. Thank God. "Thanks for inviting me to dinner."

"It's our pleasure," Emily said. "Colleen has been talking a lot about you, too. It's good to finally have a chance to get to know you."

Nat wrapped her arm around Emily's middle. "On that note, if everyone wants to take a seat, dinner is ready. I just need to serve it."

"I'll help you." Colleen stepped between Emily and Kenji, touching Nat's arm. When Nat released Emily to walk to the kitchen, Colleen stopped her with another tentative touch. Then she gave her a quick hug. "It's really good to see you, Nat."

Nat met Emily's eyes over Colleen's shoulder, clearly as surprised by the spontaneous show of affection as Emily was. Though Colleen and Nat had gotten along well since their second meeting, this was a new level of comfort. "Thanks, Col." Nat hugged her back. "Same here."

Stupidly happy, Emily watched them walk to the kitchen arm in arm. Colleen's acceptance of Nat—and the surprisingly fast friendship that had formed between them—had been unexpected. It was also the reason that six months with Nat somehow felt more like six years. All the worrying she'd done in the beginning of their relationship seemed silly now. Being with Nat felt so easy, and so right. Even when they disagreed, they managed to do so in a way that strengthened Emily's faith in their bond.

Emily turned back to Kenji, softening at his nervous expression. "How about we sit down?"

Kenji nodded. "Lead the way."

As Emily sat across the dining room table from Kenji, Colleen and Nat's raucous laughter poured out of the kitchen. Emily smiled on instinct, catching Kenji's gaze as he did the same. He cleared his throat, then exhaled in a rush.

"I hope this isn't too forward, but I wanted to tell you how much I admire you. Colleen told me all about her childhood, your parents..." Kenji was clearly flustered by her sustained eye contact. He stared down at the tabletop. "Anyway, she's a really great girl, and it's obvious that you had a lot to do with how she's turned out."

"Well, thank you." Emily's face heated, as it always did when someone expressed admiration for what never felt like a choice. "I did my best."

"You did awesome. Colleen is really special." Clearing his throat again, Kenji managed to meet her gaze. "My parents are physicians, and my brother and I had the most over-scheduled, privileged childhood you can imagine. Meeting Colleen has really opened my eyes. She makes me a better person." He winced. "I know we haven't been together long, and I'm probably crazy for even telling you all this—"

"No, I get it." Inexplicably, Emily's resistance to the idea of Colleen having a steady boyfriend melted away. She recognized the light in Kenji's eyes when he spoke about Colleen. "I fell in love with Nat almost immediately. It took me a little while to admit it, but when you meet the right person, sometimes you just know."

Kenji beamed at her. "Totally." He shrugged, seeming to relax. "Actually, your situation—raising a sibling—has inspired an idea for a new graphic novel I want to write. Colleen has agreed to collaborate with me on the story. I think it'll be amazing."

So Colleen had managed to find someone to create with her. Emily's affection for the boy bubbled over. "Well, I'd love to read it."

Kenji's expression turned sheepish. "I hope you like zombies."

Emily stifled a laugh. Of course there had to be zombies. "I'll try almost anything once."

❖

By the time Colleen and Kenji left a little more than three hours later, Emily's throat and belly ached from all their laughing over dinner. Colleen and Nat had been in rare form, trading stories and amusing barbs, while Kenji interjected every so often with surprisingly funny comments. He was a charming guy, and she could honestly say that she was cautiously optimistic about his suitability for Colleen.

As though echoing her thoughts, Nat turned to her as soon as they shut the front door behind Colleen and Kenji. "I like him."

"He's okay," Emily said, then gave Nat a helpless shrug. "He seems like a nice kid."

"It sounds like he comes from a good family." Nat took her hand, leading her to the couch. She sat and pulled Emily onto her lap, slipping a hand beneath her shirt to stroke her bare side. "I get the feeling he treats her very well."

"He'd better. Or else I'll send you after him."

"Damn straight," Nat muttered.

Emily nuzzled Nat's neck, exhaling as her entire body relaxed. "You and Colleen were adorable tonight."

"It was fun hanging out with her. Now that she doesn't think I'm a sister-beating asshole, we actually seem to get along pretty well." Nat's hands roamed her body, smoothing over her stomach before settling on her back. "I think she knows how much I love her big sister."

"I love you, too." Emily looped her arms around Nat's shoulders and rested her head against her chest. Closing her eyes, she focused on the steady thrum of Nat's heartbeat. "She knows. She can see how happy I am."

"I'm happy, too." Nat's hands moved around to cover her breasts. "Ecstatic, actually."

"Me, too." Emily's breath hitched as Nat's thumbs rubbed over her nipples. Still sore from the clamps she'd worn last night, the rough contact made them sting. "Can I do anything to make you even happier?"

"You could let me take you to bed." Sharp teeth nipped at her earlobe. "And then you could just let me *take* you."

Emily drew back and batted her eyelashes. "Seems to me that if you wanted to take me, you shouldn't be asking my permission." Excited for the play she was about to initiate, she whispered, "*Unicorn*, right?"

Nat's expression hardened even as her eyes glittered. "Come on then, bad girl." Moving quickly, she stood and hefted Emily over her shoulder like she weighed nothing. Then she brought her palm down onto Emily's bottom with a thunderous *slap*. "I've got plans for you."

Emily bit her lip against the delicious pain Nat delivered to her already aching body, then broke into a grin. She couldn't wait.

THE END

About the Author

Meghan O'Brien grew up near Detroit, Michigan, and now resides in beautiful Sonoma County, California. She and her partner Angie share their lives with an amazing son, two dogs, three cats, and assorted fish, reptiles, and even a tarantula. Somewhere in all this chaos, she finds time to indulge in her favorite things: video games, science-fiction television, and (of course) writing. By day, she works as a web and database developer.

Books Available From Bold Strokes Books

Oath of Honor by Radclyffe. A First Responders novel. First do no harm…First Physician of the United States, Wes Masters, discovers that being the president's doctor demands more than brains and personal sacrifice—especially when politics is the order of the day. (978-1-60282-671-7)

A Question of Ghosts by Cate Culpepper. Becca Healy hopes Dr. Joanne Call can help her learn if her mother really committed suicide—but she's not sure she can handle her mother's ghost, a decades-old mystery, and lusting after the difficult Dr. Call without some serious chocolate consumption. (978-1-60282-672-4)

The Night Off by Meghan O'Brien. When Emily Parker pays for a taboo role-playing fantasy encounter from the Xtreme Encounters escort agency, she expects to surrender control—but never imagines losing her heart to dangerous butch, Nat Swayne. (978-1-60282-673-1)

Sara by Greg Herren. A mysterious and beautiful new student at Southern Heights High School stirs things up when students start dying. (978-1-60282-674-8)

Fontana by Joshua Martino. Fame, obsession, and vengeance collide in a novel that asks: What if America's greatest hero was gay? (978-1-60282-675-5)

Lemon Reef by Robin Silverman. What would you risk for the memory of your first love? When Jenna Ross learns her high school love Del Soto died on Lemon Reef, she refuses to accept the medical examiner's report of a death from natural causes and risks everything to find the truth. (978-1-60282-676-2)

The Dirty Diner: Gay Erotica on the Menu edited by Jerry Wheeler. Gay erotica set in restaurants, featuring food, sex, and men—could you really ask for anything more? (978-1-60282-677-9)

Slingshot by Carsen Taite. Bounty hunter Luca Bennett takes on a seemingly simple job for defense attorney Ronnie Moreno, but the job quickly turns complicated and dangerous, as does her attraction to the elusive Ronnie Moreno. (978-1-60282-666-3)

Touch Me Gently by D. Jackson Leigh. Secrets have always meant heartbreak and banishment to Salem Lacey until she meets the beautiful and mysterious Knox Bolander and learns some secrets are necessary. (978-1-60282-667-0)

Missing by P.J. Trebelhorn. FBI agent Olivia Andrews knows exactly what she wants out of life, but then she's forced to rethink everything when she meets fellow agent Sophie Kane while investigating a child abduction. (978-1-60282-668-7)

Sweat: Gay Jock Erotica edited by Todd Gregory. Sizzling tales of smoking-hot sex with the athletic studs everyone fantasizes about. (978-1-60282-669-4)

The Marrying Kind by Ken O'Neill. Just when successful wedding planner Adam More decides to protest inequality by quitting the business and boycotting marriage entirely, his only sibling announces her engagement. (978-1-60282-670-0)

Dark Wings Descending by Lesley Davis. What if the demons you face in life are real? Chicago detective Rafe Douglas is about to find out. (978-1-60282-660-1)

sunfall by Nell Stark and Trinity Tam. The final installment of the everafter series. Valentine Darrow and Alexa Newland work to rebuild their relationship even as they find themselves at the heart of the struggle that will determine a new world order for vampires and wereshifters. (978-1-60282-661-8)

Mission of Desire by Terri Richards. Nicole Kennedy finds herself in Africa at the center of an international conspiracy and being rescued by beautiful but arrogant government agent Kira Anthony, but is Kira someone Nicole can trust or is she blinded by desire? (978-1-60282-662-5)

Boys of Summer edited by Steve Berman. Stories of young love and adventure, when the sky's ceiling is a bright blue marvel, when another boy's laughter at the beach can distract from dull summer jobs. (978-1-60282-663-2)

The Locket and the Flintlock by Rebecca S. Buck. When Regency gentlewoman Lucia Foxe is robbed on the highway, will the masked outlaw who stole Lucia's precious locket also claim her heart? (978-1-60282-664-9)

Calendar Boys by Logan Zachary. A man a month will keep you excited year round. (978-1-60282-665-6)